For all who supported my first novel
and asked for more!

Grave Relations

Kevin Shurvinton

Chapter 1

An eerie silence cast over the decaying fleet of motor vehicles, broken only by the distant drone of an outlying freeway. Hammer cocked, the deadly weapon drawn, Hill braved a peak. Hidden safely behind the sanctuary of a rusting trucker's cab he peered out as far as he dared. While offering some degree of protection, as a vantage point, it was frustratingly restricted. The target's current position unknown. Against all sense of self-preservation, Hill braved progressing out a few extra inches. Far off subtle movement caught his attention. The source, quickly identified as a ripped section of tarpaulin, flapping. Taken in the breeze. A scan beyond detected no information of interest. Hill faced a quandary. The assailant may have obtained a means of escape, in the far corner of the fenced junkyard, gaining crucial distance between them both. Or just as likely, remaining cornered, he would retreat back past Hill's makeshift sentry post. Feasibly the perpetrator could already be wise to Hill's position. His firearm trained firmly on the decaying cab, biding his time for the clear shot.

Considering the thought, Hill immediately retracted his head. It was not a favorable prospect. Instead, he took a moment to weigh up his options. Backup would arrive imminently. The sensible choice was just to wait it out. Yet despite all logic and regard for survival, the contemplation of this scourge of society escaping niggled. Hill returned directly behind the cover of the oversized front wheel. The surrounding area remained

1

carpeted in wet mud from an overnight rainstorm. Despite the unrelenting Californian sun, the surface had not yet returned to its dry dusty norm. In his suited attire, Hill carefully lowered himself down into the muck to acquire a position looking directly underneath the cab. The sensation of moist sludge coldly soaking into his clothing registered. *Better than blood*, he reasoned. Hill aimed his firearm forward, steadying his breathing. Nothing of interest was viewable through the narrow portal. *Damn*. Soiled for no good reason.

Lying prone in his slurry filled shroud, Hill considered his next option. Unexpected movement off to the far left of the constricted portal, caught in his peripheral vision. Silently he adjusted his aim. Anticipating. Waiting. Nothing. Hill eventually let out a silent breath, realizing he had halted his breathing for some time. Doubting himself, Hill questioned whether he had imagined the movement, or had another inanimate object taken in the breeze? With a shortlist of other sensible options at this point, Hill elected to wait it out. Despite the looming threat, the unpleasant sensation of slurry soaking further into his clothing began to dominate Hill's thoughts. He cursed himself for the spontaneous decision, all seemingly to no avail, when further movement substantiated the original suspicion. Hill refocused both mind and aim alike.

Sure enough, from the limited view point a pair of boots briefly appeared moving from behind one stripped-out derelict vehicle on to the next. Clearly escape in the far corner of the lot had not been possible, now he was attempting to sneak past Hill to accomplish his getaway.

The detective's chess player mentality, working several moves ahead permitted Hill to recognize the gap to the next prospective metallic safety shield was short, fully in the outlaw's favor. The next, a different story. Hill readjusted his aim again, off to the far right of the breach in the anticipated route. He waited. Sure enough, the boots scuttled to the next makeshift buffer. Then nothing. No further movement. Hill deduced the assailant now faced the same conundrum as he himself had previously contemplated. Was the risk of progression worth the consequence of waiting it out. Hill was safe in the knowledge it was only a matter of time before the cavalry arrived in his aid. The other man did not retain the same luxury. He was on his own. Escape, the only option. Taking Hill's life to attain this, merely a detail.

Hill knew this, making the predictability of his target straightforward. He would take the risk. He had to. Once backup appeared on the scene, the odds of escape plummeted to near zero. The current scenario, one against one, was a fifty-fifty outcome. Sure enough the boots suddenly scampered into view. Just as they reached the point of no return Hill acted.

"Police. Freeze." He called out. The boots stuttered briefly as the perpetrator momentarily considered retreat. Then all out progression to the next abandoned vehicle was attempted. Directly into the line of sight. Bang-bang. A double shot rang out. One scuffing the left heel of his boot, the other smashing directly into the right ankle, bringing the fugitive down to the ground in a cry of pain. Adrenaline pumping, the wounded outlaw trained his gun towards the underside of the truck, where the shot had originated from. Nobody in view. Before another conscious thought could materialize, the criminal detected the sound of fast approaching footsteps. Instantly followed by the searing pain of a forceful, solid impact to the head.

Hill had wasted no time from firing to getting to his feet and taking a commanding position. Racing around, he thumped the butt of his gun hard against his recipient's head. Without pause, Hill stamped his foot directly on the gun wielding hand of his victim. The firearm was involuntarily relinquished from grip and kicked clear in an instant. Hill wasted no time in dropping his knee firmly into his captive's lower back swiftly followed by producing a set of handcuffs from his dripping suit jacket. As he ratcheted them on his wrists, Hill could not resist applying more pressure with his knee than required.

"Arh, that hurts." The assailant cried out.

"Not as much as my dry-cleaning bill is going to hurt me." Hill returned unsympathetically.

Hours later Hill sat uncomfortably in Chief Lance's office. While Hill held the pinnacle officer in high regard, it did not mean he had to like him. Hill was also aware the feeling was more than mutual. The chief's obsession with budgets, limiting resources and making the books balance, was infuriating. Hill was an all-out, get the bad guy and never mind the consequences maverick detective. He bought home the goods, made the arrests, took evil off the streets. When did labor costs and overtime budgets supersede that objective?

The door suddenly sprang open with force, Lance storming through, slamming it back closed behind him. In his hands was an oversized file, which he proceeded to crash down onto the desk in front of Hill. The expression on Lance's face confirmed his presence had not been requested to congratulate him on cracking the case. Bringing a double homicide meth dealer to justice. No. This was going to be another berating.

"Good afternoon Chief." Hill coolly greeted in the face of the toxic atmosphere radiating from his boss and commander. For an enduring moment, Lance held a stare of contempt directly at his detective. Hill returned an unphased gaze. Playing with fire.

"Don't." The chief muttered before taking his seat. For a long time the two men just sat staring in some metaphorical display of derision towards the other. Lance filled with anger, Hill with a mocking defiance. "We've been here before detective."

"Is there a problem?"

"Yes there is a problem. Where the hell do you get off?" *Here we go*, Hill thought to himself. It was time for the chief to unload. Hill fidgeted slightly, making himself comfortable. "Do you think this police department operates around you? That your priorities take precedence over every other fucking thing? That we are able to operate without any consideration for cost? Professionalism? Any sense of civic responsibility towards the people we are hired to protect and serve? Or is it go all out to get the arrest, never mind who gets in the way?" Lance rose back to his feet as anger surged within him. "Do you have any idea what it's like to run this operation? To balance out all the resources appropriately? Here I am working seventy to eighty hours a week, I can't even take a shit without my phone pinging with the next issue. But I try. I do my best to ensure every patrol officer is looked after. Every traffic cop is valued, the detective team wants for nothing, all the auxiliary staff are hired and trained. I oversee this whole god damn operation and somehow make it work."

"It's a tough job." Hill agreed.

"Damn right its tough." Lance fired back, raising his voice. "Tough even without you. But I don't have that luxury, do I? I've got to manage your renegade kamikaze behavior. Where every villain has to be taken down as soon as possible, fuck the overtime budgets."

"I've never claimed a cent in overtime."

"No, but the army of officers you commandeer at will, with no regard for protocol do. Working them around the clock, all in aid of your single objective. Then there's the damage to the city. In your little pursuit today, forty-three cars were damaged. Forty-fucking-three. Plus buildings, fire hydrants, bus shelters, the list just goes on."

"Isn't it covered by insurance?"

"Do you have any idea what happens to our premiums when our risk profile is classed as apocalyptic?"

"You're right. That's above my paygrade. I don't know what it's like to walk in your shoes." Hill conceded, lacking regret in both voice and mind.

"I can't even assign you a partner. No other detective is interested in working with you. The most proficient detective in the fucking building and not a soul wants anything to do with you. Doesn't that tell you something?"

"I prefer to work alone." Hill shrugged.

"Well, that's just not true, is it? You tie up half my force every time you get a sniff of a breakthrough. No, you do not prefer to work alone, you just don't want anyone else involved with equal authority, somebody who can make you accountable, stand in your way, slow you down?"

"I would like to argue chief, but we both know you're right." Hill finally relinquished his high ground. "Look, I am what I am. I'm never gonna be a textbook law enforcer, but I can understand your points. I'll try to reign it in, be more of a team player." Lance raised a suspicious eyebrow. "I'll do my best."

"Get the fuck out of my sight." Hill did not wait to check if his berating was actually concluded, he hot-footed it straight out of the door.

"Hill." The Chief called just before he completed the getaway. The detective meekly peered back around the door. "Despite the antics, it was a good arrest. Glad to see that piece of scum off the streets."

"Thanks Chief."

Chapter 2

Late afternoon sunlight flared vividly across the office. The dominant beam, bestowing a distinctive brilliance to any objects trapped within its rays. Katelyn's blond hair glittered in the glaring light. Watching beyond the monitors of his private office, Chris was captivated. Unable to remove his gaze from the image before him. Her natural radiance remaining the brightest entity in the dull, sterile office.

Abruptly the visual advent waned away. A colleague electing to close the motorized blinds. Organic light receded, replaced by unattractive artificial neon illumination. The solitary exception was the enduring radiance emitted from Katelyn as Chris continued his fixation. Her hair supporting a muted level of shine, despite the softer environment, sweeping perfectly down to her shoulders. Her eyebrows were much darker, giving a stark contrast against her fair golden hair and ocean green eyes. The remainder of her face encompassed soft gentle features providing Katelyn with a perfectly balanced and beautiful look, completely organic in appearance. Chris failed to identify with the modern generation of manufactured fake beauty, sweeping in like a plague across their generation. Katelyn was, in his mind, totally unflawed.

Chris, recently promoted to the purchasing manager role, a valid achievement in the cutthroat environment of Haskins & Wilcox. This was a senior management position and at twenty-seven years of age, he was the youngest at this level by some fifteen years. Katelyn had been a close friend since her first day, eight months previously. Back when Chris was based in the goldfish bowl of the main open-plan office. His unaccustomed senior position now beginning to exclude him from the strong camaraderie which existed within the team.

With attainment comes sacrifice. Foregoing his peers was a price he had to pay. "Be Friendly, but not a friend." The Managing Director, Norman had advised regarding his relationship with his former team. Coupled with the stark isolation of his own office, the special connection with Katelyn withered before his eyes. He cursed himself for not making a move sooner. Opportunities were bountiful back when they were shooting the shit to pass the working day. An opportunity to now make a move, fading into the ether.

Chris considered tonight's leaving drinks for Sarah from admin. It was Friday and knowing Sarah, it would be a boozy affair. He had elected to attend for a few drinks, then make his excuses. Chris did not want the office staff witnessing him intoxicated, doing something stupid. It all returning on Monday morning to haunt him. He appreciated an undisclosed resentment simmered throughout his former team. As much as he was still welcome within the fold, a few would take great delight in spectating at his demise.

Katelyn rose from her desk snapping Chris from his rumination. As she walked past his office, he gave a friendly wave and beckoned her to enter. Katelyn smiled, opening the door.

"Hiya," She instantly greeted upon stepping in.

"How's life in the rock and roll world of accounting?" Chris jested.

"Getting ready to turn the volume to eleven."

"Glad to hear it." A pause followed, lasting long enough for Katelyn to look uncomfortable. Chris mentally noted such an occurrence never happened before. Back when their desks were a few feet apart.

"So, what'd ya want boss?" She quipped, breaking the silence.

"Just wondering if you're coming tonight? For Sarah's do? And please don't call me that."

"Sure am, boss." Chris threw a sarcastic smile at the retort. "I take it you'll be in attendance?" Chris nodded to confirm. "So, are you out, or are you out, out?"

"Maybe." Chris paused while he inwardly considered the question. "Let say we'll see how the night goes."

"Come on, don't be a killjoy boss."

"I'll do you a deal." Chris began with a wry smile. "You stop calling me that and I'll stay out longer."

"Deal." Katelyn returned a childish flirtatious grin. They held each other's gaze for an extended period. This time the hiatus was anything but awkward. Katelyn, still smirking, span to exit his office. "Later, boss." And with that she was gone.

A charcoal grey Ford Taurus pulled up outside the gloomy apartment block, darkened in the dusky evening shadows. It shut off its lights and engine with urgency, attempting to dissipate from noticeable view. The driver glanced up at the building. A complete eyesore, desperately overdue a

10

major facelift. The regeneration of Santa Rosa was generally impressive, making the shortfall of this block apparent. The driver looked forward along both sidewalks. Clear. A glance in the wing mirrors confirmed the reverse inspection as free of potential witnesses.

Setting the interior courtesy light to off, the driver departed the vehicle in twilight obscurity. After selecting the required call-bell out of the tapestry of choices, layered beside the foyer door, the driver nervously rechecked up and down the street. The sensation of exposure was overwhelming, giving rise to a muted level of panic. So distracted by the effort to be vigilant, the driver jumped back in surprise when the entrance door suddenly swung open. Now greeted by the silhouette of a female figure, the driver took a breath and attempted to maintain a degree of calm.

"Here." She whispered in an abrupt hushed tone, her hand extending out offering a small black oval object. The driver cautiously took the item, inserting it straight into their pocket and out of sight.

"How do I get into the house?" The driver nervously enquired.

"Go around the left-hand side of the building, the first door you come to around the back will be unlocked. Once inside, turn left and look for a TV lounge. He'll be in there." Without hesitation or further word, the lady stepped back and began to close the door.

"Wait." The driver instructed, louder than had been intended. The female froze with the door halfway closed. Despite the darkness, a mixture of irritation and confusion was distinctly engraved on her face. The driver failed to add to the flustered command and just stood blankly facing the lady.

"What?" She eventually prompted.

"Are you sure you want me to do this?" The driver eventually spat out, stepping towards the female figure. The tone closer to pleading than asking. If the driver had been hoping for mutual indecision, or apprehensive reconsideration, it was not offered. The female stared back coldly, harboring a detached conviction.

"Bye." She plainly returned, upholding the glare until the door was closed on the driver. Alone once again, the driver silently returned to the Ford. Engine fired; a short prayer was hastily uttered for the ensuing mortal sin. Imploring spiritual forgiveness, the vehicle and its owner sped off into the dusky evening.

Chris entered the bar at eight, after spending an eternity selecting his outfit. He settled on smart jeans, an affluent shirt, and his favorite tan color shoes. A dark blue suit jacket to complete the look.

It was an hour after the official meet time, Chris expected many of his colleagues to already be on their way to inebriation. His assumption was spot-on. Rowdy clusters of Haskins & Wilcox employees were scattered across the room, deep in loud conversations of complete nonsense. The noise they collectively generated was impressive. Chris had caught note of it on his approach, far down the street.

He scanned the room for Katelyn. If tonight was the night, he intended to complete some groundwork immediately. No sign of her. Sarah was visible at the bar cackling loudly and downing shots. *No way she's going to last the night*, Chris thought to himself. After another assessment of the room, he opted to get a drink.

He walked purposefully to the bar, where upon reaching it, Sarah noticed him.

"Chris, you made it." She raucously announced at high volume, although he was only a couple of feet away.

"Hi Sarah." Before he could add to the greeting Sarah clumsily burst through a couple of intervening colleagues and drunkenly embraced him. Chris hugged her back, albeit in a slightly more refined manner. Eventually she let Chris go. "Would you like a drink? Tap water maybe?"

Sarah's face briefly contorted in confusion before she burst into laughter.

"Yeah, good one Chris. I'll have a gin and tonic, make it a double."

"Sure thing." Chris returned broaching a warm smile. With that, Sarah hugged him again.

"I'm gonna miss you Chris." A drunken sincerity in her tone.

"Yeah, that's what they all say." With a wink he turned to the bar and ordered the drinks.

Chris was finally able to slip from Sarah's clutches. A beer in hand, he circulated around the room in search of Katelyn. He would greet colleagues and co-workers as he did so, being careful not to get drawn into conversation. Eventually Chris was able to confirm what he first suspected. Katelyn was not present. Having made short work of his first drink he decided to refresh his beverage. Stood again at the bar, mild irritation crept up inside Chris.

He was only here for one reason and that certainly was not Sarah. Once his drink was served, Chris checked his phone. No messages. The time was coming up to half eight. It was probable she was just running late.

Chris allowed himself to get into conversation with the marketing team who were camped out at the bar as if guarding their basilica of inebriation. Chris partially relaxed as the drinks began to flow. Although he positioned himself to face the door, keeping a track of all who entered. Once nine came Chris elected to send Katelyn a message asking where she was.

From building disappointment, he entered into a pattern of frequent cell inspection. No response. He opened the sent text. It had been delivered but not yet read. *Where is she?* Chris contemplated this self-posed question over and over. From underlying annoyance, Chris began to speed drink, subsequently permitting further irritation within. He did not want to be blind drunk trying to make his move on a stone-cold sober Katelyn. That was not a winning combination.

"Drink up, we're moving." The call came loud and clear across the room. Instantly everybody began emptying their glasses. Chris cursed to himself as he was simultaneously handed a full glass of beer. The marketing team had just bought another round. All with full glasses, they set to work on downing the entire drink in one. Chris followed suit.

Within minutes the entire workforce was fifty yards down the road at O'Neil's Irish Bar. Chris opened his phone to message Katelyn their new location. Initially he was pleased to see the first message had now been read.

Soon reminded by the marketing crew it was now his round, he quickly sent the new location and fought his way to get served.

Once the drinks were purchased, he looked again. No reply. Bizarre. Chris scanned the bar for any sign of her. O'Neil's was already teeming with inhabitants. The influx of Haskins & Wilcox employees was making the challenge of picking out an individual, who in all likelihood wasn't even present, extremely challenging. Chris returned to studying his phone. He opened the texts again. He could see the latest addition had now been read. As he considered this, the recipient typing symbol appeared. Chris stood glued to the screen waiting in anticipation of the reply. Then without explanation the symbol vanished, and no riposte came. He elected to phone her to find out what the hell was happening. Walking to the door still transfixed on the cell, the doorman stopped him.

"No glass drinks outside, sir." He belted with an over-the-top commanding tone. The addition of a polite reference at the end of the directive was completely out of place, to the point of being condescending. Chris shot him a dirty look by way of response. After setting it down at the nearest suitable location, he made his way outdoors.

Away from the noise and hustle of the bar, Chris attempted to make the call. It rang several times before switching to voicemail. Chris recognized Katelyn must have selected the decline call feature due to the short number of rings before the voicemail. This made no sense. All he knew for sure; tonight, was turning out to be a total bust.

Several parties of drunk individuals were clustered outside, their drinks in plastic glasses. All were engaged in rowdy conversation, smoking or vaping. Several tables and chairs were provided to cater for these supposably antisocial patrons. However, judging by the exultant atmosphere, they were anything but.

Chris helped himself to a seat, still engrossed in his cellphone. He desperately wanted to type another message demanding an explanation, but also did not want to be the kind of guy who sends a barrage of unanswered texts and phone calls. Not the preamble for making a move on a girl you have been in love with for the last eight months. Locking his phone, Chris hung his head despondently.

"Been stood up have ya?" A voice spoke from across the table. Chris looked up in surprise. A young lady sat opposite, quietly observing Chris with interest. So engrossed, he had failed to notice her presence.

"Yeah, er, no. not really." Chris answered clumsily.

"Never mind Sugar, it's her loss." She cheerfully responded. Chris went to answer but no words came. She rescued him with a playful laugh. Chris could not help but lighten up and laugh back. "That's the spirit, you'll be back knocking them dead in no time."

"Honestly I'm fine." Chris raised his hands in mock protest. He studied the mystery Samaritan. Roughly his age, late twenties or so. She had a prettiness about her, but also a hard, streetwise look. Not really Chris's type. He preferred delicate flowers, this girl oozed confidence and strength. "I'm gonna go back in, nice to meet you...?"

"Debs" She extended her hand as she answered. As he stood Chris shook it.

16

"Chris. Thanks Debs." After another exchange of congenial smiles, he disappeared back into the melee.

Chris recovered his abandoned drink. He elected to finish it quickly, then make his excuses before the night took a different direction. Angry and upset, further participation in alcohol abuse was not going to end well. He reconnected with the marketing team, and before he knew it, was roped into multiple tequila slammers. The best made plans to make a sensible exit disappeared as quickly as the shots presented before him.

The driver stared blankly at the road ahead, mindful to hold concentration and avoid any possibility of a traffic collision. Evidence of this visit to Santa Rosa would be extremely damaging. Yet the driver's mind conversely disconnected from conscious thought, endeavoring to block out reflections, too abhorrent to administer. The driver fought to maintain a stable breathing cycle, identifying the cusp of a full-blown panic attack lingered precariously close. Instead, as a self-administered coping mechanism, thoughts were focused exclusively on the operation of driving. As if a robot, nothing beyond this processed.

The echoing reproductions of endless streetlamps finally ceased sweeping over the windshield. *Leaving the city limits*, the driver considered. A futile attempt to acquire a sensation of safety. Although knowing the reality of the act accomplished shortly before, would pursue the driver whatever road was taken. No distance achieved could prevent it from ultimately reeling the driver back to face the demons of accountability.

Hours later Chris stumbled out of O'Neil's. Many of the work attendees had already departed including Sarah, who by all reports had vomited all over herself in the lady's bathroom. As Chris staggered towards the nearest taxi rank the smell of cooking food enticed him. Almost on autopilot he made his way into the Turkish kebab shop in search of food made infinitely more inviting after several drinks too many. He ordered and stood blearily against the counter waiting for his prize to be delivered.

"Hi sugar." A familiar voice spoke directly behind him, Chris turned to the source.

"Hi Debs." He replied with a smile.

"You remembered my name."

"I'm not that drunk, do you remember mine?" Debbie pulled a face of concentration.

"Bob." She announced with certainty. Chris burst into a roar of laughter. Debbie extended her hand letting it gently rest on the side of Chris's face. She bought her gaze to meet his. "It's Chris. I remember."

For a period of time they stood, eyes locked on each other. Her hand softly placed against his cheek.

"Kebab an' fries for Chris." A heavily accented voice called from behind the counter. Chris gradually broke free of the symbolized embrace and collected his food. Unwrapping it as he stepped out the door, Debbie following close behind. Once outside, without asking, she helped herself to a handful of his fries, flashing Chris a naughty smile.

"Help yourself." He muttered with fake annoyance before returning the smile. The area was completely pedestrianized. Both residing on a nearby empty bench, Chris endeavored to consume his food as daintily as possible. Not an easy task with an overflowing meat, salad and sauce kebab. Adding in the copious amount of alcohol consumed it was not possible to enter into refined dining at this point. Electing to share the food allowed him to relax. Debbie certainly appeared pleased to help Chris with the task and did not require a second invitation.

"So how was it, being stood up then? Think you'll survive?" She asked playfully.

"Not stood up." Chris quickly answered with a mouthful of pitta and lamb donna meat. He gestured with his hand he had more to add once the food was swallowed. "I was planning on making a friend, more than a friend. But she never showed." He eventually got out.

"Hmmm, do you think she knew that was your intention?"

"I don't think so." Chris contemplated this for a second. "Maybe."

"That doesn't bode well." She observed. Chris was uncommunicative for a time before giving a slight nod.

"I honestly don't know." With that he pulled his phone out and checked for any activity from Katelyn. Nothing. "Not heard from her all evening."

"Do you mind if I borrow your cell a second? I need to make a quick call." With phone to hand Chris just gave it over without really thinking about it. Instantly Debbie typed in a number. Seconds later her own phone rang. Debbie hung up, handing Chris's cell back to him. He gave Debbie a confused look but did not say anything. His attention turned back to the food.

"Look my place is five minutes' walk from here. Do you fancy a coffee before you head home?"

"Debs, I don't know if that's a good idea. I really like this girl." Chris answered honestly.

"That's fine, I understand. Come for a coffee anyway." Debbie stood up extending her hand to him. Before Chris could really consider the possible ramifications, he took it, standing up unsteadily. Although a good third of the meal remained, it was deposited in a nearby trash can. Onwards Chris staggered, led by Debbie.

Shortly they arrived at a decaying dilapidated apartment block. Three stories high, no elevator and a detectible scent of sewage. The building's facade categorically uninviting with communal areas to match. Chris followed, still hand in hand, all the way up to the topflight. Into the nearest door at the summit of the stairs. He was pleased to find the apartment was clean, well decorated and bestowing a much more pleasing aroma. A far cry from the shabby exterior.

Debbie shut the door and locked it. Chris was stood in the hallway unsure what to do. Without word Debbie turned, pressing her lips on his. For a brief second Chris resisted. His defiance did not last long, surrendering to what now seemed inevitable. Chris could not remember ever being with such a forward partner, within seconds she was unbuttoning his shirt, his jacket still on. Debbie's mouth remained locked on his, completing the task of pulling off his shirt and jacket in one. Her hands delicately ran down his athletic physique, then back up. Slowly feeling every muscle, taking it all in, turning herself on. Once she reached his shoulders, she gently pushed Chris backwards causing him to step back further into the apartment. Debbie simultaneously moved forwards ensuring their lips did not part. She guided him blindly into the lounge. Suddenly she pushed hard, completely taking Chris by surprise. Drunk, he could not react quick enough and fell backwards. A large couch caught his fall, tumbling inelegantly into its soft cushions. Before he could even think about what had happened, Debbie dropped to her knees before him, rubbing her mouth and face against his clothed manhood. Despite the limitations of inebriation, Chris sensed himself reacting to her teasing. As Debbie's hands moved towards his belt, he grabbed them, stopping her progression.

"We shouldn't." He rasped breathlessly. Debbie lifted her head, bestowing a devilish grin.

"I won't tell if you don't." She laughed.

"No. I don't want this." Her face unperturbed she withdrew her hands.

"Spoilsport." Debbie returned. "So, what do you want?"

"How about that coffee?"

Chris identified a buzzing, blurrily he opened his eyes, no idea where he was. Laid on a strange bed in a room he did not know. Behind the window blind, sunlight forced its way around the edge. A couple of seconds passed as Chris got himself into a state of consciousness. The buzzing, he now realized was his cellphone. Previously set to silent mode to amplify the severity of the vibration. Useful when you are waiting for a call in a noisy bar. However, this enlightenment now eluded him. Chris had no idea what had transpired to reach this current situation.

He pulled the buzzing cell out of his jeans, strewn on the floor beside him. The caller notification read *Katelyn*. Chris stared at it without action. A sixth sense told him it was better not to answer at this moment in time. Pressing the side button, he cut the vibration but not the call. Turning his head slowly sidewards, he realized he was not alone. A half-naked figure laid beside him, breathing heavily and completely asleep. He looked at her carefully, trying to remember how he had arrived at this point. Memories came flooding back like a tidal wave, splashing him back into full reality.

Chris looked back at the cell as it rang off. Without further contemplation he silently eased himself off the bed. Devoid of underwear, Chris slid on his jeans. He Crept quietly out of the unfamiliar room, no clue of where he was going. Chris desperately needed to visit the bathroom but that was not a good move right now. Priority one, to get out of here and think. He staggered into the lounge, locating his shoes. Quickly he slipped them on minus socks.

The location by the couch provided a wave of memories. Chris quickly disregarded them, looking around desperately for his shirt and jacket. Simultaneously patting his pockets for the standard idiot check – wallet, keys, cell. They were all present much to his relief, but shirt and jacket were nowhere to be seen. A sense of panic filled his body, opting to leave without them. The cost of the suit, the jacket had been purloined from flashed across his mind. But this was not enough of a deterrent to stop this act of escape. As he left the lounge into what appeared to be the exit route out of the apartment, he was presented with the remainder of his clothes, discarded inelegantly on the floor.

A sense of both relief and triumph rose within Chris. He hurriedly donned the remaining attire and without pause, headed for the door. Locked.

"Shit." Chris muttered under his breath. A key lock with no possible way to free himself without sourcing them. Chris visually searched the hallway, nothing. Retreating back into the lounge he scanned desperately for the prized bunch of metal breakout tools. They were nowhere. A semi-partition revealed a small galley style kitchen. A quick scan proved fruitless.

Frustration and anxiety coursed through Chris's body, he braved creeping back into the bedroom. Scrutinizing the area like a soldier seeking his target before he himself, actually became the target. Partial success came his way. On the dresser beside the sleeping Debbie lay the all-important keys. Yet only inches away from her face.

With stealth-like capabilities, Chris the ninja, crossed the room. Attempting to keep the bunch locked in their arranged position, he deftly cupped his hand around them. Slowly the lifting process began. For a few seconds he elevated them without the escape of any perceivable sound. The apprehension within Chris suddenly peaked, he could not stop himself accelerating his moving hand.

The sudden haste upset the fragile balance causing movement between the metal apparatus. An audible chink rang out across the room, less than a foot from Debbie's ear. Chris froze like a kid with his hand in the cookie jar. Debbie's eyes flicked open, for a moment the room was motionless. Without her body moving, Debbie spoke.

"Where are you going?" Surprise wrapped in an element of hurt tinged her question. Chris awkwardly straightened up, the offending item still within his grasp. Continuing to play the part of a child caught red handed, he failed to provide any explanation. Eventually Debbie turned her head to face him, her eyes filled with anger or pain, Chris could not decide which. Eventually he caught his tongue.

"I need to be going, I have to get to work." He lied.

"Weren't you even going to say goodbye?" she fired back, her voice growing in anger with every word.

"I didn't want to wake you. I was going to leave you a note." And the academy award goes to…

"You were just going to leave?" Debbie shot out as if the words were leaving a bad taste in her mouth. She sat up, Chris remained motionless. "You stick your dick in me and then you want to just fuck off?" Anger clear in the volume. In her tone.

"No, it's not like that. You came onto me." Chris regretted saying the second part instantly.

"Fuck you." She shouted. Her gaze centered on Chris. "Fuck you, you bastard."

"Hey, calm down." He appealed.

"I thought we had a connection." Debbie ranted not listening to Chris. "I can't believe you weren't even gonna

24

say goodbye." Debbie's rage was clearly escalating. Chris reasoned there was no conceivable benefit in continuing with this debate. Nothing he could say now would decrease the volatility. He made a decision.

"I'm sorry. Thank you for a good night." With that said, he turned and rushed for the door. He could hear Debbie hastily dismounting the bed, following after him. Reaching the door, he was thankful it was obvious which key was cut for the lock in front of him. Desperation peaking, he unlocked it, swung the door open and rushed out. So frantic was his haste he nearly fell down the steps, immediately to the right of him.

Chris gathered himself and made a start for the stairs. Instantaneously the partially closed door swung back fully open, spilling out his half naked pursuer. She made a grab for his arm. As the connection was made, Chris pulled it forward preventing her attaining an adequate grasp. Broken free, Chris hit the first flight as if running for his life. Debbie briefly gave chase but soon realized it was pointless. The whole way down and out of the door, all Chris heard was hollering and obscenities.

Chapter 3

Chris arrived back at his place. Sat for the entire taxi ride completely shellshocked. Disbelief of the reaction. Anger at himself for the situation he had participated in. Wisely electing to wait to reach the sanctuary of his contemporary loft apartment before attempting to call Katelyn back. If she asked, he did not want to explain why he was on the move so early.

He locked his door and walked in. Chris Filled a large glass of water in the kitchen and thirstily gulped it back. After pouring himself a second, he sat at his breakfast bar pulling his cell out. The missed call from Katelyn was displayed on the notifications. He quickly inspected the call history to check if she had attempted to ring previously. He could see his call to her at just after nine. He had also rung a number not in his contacts list. Dialed at twelve thirty-two. Confusion filled him. Chris spent some time trying to understand why he had called the number. Nothing but haze came back to him. He vaguely recalled the fast-food takeout and meeting Debs. His mind skipped forward to the encounter on her couch. Shame and regret consumed him.

He recalled Debbie making him the promised coffee, after her seduction attempt had been prematurely concluded. He planned to finish it quickly and go. But then everything afterwards was completely fogged out. He certainly did not recall getting into her bed fully naked, or what might have taken place once in there.

Chris hovered his thumb over the call button for Katelyn. He told himself there was no way she could know anything about what had transpired. Nobody else from work would have seen him disappearing off with Debs either. It was fair to surmise Chris did not feel in any way proud of what he had participated in, but on the same measure he had not done anything wrong. He was a single man who hooked up with a stranger for drunken relations.

Despite the over-the-top reaction from Debbie, Chris considered his cowardly exit. Completely uncalled for. He could have at least paid Debbie the respect of waking and thanking her for a great night. Then made his excuses and left. As Chris pondered his actions from Debbie's point of view, his thumb still hovering over the call button, his phone suddenly changed to an incoming call screen. The number displayed appeared to be the number he called past midnight. Chris accepted the call and put the phone to his ear.

"Hello?" He asked in genuine confusion.

"Hello Sugar." The voice returned. Chris instantly recognized it was Debbie. *How the hell did she get this number?* All at once the recognition hit. She had dialed her number from his phone outside the kebab take out. It had been a trick to get his number without asking for it. Chris could not contemplate the motivations or ramifications for this underhanded move from her. He did recognize it was not good for him. The pause seemed to go on forever.

"I'm sorry about how I behaved this morning Sugar." Debbie eventually offered. Chris unsure what to say just sat there in silence. "I completely overreacted." He took a few seconds to find his voice.

"No, I'm the one who should be sorry. I should have woken you."

"Can we agree we're both sorry?" She ventured.

"Agreed."

"Good. I feel better now."

"Me too."

"Hey Sugar, do you fancy catching a movie at the cinema later?" She asked hopefully. Chris, surprised she was now pursuing a continuation of this fling, did not want to entertain any false hope.

"Debs, you're a great girl and I really enjoyed last night, but things are complicated for me right now. It's not a good time for me to get into anything." Chris spoke diplomatically, with a soft undertone.

"You're not married, are you?" She quickly came back. A detectable harshness entered her tone.

"No, I'm not married, not in a relationship. I'm just not looking for anything currently."

"Okay. Let's just go as friends then."

"I don't think that's a good idea Debs." *Take the hint*, he thought.

"Okay Sugar." She conceded, deflation engulfing her words. Another long pause held station over the awkward conversation. Chris desperately tried to find the words to end it without sounding callous. "Look if you ever change your mind Sugar, you have my number."

"Yes, thanks." Chris acknowledged. *Given under deception*, he thought to himself.

"See you, Sugar."

"Bye Debbie." Without hesitation Chris ended the call. A sense of relief washed over him. *Now, draw a line under this and get yourself together.* Allowing a few minutes to compose himself, he then called Katelyn. After a few rings she answered.

"Hi Chris." Katelyn's voice answered. A strong element of upset was evident in her voice. A sliver of panic hit Chris. *Did she know?* He continued regardless.

"Hi Katelyn, you ok?"

"Not really. It's my father. He had a seizure yesterday evening." She stopped, but Chris understood there was more to come and did not interrupt. "Chris, he's dead." Chris sat opened mouthed at his breakfast bar.

"Oh shit. Katelyn, I'm so sorry." He uttered with a hollow voice. A long pause passed with only the sound of Katelyn's gentle crying, departing Chris's speaker. Chris remembered Katelyn had mentioned her father was epileptic. She did not talk much about it, but had once mentioned his attacks, though rare, were always severe.

"Sorry I didn't answer last night, but..." She did not finish the sentence.

"Don't worry about that. What can I do? Do you want me to come over?"

"No." Katelyn replied firmly "Don't come here, it's not good at the moment." After some thought she added. "Maybe tomorrow, we could just go for a drive?"

"Sure, anything you want." Katelyn continued to softly weep. Chris sat searching for words that did not exist. At that point he heard the ping of a received text message. He ignored it, his only priority was to be available for Katelyn. As he continued to listen to her tender sobs, guilt reignited within Chris. While he was out last night getting drunk and angry with Katelyn for standing him up, she was out there grieving for her father. And what had he done? Apparently slept with the first girl who came along. Too drunk to even remember it. *Some friend he was.*

"I'm going to go now. I'll message you tomorrow if I'm available."

"Okay Katelyn. I'm so sorry. If you need anything, anything at all, let me know."

"Thanks, bye."

"Bye." With that she hung up. Chris sat with the cell still to his ear, frozen by the revelation, coupled with the accountability of his own personal actions. Eventually putting the phone on the countertop, lowering his head in shame. Only then recalling he had received a text. Chris grabbed the cell, unlocking it. Straight away he recognized the number of the sender.

"Shit." He muttered to himself. He opened it.

Hi Sugar. I know you said you didn't want to go, but I purchased two tickets for the new Jon Wiser film at the Long Road Cinema for tomorrow afternoon at 4. I wanted to watch it anyway so if you don't come it don't matter. Would be great to have some company, only as friends. Hope to see you outside? Please don't be cross. Debs X

"Unbelievable." He told his cellphone. Chris started to write a reply, anger beginning to rise within him. Halfway through he stopped, looked back at what he had written, then deleted it all. He locked his cell, chucking it down on the counter. "Can't this woman take a hint?"

After a shower, Chris spent an hour looking through the sports news, He followed that with a couple of hours work from his newly created home office. Now he considered himself important enough to the company to warrant a dedicated space for homeworking, he recently purchased a desk, new monitors and an ergonomic mouse and keyboard. Gone were the days of typing hunched over, on the couch. Despite the investment, today he could not really concentrate. Thoughts constantly turned to Katelyn. He gave up on that idea.

Chris continued to mooch but could not settle. He attempted to occupy his mind with television, spending more fruitless time flicking from channel to channel. Nothing grabbed him. He considered going for a run, but the hangover and the previous night's poor-quality sleep had robbed him of physical energy. A run would not be a good idea. Just then his phone pinged. Chris quickly grabbed it wondering if it was Katelyn. Dismay hit him when he inspected the sender.

"I don't believe this." He muttered, opening the message.

Hi Sugar. I was out shopping for groceries and decided to cook a Thai meal tonight. I do an amazing green curry! Do you want to come over to try??? Or if you'd like, I could come over to yours and cook there? LMK Sugar. Debs X

This is getting scary now, he thought to himself. *This girl is seriously nuts.* He considered several options for reply from gentle and polite to harsh and nasty. In the end he elected to maintain the silence. Answering might feed this behavior. Providing no ammunition or reaction might suppress her interest. Half an hour later she sent a picture message. Chris opened it to reveal a picture of Debbie taken by herself in front of a full-length mirror wearing a skimpy silk night shirt and high heels. She was pouting at the camera like a typical Instagram selfie. Chris could not deny she had a great body and looked hot in her attire, but the manufactured pose was a definite turn off for him. This was not the kind of girl he liked.

Shortly after, she phoned him. Chris sat watching the phone on his coffee table vibrating, her number scrolling across the screen. Eventually it went to voicemail. Chris was at least thankful she didn't leave a message. Within five minutes she called again.

"Enough." Chris called out. He grabbed the cell, rejecting the call. He deleted all the texts and the picture message. Finally opening the call history, he highlighted her number, and selected the *Block Number* option. He prayed that was finally the end of it. Despite the decisive act, waves of trepidation washed over him for the rest of the day.

Chapter 4

As instructed Chris pulled his vehicle up at the bottom of Katelyn's long sweeping driveway. Formidable wrought iron gates stood before him, encased within a wall so high, grappling hooks would be required to scale it. Katelyn's family home sat beyond the brick and metal security. Located much further back, completely out of view of the gate. Her father Stan had been a successful investment banker in a former life. More recently the family had relocated here, Santa Rosa, nestled in Mid-California. Supposedly for Stan to retire. Although by all accounts, he never really did.

Katelyn obtained an accounting clerk position at Haskins & Wilcox. Chris, besotted from her first day. Eight months later he still hadn't plucked up the courage to ask her out. Now Stan was dead, completely out of the blue. Despite his workaholic tendencies, they appeared a close family unit. Katelyn adored her father. She would be crushed.

It was just before three on Sunday afternoon, Chris had received a text from Katelyn an hour earlier asking him to meet her at the bottom of her drive. He had heard nothing more from Debs since blocking her number. His attentions were now fixated squarely on his friend, hoping to provide genuine support. If this was to facilitate bringing them even closer together as a biproduct, then sobeit.

A motorized buzzing noise suddenly commenced. Following an audible clunk, the two gates began to creep backward, turning on their hinge points to create an ever-widening gap in the middle. Chris watched them slowly sweep back into the property. His gaze continued beyond, until he observed Katelyn walking down the driveway, coming into view. Dressed in sweats and scuffed trainers, no makeup applied, hair roughly tied back. She still looked a vision in her own right.

Chris watched her carefully as she approached the car, clearly carrying the weight of the world on her slender shoulders, she appeared tired and defeated. Katelyn jumped in without word. She closed the door, sitting staring directly ahead, as if Chris was not even present. He turned to face her, not totally sure what to say or do. A single tear ran slowly down her cheek. Chris reached out, gently brushing it away with his fingertips. With that Katelyn threw her head into Chris's chest and began loudly sobbing. He closed his arms protectively around her, lowering his head so his lips nestled on top of her head. Chris tightened his grip around her. Katelyn responded by burying herself deeper into his torso.

The moment was comforting for both participants in equal measure. They held it a long time, neither wishing to relinquish the sensation. Still within his grasp, Katelyn eventually spoke.

"Can we go somewhere?" She whispered. "I need to get out of here for a while."

"Of course." Chris softly replied. They slowly untangled, Katelyn glanced at Chris throwing a brief courtesy smile, she immediately turned her gaze back straight ahead. He started the car and pulled away.

◆ ◆ ◆

A short time after, they reached Riverfront Reginal Park. A large parkland encompassing several lakes and woodland. Although inhabited by numerous tourists and visitors on a warm Sunday afternoon, its large expanse meant it was possible to easily be alone and undisturbed.

Chris parked the car. Both got out. He knew the beauty spot well, having regularly cycled out here for exercise with scenery. Chris led Katelyn out to a completely secluded spot, bestowed with majestic views that elevated over Lake Wilson. He had discovered this by chance last year, returning numerous times during recovery breaks from his biking.

A solitary bench sat overlooking the expanse. Trees provided thick cover from either flank or behind. They were totally invisible from the outside world, while the most serene view sat directly in front. Sat in silence, both just took in the spectacle before them.

"This is beautiful, Chris."

"Thanks." They continued to sit and stare.

"I just had to get out of that house." Katelyn eventually offered. "Mom is in pieces, I'm not much better. It's all such a mess." Chris placed his hand on Katelyn's back, rubbing slowly up and down. "I won't be at work tomorrow. We've got to apply for the death certificate, sort the funeral arrangements. We have to wait to get my father back. They are going to do a postmortem. I don't even want to think about that. I guess I'll be back Tuesday if all the things we need to do are sorted."

36

"Don't worry about work, that's not important right now."

"Yeah, I know." Katelyn looked down at her feet then back up at the charismatic depiction ahead. "Do you mind if we just sit here and don't talk?"

"Of course, I'm here for you. Whatever you want to do." Chris turned to her, offering a passive smile and his arm. Katelyn returned the smile, moving across to engage in his embrace. They continued to take respite in this temporary breach from reality. Both procuring in the view before them, emptying their minds.

The continuation of the tranquility was abruptly cut short. Chris's cell phone chimed to life. As it started to ring, he cursed loudly. Throwing Katelyn an apologetic glance before pulling it out of his pocket. It read *No Caller ID*. *Shit*, Chris thought. *Could this be Debbie?* He did not dare answer it and sat motionless.

"You can answer it, it's okay." Katelyn instructed. Without further consideration Chris rejected the call.

"Nah." He switched it onto do not disturb and slid it back into his pocket.

"Who was it?"

"No Caller ID, so who knows?" Chris replied. "Who cares?" he added, attempting to keep his voice as level as possible. Katelyn appeared to agree, she nestled her head back into Chris.

They remained statue still for an impossibly long time, not a word spoken between them. Chris tried not to think about the phone call and what it could possibly mean. Nothing else disturbed the tranquility of the moment until Katelyn let out a long sigh.

37

"I think I probably need to get back home." She groaned. "I told Mom I'd be an hour or so. She might be worrying." Katelyn didn't attempt to move, holding onto the moment for as long as she could. Eventually Katelyn braved a glance at her watch, telling her the time to move had been and gone some time ago. With another loud exhale she eventually separated herself from Chris. "Let's go."

As they started walking back to the car, Chris discreetly peaked a glance at his phone. *Forty-five missed calls* read the notifications banner. His heart sank. This issue clearly was not over. Chris tried his best to bury the concern until after he had dropped Katelyn off.

The drive back was mostly silent. Katelyn preparing herself for the return home, Chris inwardly panicking about what Debbie was going to do next. Reaching the bottom of her driveway, Chris pulled up and shut off the engine. After a long pause Katelyn eventually spoke.

"Thank you, Chris. I really needed this. I can't tell you how much this helped." Chris turned to face her, returning the look she bestowed upon him. Some of Katelyn's blond locks had dislodged from her ponytail tie. They sat clumsily in front of her subtle features. Chris lifted his hand, carefully moving the hair back away to reveal her appearance in all its beauty. Chris brushed his hand along her cheek, slowly withdrawing. Katelyn's eyes were wide, rich in engagement. She moved her head towards Chris, her intention clear. Chris fought his instinct, backing away.

"This isn't the right time." He whispered. "You're grieving. I don't want to take advantage." Nothing changed in Katelyn's persona. Clearly Chris's plea failed to register. She moved in once again. Before he could think further her lips gently rested on his. The kiss felt wonderful, despite the circumstances and the array of troubles in both their lives. Katelyn eventually took decisive action, backing her head away, cutting the moment she created short.

"Chris..." She started.

"I'm sorry." He interrupted. They looked at each other, both pairs of eyes conveying unspoken words.

"Don't apologize. I want this. I really do. You are right though, now is not the best time. Let me sort my head out first, okay?"

"Sure." Chris felt a concoction of emotions, but primarily joy at the admission she shared his feelings. They hugged one more time before Katelyn got out. Using her fob, she commenced the dramatic gate opening sequence. Standing with her back to Chris, she waited until the gates had parted enough for her to slip through. After a few steps into the estate, she turned and gave Chris a farewell wave and smile. Chris returned them, and then she was gone.

He started the car, pulling out his cell before doing anything further. The notifications now read *sixty-three missed calls*. Chris sighed and threw his phone on the now vacant passenger seat. Put the car in drive and pulled away.

Chapter 5

Chris reached his apartment. He sat tensely on the couch with his cellphone in front of him, placed on the coffee table. There were now over one hundred missed calls. The caller clearly in a repetitive pattern of ringing until it transferred to voicemail, not leaving a message and then instantly ringing again. Chris switched his cell completely off and laid back on the couch. He stared at the ceiling for a long time, thoughts running through his mind of what he could do to stop this.

Paranoia soon crept in. For all he knew Katelyn could be trying to get hold of him. She might have sent him a message about what had just happened. He did not want there to be any delay in his response, or to miss a call from her. He left the phone off for an hour, but that was as long as he could stand. He switched it back on impatiently waiting for it to reconnect to his network. Within seconds of the connection being fulfilled it rang. *No Caller ID*.

"My god, what is her problem?" He shouted at the phone in complete dismay. After some thought, he elected to dial his service provider for advice. Once he navigated endless menu screens, Chris was put on hold waiting to speak to an operator. Enduring twenty minutes of Green Sleeves and such like, before he was finally connected.

"Good evening, my name is Tracy and I'll be your call handler today." Sounded a bright and enthusiastic voice. Tracy took Chris through a range of security questions before finally permitting him to explain his issue.

"I have a nuisance caller who won't stop ringing me."

"Have you blocked the caller's number?" Tracy asked.

"Yes, I did that yesterday, but now I keep getting No Caller ID."

"It would have to be another user, device or SIM card if you had blocked the original number. It would not permit the call, even if the user switched to remove the caller identity."

"Well, it's still the same caller and they won't stop."

"Okay, there is not much we can do at this point if the caller is blocking their number from being displayed. I can help you set your phone to block any call without an identity?" Chris considered this but decided against it. He often received calls without an ID which he would not want to cut out. He declined the offer. "Okay at this point the best option is to get in contact with your local law enforcement. Do you know who the caller is?"

"Yes. Kind of."

"Okay my advice is to report this individual and let the police deal with it."

"There's nothing more you can do?" Exasperation filled the question.

"Sorry sir, but without a legal warrant there is nothing more we can lawfully do to help you." Chris gave an inaudible mumble by way of response. "The other option is to change your number. I can send out a new SIM card with a new number if you would like?"

"No, don't do that. I really don't want to change my number."

"Okay sir. Is there anything else I can help you with today?"

"No, thank you." He answered dejectedly.

"Okay sir. Well thank you for the call and I hope you have a pleasant remainder of your evening." Chris hung up the phone without further response.

"Like you care." He muttered.

The phone, still with the do not disturb feature activated, continued to silently light up to acknowledge an incoming call was happening. Chris concluded he had two options at this point. Either continue to ignore the calls in the hope she would just give up. Or answer one and make his feelings crystal clear to Debs. Option one was not faring well, he chose to go for number two.

"Hello?" He barked as he answered.

"Where were you? You missed our date at the cinema." Debbie returned without hesitation. Anger filling her voice.

"We don't have a date. I told you I wasn't going."

"I thought you might change your mind. We can't deny our feelings for each other forever. We should just give into them."

"My God, are you crazy? I don't have any feelings for you." Chris's temperament and volume escalated as he spoke. That was nothing compared to the response.

"Don't you fucking tell me you don't have feelings for me, you lying bastard. You stick your dick in me and give me your seed. You gave me that because you love me." She screeched harshly back down the phone.

"Love you? Christ, you're absolutely mental. I fucking hate you. Just stop calling me. Leave me the fuck alone. I'm calling the police."

"You do love me. You can't just make love to me then walk away. It doesn't work like that."

"Make love? That wasn't making love. It was a drunken kiss, nothing more. I don't even remember what occurred after that. Whatever happened, I regretted it yesterday and despise it now." Chris quickly obtaining the upper hand in the anger stakes.

"Don't say that Sugar." Debbie pleaded. "You do love me, and I love you."

"Fuck off." He screamed before ending the call, sat in total disbelief. *What the hell is happening? She's completely nuts.* He looked down at the phone, still in his hand. It was lit up with an incoming call. *No Caller ID.*

Chris, realizing he was devoid of options, looked up the Santa Rosa Police Department. He called the non-emergency number. Once the obligatory menu screen was successfully navigated, Chris was pleased to be put straight through to a call handler. He gave a brief account of what had taken place. The call handler advised he would have to come into the station to file a report. Not in the mood to waste any further time, he left immediately.

Chris parked outside the police department. Previously passing the building in his car multiple times, the precinct and neighboring fire department had a distinctive double sloped roof, catching his eye on every occasion. This was the first time he had ever needed to enter it.

After passing through a security station and metal detector, he walked up to the manned enquiry desk. The officer on duty took a handful of vague details and began filling out a report. Once the initial information was gathered, he invited Chris to take a seat. Someone would speak with him shortly. He sat in the waiting area with a mix of people. All clearly harboring their own range of personal issues. It was not a particularly pleasant place to spend his Sunday evening. Nearly ninety minutes later, a stocky young black officer came into the waiting area and called his name. He took Chris into a side room, offering him a seat one side of a fixed table. The officer sat opposite pulling out the preliminary report Chris had completed earlier.

"Evening Mr. Brooke, I'm Officer Rufus. I need to go back through this." Gesturing to the written report. "Take a statement to establish the full details. I can then give you the options and any course of action I will take." They went over the whole sequence of events from the first meeting on the Friday night, up until the phone call Chris answered shortly before. Chris noticed the officer was careful not to give any of his own thoughts or opinions. He gathered the facts as Chris reported them but appeared to be keeping an open mind on the one-sided account provided. Chris mentally kicked himself when asked to produce the texts and picture message. He had deleted it all in frustration. His only hard evidence wiped.

Chris chose to validate his account by putting his phone on the table in front of them both. Still set on the do not disturb feature, the latest call with *No Caller ID* was occurring. It rang off and the screen went black.

"Give it a few seconds." He told Officer Rufus. Sure enough the screen relit with an incoming call, *No Caller ID* clearly displayed on the screen. Chris looked expectantly at the officer.

"Do you mind if I answer and speak with her?" He asked.

"Not at all." Chris was pleased he was prepared to act there and then. Chris unlocked the phone before Officer Rufus answered.

"Hello." Rufus said. After a short pause he continued. "I'm Officer Rufus of the Santa Rosa Police Department. I'm currently here with Mr. Brooke who is claiming you are harassing him and continuously dialing his phone." Chris inwardly screamed. *Great, now she knows my last name*, he thought. He could just about hear the muffled tone of Debbie's voice on the other end but was unable to ascertain what she was saying. She spoke for a short while, the officer listening intently. He took some notes as he did this. Chris tried to read the upside-down scribbles but from his distance it was impossible to make out the content. He did not want to be noticed craning his neck to get a better view, so Chris elected to sit tight.

Eventually the officer asked for her full name, address, and other contact details. He could make out Debbie's full name as he wrote it down. Deborah Green. Eventually the officer switched his tone to polite but firm.

"Ms. Green, whatever the circumstances, I am instructing you to stop calling Mr. Brooke, right now. If you persist, I will arrest you for harassment. I will bring you in for questioning and I will seek to charge you. Am I making myself clear?" There was a pause as she responded. Again, Chris could not grasp the content, but her tone appeared calm. "Thank you, Ms. Green. Have a pleasant evening. I sincerely hope we don't have to speak again." He ended the call and handed the phone back to Chris. "Hopefully that will put an end to the matter. I'll enter the report. If it continues you can file a civil restraining order. I'll grab you the victim petition form in case you need it. You will have to get it notarized. Your bank should have someone who can do it." Chris nodded as he took in information never previously required. "Once complete, you can file it with a clerk at the Civil Court. They'll take you through the rest of the process. A judge will determine the terms of the restraining order. Evidence will help significantly so don't delete any further messages. The standard one will keep her at least one hundred yards away and prevent her from contacting you."

"Thanks, you've been brilliant." Chris acknowledged. Rufus gave a small smile.

"I'll get the forms."

Just before ten in the late evening, Chris finally departed the building. Hopeful this was finally the end of his encounter with Debbie. The calls had ceased, and Chris had set the wheels in motion on the restraining order. It was a long night, but he left feeling optimistic.

Chapter 6

The Monday morning office was alive with tales of what had taken place on Friday night. Chris, devoid of much of the gossip on account of his private office, had still gotten wind of several employees engaging in numerous acts of inappropriate behavior. The usual post office night out chatter, rang around the goldfish bowl. There had been no mention by anyone about Chris's antics, so now he felt totally assured he had not been spotted walking away with Debs by some rogue, appropriately placed employee.

Since speaking with Officer Rufus, the calls had ceased. Chris heard many times previously how ineffective the local law enforcement was. Judging by this experience, the complaints appeared somewhat unfair. Chris looked across at Katelyn's empty desk. A couple of employees had enquired where she was, but this was not Chris's news to give. He answered that he was as clueless as them.

It was coming up to ten-thirty, Chris was attending the senior management meeting at eleven. He still had several reports to run that would be required. He focused himself, getting his head down.

The meeting was late to kick off. This was due as always to Frank, the Sales Director, arriving late. Never on time but would get right on his soap box if the meeting began without him. A genuine attempt to demonstrate how important he was. *Complete insecurity*, Chris mused to himself. Next, they listened to the MD give his over-passioned speech about everything that was wrong at Haskins & Wilcox. This was an obligatory offering. Served at every management meeting, despite the fact the Santa Rosa facility was without argument the best performing division in the entire organization.

Once these formalities were complete, the actual meeting could begin. Each department manager and company director would provide a report on the headline aspects of their professional world. Accompanied by a set of standardized graphs to track performance. The weekly meeting was the brainchild of the Managing Director, and he was very proud of it. Attendance was mandatory, your graphs must be up to date and punctuality was paramount – unless your name was Frank. Most of the attendees considered it a complete waste of time. Chris could see some merits; it was a powerful communication tool. However, it had a tendency to drag on and on. Monday was a day for a big breakfast.

The previous thirty minutes had been very stressful for Chris. Two hours of preparation work he had intended to complete at his leisure over the weekend were condensed into the previous half hour slot as a consequence of everything that had taken place since he left the office on Friday. He had pulled it off, with the bonus his figures were fresh in his mind. Despite the fraught finish, Chris considered himself prepared for his slot.

When the time came, Chris took his place at the massive wall mounted screen. He provided a factual, but brief account of the dealings within purchasing. He summarized the challenges in the forecast, fluently from memory. Concluding by smoothly transferring into the department reporting graphs. As he finished, he briefly glanced towards his MD, Norman. A slight spindly man, sharp as a tack and as furious as a bear when needed. At this level you never presented weakness to him. Worst of all, was attempting to bluff him when you did not know the answer to one of his questions. If either manifested, Norman took great delight in ripping you apart. Other than that, he was a teddy bear. Chris caught his eyes. Norman gave a slight nod, barely detectable, but all that was required. Chris had done well, and Norman approved. Chris retook his seat away from the one-hundred-inch wall monitor of death, displaying his department's performance for all to see. Now he could relax and watch others walk the tightrope.

The meeting was intended to conclude at one, ready for lunch break. That never happened. For the senior managers this did not make a difference. The standard unwritten rule was senior managers did not stop for lunch. They just powered through, consuming some food, if any, at their desks. For the directors it was a different story. Officially they had an hour, but that was adopted as a suggestion by all, apart from Norman.

It finally broke at five past two. It was likely the directors would not be doing much more today. Chris did not learn much he was not already aware of. Susan the human resources manager reported they had a strong application submitted for the newly vacant admin role left by Sarah. The candidate could start immediately. They were interviewing her this afternoon and if she came across well, the job would be hers. Other than that, it was a fruitless three-hour slog.

Chris walked back to his office from the conference room. His venetian blinds were down but open, in their usual position. This enabled him to clearly look out, but partially obscure himself from the goldfish bowl. Helpful when he spent long periods watching Katelyn without attracting the attention of others. As he approached, Chris immediately observed a large object placed on his desk. The semi seclusion of the open blinds prevented him from making out exactly what it was. Spotting Chris as he advanced, several female employees possessing eager smiles, excitedly flicked their eyes from Chris to his office and back.

Anxiety rose within, still unable to identify the object that was clearly creating interest in the bowl. He reached the doorway, ignoring the stares and hushed whispers, walking straight in without breaking stride. Before him lay a huge muffin basket, literally overflowing with the sweet treats. It was clearly a professionally made affair and looked very expensive. Speared through the center of the basket was a wooden stake with a large cardboard printed sheep. It read in big bright red letters across the ewe, "I'm feeling very sheepish."

Chris stood for a second or two staring at the cake monstrosity in absolute disbelief. Distinct whispering and muted laughter continued behind him. Without hesitation Chris shut his door. He considered closing the blinds, but quickly decided against it, knowing that would attract further attention, heightening the interest of his unwanted audience.

With a prolonged sigh, Chris sat at his desk examining the mystery offering. A small envelope was taped to the back of the cardboard sheep. Chris discreetly removed it and pulled out a message card from inside. Within reading the first two words Chris's worst fears were confirmed.

Chapter 7

Hi Sugar,
I've been really unfair. I'm so sorry I rushed
you. I can see now I came on too strong. It's
just I've never met someone like you before
and I'm completely love stoned. Lets take it
much slower, to give you chance to catch
up. How about a cheeky beer after you
finish work? I promise only to use my lips
for talking, this time!!! I'll wait in Prestons
across the street.

Catch you Later.
Debs x x x x

"This isn't going to stop." Chris whispered to himself.
For a period of time, he just sat reading the card over and
over, trying to compute why this woman was so intent on
targeting him. No reasoning came, only further feelings of
dread. Chris glanced above the top of the card into the
goldfish bowl from his blind's castle arrowslits. The usual
office gossips were in full speculation regarding Chris's
unidentified delivery. All talking in shushed voices,
frequent flashes of eyes in his direction. Clearly the muffin
basket arrival while Chris was otherwise engaged, had
superseded the Friday night gossip, which had already
been flogged to death. Now there was fresh meat on the
chopping block and the organization's vultures were ready
to feast.

Chris, aware he was being spied on, calmly got up. He withdrew the long wooden stake and swiftly pulled the sheep off. The stick was deposited into the trash. A much worse fate was waiting for the poor cardboard farm animal. Straight into the shredder it went, closely followed by the mini love note. Nobody would be inspecting his rubbish after hours to get the inside scoop. Moments later, the realization hit him that once again he had just destroyed evidence. *Stupid. Really stupid.* Although on its own, it wasn't substantial enough to accurately convey the actual level of harassment.

He carried the oversized basket out into the goldfish bowl, placing it centrally in the oversized office.

"Help yourself all." Chris openly announced to the room. Without further explanation he returned towards his safe haven. Before Chris could make it, Claire, who just couldn't help herself, loudly asked the question everyone wanted to know.

"Who they from Chris? You got a secret admirer or something?"

"Something." Chris flatly responded without breaking stride. He could not shut his door soon enough.

Five O'clock arrived. The main office exodus ensued, leaving the usual faces still at their workstations. Some genuinely wishing to complete their work before calling it a day, some to curry favor with any high-ranking employee departing before them. Soon enough these thinned out until Chris was alone.

His extended session was not out of a desire to get extra work done. With his mind so preoccupied on other events, he had barely achieved anything today. Truthfully, he was petrified of leaving the building. Without setting off the emergency alarm to use a fire escape or leaving via dispatch which would definitely set tongues wagging as it was manned until eight by the worst rumormongers in the building, his only exit was the lobby. Straight opposite the large glass windows of Prestons Bar and Grill.

For the hundredth time Chris asked himself how she could have uncovered his place of employment. He did not know for sure, but the leading suspicion was Debbie had set her sights on Chris before the kebab takeout. Most likely after their initial conversation outside O'Neil's. The bar was packed with Haskins & Wilcox employees. It would not take much effort to source such information in the fray of a drunken leaving party.

What was certain, if necessary, she would remain in the bar all night. He could not wait this out. He thought about phoning the police. If he could speak to Officer Rufus, he was sure the inevitable confrontation could be avoided. Yet the thought of police involvement at his place of work was highly undesirable. He did not want to be the center of a workplace scandal and certainly did not want any of this leaking back to Katelyn. It was not a feasible option.

As Chris sat back in his chair, massaging his stressed forehead, his phone pinged.

"Here we go." He told himself, attempting to mentally prepare himself for the content. The idea it could have been sent from anyone other than Debbie never entered his head. Complete surprise hit him when Katelyn's name appeared in the notification box.

> *"Hi Chris, it's been a shit day, but we got loads sorted out. I haven't been able to stop thinking about yesterday. Do you mind if I come over this evening to get away for a while?*

Chris had almost forgotten the momentous occurrence yesterday. Something he had waited all this time for. Yet the transpiring relationship was entirely tainted by Debbie. Chris quickly responded. He asked Katelyn to give him an hour adding he had also been thinking non-stop about yesterday. The content felt a touch cringeworthy but there was no time to compose his words. He had to escape and quickly.

Chris arrived in the lobby. The office parking lot was located in a neighboring street. It was half-six and the sun had begun its descent, still shining brightly straight into the entrance. Despite the tinted glass, the glare was completely obstructive as Chris attempted to gauge the threat across the street. It was impossible to tell with the dazzling sun upon him if Debbie was watching, ready to pounce. With head lowered in some inadequate attempt to conceal his identity, he made his exit. Forcing the door hard, Chris hit the street at an intense pace. It was short of breaking out into a run, but pretty close.

To his annoyance, other pedestrians created moving obstacles to hastily navigate. Every few seconds he braved a glance behind him fully expecting to see Debbie at full sprint closing him down. Yet she was nowhere to be seen. Was she that deluded that she might actually be expecting him to join her in the bar? Quite possibly. Such details were peripheral at this point. Reaching the car was the imperative objective.

Chris arrived at the end of the street, making a hard right turn. He gave one final glance as the establishment of terror disappeared from view. It was another one hundred and fifty yards to the parking lot entrance. The distance only previously observable when it was raining. In Santa Rosa this was an infrequent event. Chris was noticing it now. He fought the instinct to break out into full sprint, trying to preserve some measure of personal dignity.

Finally, he reached the opening to the lot. While simultaneously searching for his keys and taking another hard right through the entrance, he swung his head back to look back up the road. Still clear. He recovered his keys deep in his pants pocket, immediately hitting the unlock button. Readying himself to jump into the car without a break in motion. As Chris returned his gaze forward into the near empty lot, he practically stopped in his tracks.

There, as large as life, stood Debbie, right next to his car. She looked relaxed with a welcoming smile on her face.

"Hi Sugar, I've been waiting for you."

"Leave me the fuck alone." Chris snarled like a junk yard dog.

"Sugar, I just want to talk." She pleaded softly.

"No." Chris headed for the driver door. Debbie took a quick sidestep to stand right in front of it, blocking Chris. He considered grabbing her, pulling her clean out of the way. Somehow, even after everything that had happened, using physical force did not seem appropriate. "Move. Now." He growled.

"Sugar, just hear me out. Let me say my piece then I'll go. I promise you'll never see me again." Debbie's voice remained calm. Chris briefly considered the proposal but soon reached the conclusion that whatever she promised would soon be forgotten.

"No. Just let me leave. I'll call the cops."

"I just want to talk." A tang of desperation now entered her tone. The sensible option for Chris was to hot foot it back to the office and call the law enforcement. But what would it achieve? Debbie would almost certainly be gone by the time they arrived. Chris would have to give a statement. He wouldn't get back in time for Katelyn. There would be questions from her. No. Chris without warning flanked Debbie, charging straight past her to the passenger door. Debbie briefly moved towards him but quickly realizing she wouldn't make it, doubled back towards the driver's door. Chris leapt into the vehicle hitting the door lock on the driver's side in a single movement. Debbie got her hand to the door handle but was a split second too late.

She then elected to race around, although Chris had ample time to shut the passenger door and press the central locking button. He was briefly safe but didn't want to hang around to find out what her next move would be. Ungainly clambering himself into the driver's seat, he started the engine. Debbie was down, but not yet beaten. The car was backed into a space with the perimeter fence directly behind. Chris could only move the car forward to get away. Debbie stood directly in front of the vehicle to block this avenue. Staring directly into her eyes Chris only saw anger and determination. This was absolutely terrifying. He selected drive and started to creep the car forward. The bumper pressing against her legs, slowly forcing her back. She placed both her hands on his hood, desperately trying to halt his progress. Chris continued the slow progression forward. Although she was powerless to prevent his advancement, it was not feasible for Chris to continue the status quo much longer. It occurred to Chris, if Debbie decided to lie down in front of the car he would be totally stuck. He had to gain enough room behind to reverse, so before she had chance to consider this tactical move Chris increased his rate of forward movement.

"Stop the car." She screamed at him through the windshield. "Stop now." He didn't, continuing to push her backwards. Gradually adding left turn on the steering wheel, Chris directed her towards the lot entrance. A quick check of his mirror told him he had just enough rearward space to back up, then race forward taking a different line. Without warning Chris hit reverse and sped backwards. Debbie, with all her weight and pressure on the hood fell forwards onto the floor with the sudden removal of her support.

Chris slammed on the brakes, inches before he reversed clean into the lot's boundary. As he reselected drive, he span his other hand clockwise desperately on the steering wheel, almost achieving full right lock before pulling sharply away.

Debbie had not remained on the floor, springing up like a gazelle and running diagonally across, towards the front of his vehicle to reacquire her control on the situation. She reached the front corner as the vehicle sharply lurched forwards. Chris heard a significant thump as it struck her knocking her down out of view. He continued forward down into the lot until she came into sight in his rear-view mirror. Debbie rested awkwardly on the hard surface. Chris stared in horror. What had he done? He could feel bile rising up in his throat as he circled the car back around to face her and the only exit.

He thought about just speeding off, but that didn't seem right. Even in these extreme circumstances, he was a caring guy. He wanted Debbie out of his life, but not hurt, or worse. Maintaining a safe distance, he crept the car closer, lowering his window. Debbie was face down and still had not moved.

"Debbie?" he called out. Nothing. "Debbie, are you okay?" Finally, she began to stir. Chris sat statue still, waiting, without any clue what to do. Eventually Debbie bought herself into a sitting position, plainly dazed and confused. She looked around aimlessly until she located Chris looking down at her from the vehicle. "Are you ok?" He repeated.

"You hit me." She uttered. Her voice filled with disbelief.

"I'm sorry. I didn't mean to." Chris's words trailed off. The two just stared at each other. "Where are you hurt?" Debbie didn't answer, Chris could detect her mind working overtime. From sincere concern came misgivings, she was about to try and work the situation to her advantage.

"I don't know if I can stand. Can you help me up?" Chris considered the danger. His suspicions immediately validated. At this point he was not going to leave the vehicle.

"Where are you hurt? Is it your leg?"

"Sugar, please help me up." She begged.

"I can't." Chris answered decisively. Once the words sank in, Debbie sluggishly started to move, attempting to get to her feet. Chris did not hesitate in pulling further forward, closer to the exit and further away from Debbie. He spectated uncomfortably from his wing mirror as she eventually stumbled to her feet. He could not determine whether she was genuinely hurt or making the most of the opportunity. As soon as Debbie was fully upright, she began to stagger towards Chris's vehicle.

"You bastard." She hollered. That was enough for Chris. Without another thought he rapidly departed the scene.

Chapter 8

The doorbell rang. Chris vaulted off the couch as if it were electrified. Praying it was not Debbie, that she had not been proficient enough to locate his home residence. In the present situation it was his only lasting safehold. After racing home following the parking lot confrontation, Chris had desperately attempted to get himself into a state of composure. He needed to get Debbie out of his head, focus on Katelyn.

Chris checked the spyhole, looking out on the open-air staircase leading directly to his apartment from the ground. The building, previously a civil defense administration block, disused and run down, its destiny appeared sealed to history. However, following a major firestorm back in 2017 which devastated forty-five thousand acres of the Santa Rosa territory, the building and surrounding area was completely redeveloped. This was now an up-and-coming district, a desirable location to reside. He immediately recognized Katelyn and unlocked the door.

"Welcome." He greeted, as she stepped in.

"Hi." She faintly responded. Chris studied her, she looked fatigued. Carrying a massive psychological weight. Katelyn glanced up at Chris, forming the familiar smile, albeit tinged around the edges. After a hug they took to the couch. Chris poured two glasses of wine he had readied on the coffee table. "Thanks." She offered, immediately taking a sizeable drink from the glass.

Katelyn spoke about her day, informing Chris of all the things they had arranged throughout. Chris listened intently, almost too eagerly as he attempted to block out other thoughts. Not wishing Katelyn to detect he had his own woes to manage. Besides the obvious desire to conceal the whole sordid affair, he was aware Katelyn might misinterpret his preoccupation as disinterest towards her own plight.

As she recited events her hands began to animate, as they often did. Every so often she would realize her involuntary actions and drop her hands down. Occasionally one would fall onto Chris's leg. Her touch even through suit pants was a pleasant sensation. Frequent temptation to take another much-awaited kiss manifested, the inappropriate context of discussion prevented him.

Chris noticed her glass was now empty. He picked up the bottle attempting to pour her another, but her hand moved over the glass.

"Thanks, but I'd better not. I have to drive back."

"Sure thing. Anything else I can get you?"

"A glass of ice water would be great, if it's not too much trouble?"

"No trouble at all." Chris got up from the couch and prepared the chilled beverage. As he came back into the room, he noticed Katelyn had sat forward. She was watching him intently. Something appeared more alive in her persona, he could not put his finger on it. Chris placed the drink down and returned to the couch. Katelyn taking no interest in the glass shuffled closer to Chris, making eye contact, not attempting to say anything. Undoubtedly, she had decided this was to be the moment. Moving slowly toward him, she leaned in until their lips touched. Initially the pressure was reserved and soft. Incrementally the compression increased, intensity gradually mounted. Arms became wrapped, tongues explored, tensions evaporated.

Katelyn slowly slid herself back, flicking off her sneakers with her feet as she did so. Within moments Chris was on top of her, fully laid out on the settee. Briefly he broke away from the kiss. Lifting his head, just to look at her. In the soft light directly beneath him she looked perfect. Not a thing he would change about her. Her cheeks were reddened, her mouth remained open in anticipation, breathing heavy, eyes imploring. Perfect.

Chris resumed his advance, reconnecting his mouth with hers. His hand slid slowly across her skimpy summer top, running over her breasts. Through the thin material and slender bra beneath he could feel every detail of her pertness. Reaching the area directly over her nipple he sensed the firmness through his fingers. Chris gently massaged the area, causing Katelyn to tense her entire body. He lifted his head again allowing her to release a moan of gratification. Chris lowered his head down to her bosom, replacing his fingers for his tongue, circling around her covered nipple. Squirming slightly under Chris's weight Katelyn pulled her top upwards, taking the bra with it to reveal herself. Chris dived onto the newly exposed flesh. His mouth and tongue working feverishly on the nipple. His left hand raised to tenderly caress the other. Taking his time, enjoying the moment. No thought for what came next.

Katelyn's satisfaction was palpable. Her body tensing with the lavishing of stimulation. Her hands gently caressed the back of Chris's head, letting her fingers flow through his smooth brown hair. Eventually the hands shifted their attention, moving delicately down his body. When they reached his buttocks, she gripped both cheeks, pressing towards herself powerfully. Chris lunged his body forward in unison. Through jeans and pants, she could feel his arousal against her. The sensation was startling, as if she was on the edge already. Several times she repeated the pressure squeeze. On every cycle Chris responded. The pressure and friction reaching her most intimate location with each occurrence. He bought his head up to hers, their eyes converging.

"I want you." She whispered, an odd throaty husk in her voice. "Right now."

The voice of reason jerked him from an out-of-focus trance.

"Chris, I need to get going." He lifted his head slightly, a goofy half-asleep look upon his face. Tightly entangled, completely naked on the couch, Chris returned to the here and now. Katelyn's face inches from his, her soft pale flesh merged indistinguishably with his tanned physique.

"Stay the night." Chris pleaded.

"I'd love to do that more than anything, but I have to go home now." She replied kindheartedly. Chris understood her personal situation but could not help making a final plea.

"Please don't leave." He uttered as he moved in for an uninvited kiss. Katelyn seized the kiss without hesitation, but soon her hands remonstrated, it was leading nowhere.

"I'm sorry, I really have to go." Chris sighed an exaggerated breath out, as way of concession. Slowly they untangled their naked bodies. Chris watched with interest as Katelyn sourced her discarded clothing on the floor. She made no attempt to conceal herself, indicating her comfort of totally exposing herself to Chris. Once the point of dressing covered any aspect of special curiosity, he sat up.

"I'll walk you out to your car." Chris quickly tossed on his clothing. Before letting her leave, he stole one more passionate kiss.

They quietly exited down the staircase in an air of mutual satisfaction. It was another hot sticky evening, a world away from the cool air-conditioned apartment they had just departed. Chris felt unsteadily light on his feet as he made his way down the steps to ground level. Reaching the bottom, Chris gently grabbed Katelyn, pulling her into him.

"Are you okay?" He asked, their eyes uniting yet again. Katelyn smiled and delicately touched his face.

"Yes. I am."

After another embrace, Katelyn led him to where she had parked her vehicle, seemingly a lifetime ago. When it came into view, the entire atmosphere dramatically turned on its head. As Chris struggled to fully process the scene, white hot dread plummeted into his stomach.

Chapter 9

"Oh my God." Katelyn uttered. Her voice tinged with disbelief. They both walked closer to the vehicle to inspect the damage. Every panel violently scratched, ripping through paint, primer, and bare metal alike. This wasn't the work of some mindless delinquent forcing keys up the side as they walked by. This was pure aggression. Haphazard scores were everywhere, the depth counting more as grooves than scratches. Katelyn walked around the vehicle with her hands to her mouth. Horror cemented on her face. From every angle the damage was absolute.

"Bitch." Chris murmured to himself. It came out louder than intended, causing Katelyn to glance at him. "Son of a bitch." Chris artificially corrected. Katelyn bought it, returning her attention to the defunct car.

"Who would do this?" She asked rhetorically. "I'm going to call the cops." Chris squirmed a little. His nasty little secret was getting harder to conceal. Should Officer Rufus attend, this could add to the complication. Katelyn had not waited for any confirmation from Chris, immediately dialing 911. Once the operator connected her to the police despatcher, Katelyn gave her account of what had occurred. Chris listened intently to the one-sided conversation audible to him. Soon able to gather they were not going to send a car out. She would have to go to the station to report the incident. Katelyn was clearly not pleased at this news, her emotions running high after the untimely demise of her father. She became quite animated, demanding a unit come out. All to no avail. She hung up the cell angrily.

"They're not even gonna send anyone out." Katelyn complained. "I've got to go to the station to report it." Chris shrugged his shoulders, not sure what he could say. "It's probably pointless, they won't investigate it. They're just not interested. She told me the best course of action was to claim on my insurance."

Katelyn began pacing up and down the road alongside her vehicle, clearly attempting to calm herself down. Inwardly Chris was panicking. There was one plausible explanation for the targeted attack on Katelyn. While relieved to not have direct police involvement at this specific time, he had to take action to end this assault on his freedom. No longer able to run, Debbie was at every turn. He considered coming clean to Katelyn. In her current state he wasn't sure how that influx of news would be accepted. Every which way he considered it, permanent if not terminal damage to their friendship, and now their relationship would result. He was completely boxed in.

From the intersection up the road, a vehicle turned in their direction. It was a quiet neighborhood and traffic was sporadic at this time of evening. Katelyn was still out in the street pacing up and down oblivious to the approaching headlights. Tension raised quickly within Chris, at this point anything appeared possible. He had no knowledge who was behind the wheel. Katelyn was in a vulnerable position oblivious further threat was potentially heading her way. Chris watched its approach, something about the speed of the vehicle did not sit right. It was traveling too slow. Any vehicles on these deserted roads at this time of night, either hit or exceeded the speed limit. The approaching car was not crawling but travelling noticeably beneath normal speeds.

"Katelyn. Get off the street." Chris instructed as he moved towards her. She turned her head, noticing the headlights moving her way. She did not share Chris's concern and stood motionless looking into the beams. It was now too late for her to move to safety, even if she wanted to. Chris broke into a short sprint, arriving out in front of her, attempting to offer some protection from the impact he was sure was imminent. Katelyn stepped back, putting her hands up in alarm. Chris's dramatic movement coupled with the reaction of the lone female in the road certainly attracted the attention of the driver. The vehicle abruptly stopped with an audible squeal of tires. A second later, blue and red neon lights flooded the roadway accompanied by a single wail of the distinctive siren. It was a cop car.

Katelyn gave Chris *a what the hell* bemused look, before stepping past him waving to attract the attention of the officer, despite it already being clearly achieved. The driver's door opened. A silhouetted figure moved quickly behind the door. Chris could not tell if it was Officer Rufus.

"Hands up where I can see them." He commanded in an authoritarian tone. Chris recognized the voice did not belong to Rufus. Both raised their hands above their heads. It felt a little over the top, but until the cop could ascertain what was transpiring, anyone was a direct threat. Chris could identify.

The officer swept towards them, gun still holstered, but his hand placed directly on it to react should the need arise. He patted down Chris first, then Katelyn. Once satisfied neither was harboring a concealed weapon, he backed off towards the vehicle.

"Stay where you are." He shouted. Without removing them from his line of sight he pulled his shoulder radio to his mouth and called in to dispatch. Protocol followed, he returned.

"Mam, what is happening here?"

"Someone has vandalized my car. Look." The cop gazed past her to the stricken vehicle.

"Who is this?" He asked, gesturing to Chris.

"My friend. I was visiting him. I went to go home, to find this."

"Mam, why was he grabbing you?"

"I just…" Chris started but was abruptly cut off by the officer.

"I asked her, not you."

"I honestly don't know. Possibly he thought you were going to run me down?" She answered.

"Is that correct sir?"

"Yes." Chris quickly got out. "Her car is trashed, then this car is travelling down the street, looking strange. I guess I just panicked." The cop took a few seconds, computing all the information, the corroborating evidence, the body language. Finally deciding it stacked up, and the risk of threat was low. He updated dispatch on the radio. Next, he instructed both to lower their hands while pulling out his flashlight. He walked around the vehicle, assessing the full extent of the damage.

"Someone did a real number on this." He commented, his tone dramatically different. "Have you reported it?"

"Yes." Snapped Katelyn. "They weren't interested." The cop gave a nod of recognition.

"I understand your frustration. We're just overworked and undermanned. We are interested." Katelyn nodded glumly, accepting the statement. "Any idea who did it?"

"I have no idea." She quickly responded. Chris shifted slightly but said nothing. The cop looked up from the car, directly at Chris.

"And you sir?"

"I don't know. Nothing like this happens in this area." The officer held his stare. Chris did not look away, but knew he looked guilty. Eventually the cop turned and shone his flashlight over the neighboring parked cars.

"Only this car damaged. Strange, no?"

"Yes." Katelyn slowly responded, considering this information.

"Either of you upset anyone recently."

"No." They both responded.

"Mam, when you drove over here did you have any kind of incident? Cut up another vehicle perhaps?"

"No. I don't think so. I can't recall anything."

"Okay, there's not much I can do. My advice is to take plenty of photos now before you move the vehicle. Take more photos in daylight. Report it to your insurance company and follow their instruction. They may insist you make a police report, or they may just process it anyway. If you learn of any other information, then come into the station."

"Okay." Katelyn responded. "It's just so unfair. Can't you take fingerprints or something? DNA?"

"We don't have the budget to use those resources on this kind of thing. I wish there was more I could do for you, but with no suspect or motive..." The cop's voice trailed off.

"it's just so unfair." She repeated.

"Yes, I totally agree. Sorry I can't do more. Have a good evening." He turned back towards his vehicle, the blue and red still strobing out across the nearby apartments.

"Thank you." Chris meekly offered. The light show extinguished and the police SUV pulled away into the night. Chris and Katelyn looked at each other aimlessly.

"Do you still want to go to the police station?" He asked. "I'll come with you." Despite his offer, he did not want to attend for obvious reasons. He also understood it would appear pretty callous of him not to offer.

"No. I want to go back to work tomorrow. It's late and we both need sleep. I'll call the insurance company at lunch and go from there." She threw her arms around Chris and took a comforting embrace.

"Okay Katelyn, whatever you want to do, I'm here for you."

"Thanks." After capturing a handful of photos on her phone, she got in her car and drove off. Chris, left behind at the roadside surveyed the area, looking in the shadows. *Was she out there, watching it all unfold? What was she going to do next? Where would all this end?*

Chapter 10

Chris got up before his alarm rang. Moving around the apartment as if a ghost of himself. Barely obtaining a hint of sleep all night. His mind whirring between the momentous evening with Katelyn, the parking lot incident at work, discovering Katelyn's car, and primarily what was waiting for him today. Debbie, it seemed, was capable of anything. He did not know if he was in actual danger. More concerning was he may have just moved the unsuspecting love of his life into Debbie's crosshairs. Chris looked at his home office desk, the restraining order petition forms sat under a couple of other pieces of paperwork. Deliberately concealed from Katelyn last night. He would complete them as soon as he returned later, then take time out of the office tomorrow to get it notarized and submitted.

He left for the office half an hour early. He wanted time to spare should he need it. As he pulled into the previous evening's parking lot of terror, all appeared calm. Not many vehicles in residence on account of his premature arrival. He selected a space where he was unlikely to get blocked in and shut off the engine. Scanning the area, it was abundant with potential hiding places. No way he could prevent a potential ambush. No further option but to brave the walk to the lobby.

Chris walked at a steady pace, looking all around. Part of him wanted to make a dash to the door, but the overriding instinct was to challenge Debbie if she appeared. Katelyn would shortly be following Chris on this stroll. Any confrontation should be directed at him, not her. Reaching the lobby door without incident only heightened his anxiety. Had she allowed his safe passage for other objectives?

Before Chris entertained any thoughts of switching into work mode, he made himself a strong coffee. The constant adrenaline rushes combined with nonexistent sleep were overwhelming. He took it into his office and attempted to deal with the mountain pile of unread emails.

It was hard to focus. Every time the goldfish entrance door opened, Chris looked to see who had arrived, willing it to be Katelyn. Safe and in one piece. His mind was engulfed in the stress of this repeated process, until finally the door clicked and in she stepped, looking as tired as Chris. As she walked by, she glanced into his office. Sighting Chris, she gave a warm smile. He returned it, filled with relief. Katelyn continued to her workstation as normal. After a few minutes to steady his fractured nerves, Chris was finally able to concentrate on his work. Although the sensation, it was just a matter of time before circumstances changed, never moved far from the forefront of his thoughts.

Revealing the fate of her late father to the office, the attention on Katelyn had peaked and then slowly disbursed. She hadn't mentioned last night or the incident with her vehicle to anyone.

Once the visits of concerned or sympathetic colleagues died down, Katelyn took a small pile of invoices into Chris to check before they were processed and paid. This was normal office activity and did not raise any attention. As she entered his office Katelyn discretely slid his door ajar. Closing it fully, generating a click certainly would have attracted the attention of the office gossips, hungry for the next scoop.

"Hi." Chris greeted her with a warm smile.

"Hi you."

"How are you?"

"I'm good. Totally pissed about my car, but what can you do?"

Chris shrugged his shoulders. "It's crap. Kinda took the edge off a good night."

"I really enjoyed it, until then. Fucking asshole." She agreed.

"No regrets on what we did?"

"Not at all." She gave a muted laugh. "Far from it. You?"

"The same." Chris said with a smile. "How's your mom doing?"

"Bearing up." She paused still considering the question. "It's early days. I think we need to get the funeral over with, then she can start to grieve."

"And you?"

"The same. I guess I have a good friend to support me?"

"You do." Chris confirmed with certainty.

They completed the personal chatter, Katelyn went over the invoices and then returned to her desk. Every so often one would catch the other just gazing at them. An awkward knowing smile would follow. This should be the fun, carefree stage of the newly formed relationship. For Chris it was all tinged in fear and deception.

Katelyn's lunch break was consumed by reporting last evening's incident to her insurance. She had not undertaken this task in the office. Again, avoiding the gossipmongers was always a consideration at Haskins & Wilcox. Chris watched her step out, knowing what she was doing. As previously, he was taken by the dread of Katelyn leaving the security of the office. Outside, totally at the mercy of Debbie. Not a trait she demonstrated habitually.

It was a painful, lengthy wait for her return. Eventually she did. With much of the office at lunch, Katelyn popped her head into his office.

"The insurance was really helpful. I've got some electronic forms to fill out, but I don't think they're going to make an issue of it." She said discreetly.

"Good, it's the last thing you need right now." Chris agreed. At that point Katelyn pulled a puzzled expression.

"What's this I'm told, about a muffin basket?" She quizzed.

"It was left on my desk, but there was no card. I'm not even sure if it was for me." He lied. "I just put it out there for everyone." Katelyn slowly nodded her head, mulling over the explanation. Chris hated this constant dishonesty. He was trapped within a web of lies.

"Mystery." Katelyn simply responded. She returned to her desk and the afternoon session began.

As the time clicked past half-four, nothing untoward transpired. Chris could not decide if this was a relief or more worrying. Had she reached her conclusion or was this the hiatus to something big? Either way the simmering apprehension began to subside within him. Then an instant message popped up from Katelyn on his desktop monitor. Unlike emails this communication platform could not be saved, short of taking screenshots. Many of the staff used this format for inconspicuous nonwork-related communication. Essentially gossiping and sending disparaging remarks about another employee. Chris clicked it open.

Fancy going for a drink after work? What about Prestons?

The mention of Prestons bought a chill up Chris's spine. Her message vanished as he replied.

Yes, but not there. Too close to work. I know somewhere nice. You can follow my car.

Katelyn sent back a thumbs up emoji. Chris considered the distinct possibility of Debs stood waiting for him by his car. He elected to test his luck. After no challenge all day, Chris was feeling substantially bolder. Maybe leaving her on the ground in the parking lot had finally conveyed his feelings towards her. It was too much to consider the vandalism of Katelyn's car a coincidence, but may have been her parting gift.

The time ran to quarter-past-five. Chris looked up observing many of the staff had departed as per usual. He caught Katelyn's eye. She instantly pulled a *get a move on face*. Chris gave a nod. Finished the email he was writing and sent it. As he motioned to turn off his monitors his eyes flicked through the list view of the most recent emails. A couple still unread. One from Susan, the HR manager titled *Admin New Starter, Sep-14*. Tomorrow. Quicker than normal to sort the recruitment, he thought, getting up to leave. A glance told him Katelyn was doing the same.

"Bye all." Chris called out to the few remaining in the goldfish bowl. He exited the door. It clicked shut, instantly reopening as Katelyn passed through. Chris called the elevator, the doors opening just as she caught up. Once inside with the doors closed, they were alone. Although the window of time was short before it reached the lobby, neither could refuse the opportunity for a brief passioned kiss and quick fondle. They arrived on the ground floor all too soon, both rapidly straightening themselves out before the doors opened. As they slid mechanically apart, both participants donned faces of innocence for whoever might be waiting to board. The lobby was empty. They looked at each other and burst into laughter. The moment felt good, but it didn't last for Chris. As they stepped outside, he understood he might be charging into the valley of death.

Mirroring yesterday the short journey to the parking lot went without incident. Chris attempted to appear relaxed but failed to prevent himself occasionally glancing behind.

"The office is going to find out at some point." She stated matter-of-factly, clearly picking up on the unusual behavior. Chris decided to buy into the misinterpretation.

"Does it worry you if they do?"

"Nope."

"Good."

They turned into the entrance. Just vehicles, not a soul in sight. The danger still wasn't over, but it was looking good. They both jumped in their cars. Chris pulled up to the exit and waited for Katelyn to catch up.

She followed close behind as Chris led them into the Windsor region. Chris kept a watch in his mirrors. Not so much at Katelyn and her ruined car, but for any other suspicious looking vehicles. Anyone who might look like they were giving pursuit. Eventually he pulled into a pleasant in appearance restaurant, neighboring Keiser Park.

"That was a bit of a drive." Katelyn complained as she got out.

"Trust me, it's worth it." Chris replied with a smile. "Tell you what, I'll buy you dinner."

"Okay, but its gonna cost you."

"I wouldn't expect any less." Chris laughed as he threw his arm around her, leaving his troubles behind.

"Wonder if they do lobster?" She teased as they walked arm in arm through the entrance.

Chris arrived home, already well past half-ten. The meal was great, the company even better. Once finished, they strolled across the park. Quiet and secluded at that time of evening, without discussion a suitably sheltered location was sourced and exploited.

Now back, Chris's fatigue caught up with him. He needed to catch up on some sleep desperately. Glancing over at his home office, the petition he had resolutely vowed to complete when he returned still sat there. Re-engaging his brain at this point was not an attractive option. Making a conscious decision, he washed and went straight to bed.

Chris awoke with the alarm. He had slept the moment his head touched the pillow. Following his normal morning routine, he left feeling much more like himself. The only notable difference, he was in love, and it was reciprocated. Debbie fell further down his list of thoughts. The sense of threat diminishing in the wind. Once in the office, he switched the monitors back on. Clicking open the first unread email in the list. The sender was a key supplier, with whom he was managing a significant order. The shipments were due to commence next week to feed substantial manhours of planned operational work for his organization. The email explained there had been a significant delay in production and the initial shipments were going to be delayed. *Shit*. Chris sat up in his seat. He wished he had read this yesterday. The implications could be massive. He phoned the supplier without pause. They explained all the reasons for the delay and how it was out of their control. Chris did not really care about the reasons. He had to renegotiate the delivery schedule. Haskins & Wilcox required some kind of delivery next week, even if it was a proportion of what was originally promised. Chris put pressure on the supplier to sort something out. It did not take long for him to relinquish. They agreed a new schedule for the next two weeks. Not even close to what had been formerly confirmed, but enough to keep production moving his side and enough to not completely upset their end customers who were all downright unsympathetic to delays beyond Haskin & Wilcox's control.

As soon as this was agreed, Chris sent an email marked with high importance, to the Operations Director, Production Manager & Planning Manager. He copied in Norman and Frank for good measure. He tailored the wording as positively as possible while breaking the bad news. With it sent, he next had to access the relevant purchase orders in the company accounting system to change the delivery dates. This would allow the planning manager to run Materials Required Planning to assess what he had and when, or rather what he didn't have.

Before he had chance to breathe, the Operations Director phoned Chris to rant and rave about his disgust at the newly announced delays. Chris kept his cool, stuck to the facts and pointed out what he had done to at least minimize the damage. Eventually the director calmed down. Chris was relieved to end the call amicably. The Production Manager however had been waiting for Chris's line to become free. As soon as Chris put the phone down it rang again. He had to go through a near identical conversation. The phone eventually went down and to his relief did not ring instantly again. Chris breathed out heavily and sat back in his chair. Over an hour had passed since Chris last looked outside of his office windows. The goldfish bowl was fully populated, everyone well into their working day. He watched Katelyn for a short while. She was talking on the phone, but her conversation appeared much less controversial than his last succession of heated debates. She was smiling as she talked. Chris watched in awe. So attractive, full of fun and charming to boot. The looks and personality combination does not come along often. He knew he was lucky.

Turning his concentration back to the computer screen, Chris continued through the unread list. He prayed the remainder would not contain any other unwanted surprises of the same magnitude. He opened the next, the one from HR regarding the new starter. As he read on, his chin hit the floor. This was not another piece of unwanted news of the same magnitude. The content, infinitely worse than that.

Chapter 11

Chris read the words over and over. Sat rigid in his seat, hands squeezing desperately at the arm rests.

Hi All,

FYI, we have a new starter in Admin to replace Sarah, starting Wednesday Sep 14. Her Name is Deborah Green but calls herself Debs. She has substantial previous experience, working in data administration and analysis for a pharm-aceutical development company. Many of the skills are transferable. She will hopefully be able to develop beyond her initial role. Please make her feel welcome.

Best Regards
Susan

Chris did not dare to look up in the direction of Sarah's old workstation. He could not bring himself to do it. Body physically immobile, his petrified eyes flicked left towards Katelyn. Still chatting, smiling, completely unaware. Chris forced himself to turn his eyes to the right and sure enough, there she was. Sat at a desk. A bona fide employee within his company.

Chris fused to his seat, could not move, could not think. This was unbelievable. He needed time to process how this could happen. More importantly to consider what his next move would be. The workstation was located where Debbie mostly had her back towards Chris. For her, not a great vantage point. Chris however, able to monitor her with relative ease. He was not sure how that helped but felt as if he had some kind of advantage. For everything else, clearly, she was calling the shots.

Transfixed on the shark in his boat, Chris failed to notice Katelyn get up and approach his office. As she strolled casually in, he almost leapt off his chair.

"Steady." She laughed. "Bit jumpy this morning?"

"Yeah, didn't see you coming." He replied as nonchalantly as he could manage, retaking the seat.

"Unlike last night?" She naughtily retorted in a whisper. Chris laughed nervously but failed to find a comeback. "You alright? You look shaken up." Chris hesitated. At this point he knew the game was up. No choice but to do the right thing, come clean to Katelyn. Once the charade was admitted, he could take steps to address his stalker once and for all. However, this probably wasn't the right moment to confess. He needed to buy a little more time.

"Sorry. I've had a real nightmare morning. We've been badly let down by a supplier that will have a massive knock-on effect. I'm stuck in the middle, getting all the heat." Katelyn nodded understandingly.

"Okay, I'll leave you to it. Maybe help you relieve your stress later tonight?" Clearly Katelyn was already engaging in the previous evening's conversation of not bothering to be inconspicuous about the change in their relationship status. The door was wide open, and her last comment spoken at a normal level. One of the ladies stationed closest to the door lifted her head, looked across, then turned back, as if she caught the comment.

"Speak later." Chris confirmed. Katelyn exited, then walked into the office kitchen. Chris turned his eyes back to Debbie. Still sitting there as if she were the model employee. After a breath, he picked up his phone. Finger hovering over the speed dial to Susan, the prickly HR manager. Hesitating, he slowly replaced the handset. Before acting, he needed to think this through.

Over the next few hours leading up to lunch, Chris regarded his assailant. Nervously peering over his monitors, he waited for Debbie to turn her head towards him. She remained transfixed on her own screen, quietly working through her induction training package. Seemingly oblivious to Chris's presence. A multitude of questions ran through his thoughts. All without an answer. The obvious move, to meet today with Susan. Come clean about the whole situation. Directly after work, do the same with Katelyn. Once executed he could populate the restraining order petition form, ready to action tomorrow. Whatever the fallout professionally and personally was to be. There was no choice but to face it now. Any postponement continued to leave him open, permitting inevitable further attacks.

As lunchtime hit, the goldfish bowl rapidly emptied. Katelyn rose from her desk, walking past Chris's office. With cell in hand, she pointed to it and mouthed "Car insurance." Chris nodded, watching her proceed out the door. His fervent observation soon witnessed Debbie leaving her workstation, entering the kitchen. The office was virtually empty, if Chris was going to confront her, now was the opportunity. Not a considered plan of attack, but as the chance presented itself, the opening was hard to resist.

Chris quickly stood, departing out of his private room. He glanced around, surveying the office. The few remaining in the bowl were situated at the far end, well out of ear shot. As it was lunchtime some had Bluetooth earbuds in anyway, enjoying music as they doom scrolled through social media. Chris wasted no further time, entering the kitchen. He closed the door, eyes on Debbie within the narrow galley. Her back to him, making a coffee. As the door clicked shut, she jumped, spinning around in surprise. The instant realization it was Chris broke her into a joyful smile.

"Hello Sugar." Debbie beamed.

"What the fuck are you doing?" Chris mutedly growled.

"It's my first day here Sugar, starting my new job." She replied sweetly, as if they were engaged in completely natural conversation. Chris just stared in disbelief. "Would you like a coffee? Or if we're quick I could buy you a sandwich across the road?" Chris chose to ignore the questions.

"What are you doing here?" Chris's voice rose in volume.

"Sugar, I told you. I got a job here. I think it's gonna be a great place to work." Chris struggled to fathom her level of delusion. "It's gonna be swell working together, but we've gotta be professional. No blowjobs under your desk or anything." She laughed at her own quip.

"Are you crazy? Why are you doing this to me? I'm sorry if our one-night stand hurt you, but I want nothing more to do with you."

"The door's shut." She announced, looking past him at the closed door. "We're totally alone. Do you want me to jerk you off right now Sugar?"

"No. Fuck's sake." Chris, in exasperation put his head in his hands for a moment. "I don't understand you. Stop calling me fucking Sugar." Blood boiling.

"Sugar, it's just a job. It's important for me to work right now, who knows, I might be pregnant." The comment lit the touch paper within Chris. Like a tightly coiled spring, all the pressure and tension exploded within him.

"Pack your fucking stuff up right now and fuck off." Control lost, now screaming at Debbie. "If you're still here in five minutes, I'm gonna grab you by the hair, drag you down the stairs headfirst and throw you out on the fucking street." As he concluded the idle threat, immediate regret formed. Words purely used as a venting tool, lacking any truth behind the intimidation. In the moment of pure rage, harsh vocabulary just spilt out. Debbie stood looking at him, calm. Almost a grin on her face. Chris span around, yanking the door open and stormed out.

Stood outside, clearly returning from lunch, stood Cassey and Lucy. Both opened mouthed, staring horrified at Chris. Terror welded into their faces. His heart sank. Pushing past them, Chris hit the stairs, quickly exiting the building. He ran to his car without thinking, once inside he threw his head in his hands. How could he have played this so wrong?

Chapter 12

Sat alone in the car for over an hour, fluctuating emotions flowed through Chris. Panic, anger, despair, all had visited and departed. Finally, a resolute determination filled him. This was over. One way or the other, it stopped here and now. He made a decision to stick to his original plan. Pulling out his cellphone, Chris rang Susan's direct line. The single intention to arrange a meeting with her, right now. It went straight to voicemail. *Shit*. He phoned Annika, Susan's assistant. She picked up.

"Hi Annika, its Chris."

"Hi Chris."

"I need to meet with Susan on an urgent issue, but her phone is set to voicemail." He explained calmly.

"Er, she's currently in a meeting right now."

"Can you interrupt and ask her to phone me? As I say, it's really urgent."

"Sorry Chris. I can't do that. Her blinds are down." Annika replied politely. Chris cursed inwardly. Now victim to another Haskins & Wilcox unwritten rule. Meetings could be, and were habitually disturbed, when urgency dictated. But when the blinds were down in Susan's office, it did not matter if the building was on fire, even if it was Armageddon outside, you did not interrupt.

"Please can you have her call me immediately, as soon as she becomes available? As I say it's extremely urgent."

"Yes, of course Chris."

The call ended. Aggravation bore into his stomach, desiring to act, right now. Commence this journey of resolution. Instead, he was trapped in his car accomplishing nothing. Minutes later his cell rang. He grabbed it quickly anticipating the call back from Susan. The caller was Katelyn. At this point he did not know if the office was alight with scandal at his austere riposte targeted at Debbie. Or if Cassey and Lucy had spoken directly with Debbie afterwards and kept what they had witnessed to themselves. Katelyn might be calling innocently wondering where he was. Alternatively, if the shit had hit the fan, to find out what the hell was going on. Either way he had to deal with Susan first before starting with Katelyn. He let the call ring off.

Sometime afterwards Susan finally called.

"Chris?" She asked.

"Yes, I need a meeting urgently please."

"Where are you?"

"In my car in the parking lot."

"Please come up now."

"Okay bye." The call ended. Chris could not help but notice Susan had her innate human resources voice on. The two had often chatted as friends within the relationship of colleagues. Her normal voice and manner of speaking was notably different to her professional tone. She never spoke to him in the uniformed monotone when it was just the two of them, until now.

Concerned, Chris rapidly made his way back into the building, taking the elevator to the floor above his office. The top floor, where the directors, the boardroom and the HR department were located. The corridor leading to her office was intentionally private. No desks of onlookers to observe who was coming and going out of her office. The sole exception was Annika, her desk located directly outside to act as a personal assistant and secretary combination. Chris reached Susan's office. The blinds were down, the door firmly shut. Chris glanced at Annika. She looked up at him through her thick glasses.

"You can go in." She offered.

With a lump in his throat, Chris gave the door a courtesy knock before opening. Susan was not at her desk but residing on her meeting couch. Two green leather sofas, placed to face each other with a small glass table in between, providing an intentional separation. Placed on the table, a box of tissues. Sometimes required by the person sat on the opposite couch. On Susan's side, residing in a desk chair, sat Norman. Neighboring, yet distinctly detached.

"Hi Chris, please take a seat." She instructed with a serious expression and the same flat tone. Norman's face corresponded proportionately to the atmosphere she had established. Chris quietly took a seat, sensing his breathing quickening in the knowledge whatever was impending was not good for him.

"Thank you for coming." Susan stated. *She's treating this meeting as if she summoned me*, Chris immediately thought to himself. "I've invited Norman to sit in on this meeting due to the gravity of the situation." Norman sat motionless, as if an ornament within the room.

"I'm sorry, but I'm confused." Chris interrupted. "I asked to meet you, to report a serious issue happening to me. However, it's clear before we even start, I'm being viewed as a perpetrator, not the victim." Chris had no idea what had already transpired, but he was savvy enough to gauge the mood and take steps to mitigate himself before the inevitable accusation was leveled against him.

"Chris, you are correct. A complaint was made against you this afternoon. The nature of which is very concerning." Susan spoke in a matter-of-fact patter, yet a soft undertone amalgamated her words. "I can tell you now, no conclusions have been drawn. This is your opportunity to provide your context on matters and enlighten us on your own concerns." While it all sounded very plausible and fair, Chris knew Susan and Norman would have already discussed the testimonials, drawing conclusions on the one-sided accounts. Chris would now have to prove his innocence.

Susan produced an electronic recording device, setting it on the table. "We'll have to record this meeting, in line with company policy." Chris gave a small nod of consent. He glanced again at Norman. He still hadn't moved, his eyes fixed, but on nothing. After starting the recorder, she announced the time, date, the person's present and the type of meeting. She referenced it as a disciplinary investigation meeting.

"Okay, let's get started." Susan straightened a notepad on her lap, glancing through the top page. "At two this afternoon, two employees came to me to report an incident of violent conduct they had witnessed. They said when returning to the office from lunch they overheard you angrily shouting threats and abuse against our new employee, Deborah. They commented that the level of aggression was absolutely terrifying. Both employees were extremely emotional, in such a state, I had to take the decision to give them the rest of the afternoon off work." Briefly pausing, Susan looked up from her notepad, directly at him. "That's a pretty serious accusation." Chris sat silently listening to every word. Dropping his head down, shaking it from side to side to advocate his lack of agreement on the interpretation. "Chris, can you explain to me what happened?"

"You need to understand the context of what they saw." He stated firmly.

"Okay Chris, then give us the context."

"Have you asked Debbie, about the context?"

"We have." Susan confirmed but did not elaborate.

"What did she tell you?" There was an audible bitterness in Chris's tenor. He had not intended it to show, but it did.

"That's not important right now. I want your side of this."

"Well, I want to know what lies she has told against me." He countered, further emotion seeping out.

"Chris." Susan immediately replied. Her voice, polite but her tone commanding. "Until I have all the facts and statements, I will not be divulging any information. This is your opportunity to enlighten me on what has happened. Please don't waste it." The point made, Susan sat back and waited. Chris thought for a moment, then reset himself.

"I first met Debbie on Friday night, at Sarah's leaving party. I wasn't particularly interested, but at the end of the night I was quite drunk. She talked me into coming back to her place on the promise of a coffee. When we got there, she frankly forced herself on me." Chris paused briefly. He could not have made his account sound more dubious if he tried. Susan's expression was completely blank. Norman remained in his trance like state. Chris continued. "Don't get me wrong, it wasn't like I fought her off or anything. I just wasn't seeking it. Everything is such a blur. I can't even remember if we had sex. In the morning I woke up before her, realized I'd made a big mistake, so tried to sneak out. She woke up at the last minute and got really angry. Anyway, I left without delay. Since then, she has been constantly texting me. Phoning me over and over. I had to go to the police. They spoke to her over the phone, instructing her to leave me alone. It didn't stop though. She's been constantly stalking me. She tried to harass me after work on Tuesday, then yesterday, erm." Chris paused again. He was about to disclose the vandalism of Katelyn's car. He really did not want to draw Katelyn into this, so moved on. "Then this morning, I look up and she's employed here. It's totally taking over my life. I went into the kitchen to confront her and ask her to leave me alone. But she wouldn't listen. She attempted to proposition me sexually." Even the pokerfaced Susan could not help but raise a suspicious eyebrow at the last statement. "Finally, she commented she might be pregnant." Chris looked up and caught her eyes. "I know the way I reacted was not acceptable, I just completely lost it and started screaming at her. I guess it was just a release of everything she's done to me. I stormed out. Cassey and Lucy were stood there. I ran out of the building."

"Thank you Chris." Susan responded. "I have a couple of questions."

"Okay."

"The night you went back to Debbie's apartment, you're not sure if you had sexual intercourse?"

"I can't remember, I passed out. The last I can recall; she made a full-on attempt to initiate a sexual encounter. But I stopped her. Then she made me a coffee." Bafflement materialized across Susan's face. Chris did not want to elaborate on something so personal but had to clarify. "I drank the coffee but cannot remember anything else. When I woke up, I was naked beside her in her bed"

"You don't feel it was you who instigated the sexual relations? Or that they were mutual? You feel Debbie led or tricked you into sex?"

"She didn't trick me, and I didn't completely resist, but I was very drunk. I don't know if we had sex, but she was definitely the instigator."

"Okay, thank you. Moving on, you say she stalked you with loads of texts and phone calls?"

"Yes, they were constant. She wouldn't stop."

"Okay, do you have any of her texts on your phone you can show me to validate this?"

"No." Chris sighed. "I deleted them all off in frustration. I now realize that was a mistake."

"That's a shame." Susan agreed. "Can you estimate exactly how many texts she has sent you since your first meeting?" Chris thought about it, his heart plummeted.

"About three or four." He answered honestly. "But it was more the phone calls."

"So that's what, three or four a day?" She asked, confused.

"No, total. But as I said it was more the phone calls, there was hundreds."

"Chris you just said she was constantly phoning or texting you. Now you tell me it's a maximum of four texts."

"It was constant, but mainly the phone calls. When she kept phoning, I blocked her number, but then she kept ringing with no caller identity. I guess she decided not to send texts as I could use those as proof." He reasoned.

"Did you answer the calls without a caller ID?"

"No. I didn't want to encourage it by engaging."

"So, if the caller identity was blocked, how do you know it was actually Debbie ringing each time?"

"I answered once and it was her, and the cop answered when I was reporting it at the station. He told her to leave me alone."

"But you have no proof, any of the other calls were from her? It's just your assumption?"

"I know it was her." Chris sat forward, validating his previous claim.

"Okay. Let's move on. What can you tell me about an incident in the employee parking lot on Tuesday?"

"As I said, she tried to harass me after work on Tuesday. She was waiting for me by my car. She wouldn't let me get in, then she tried to block me from driving off. She's a lunatic." Chris was beginning to raise his voice as the excitement took control. He stopped and inwardly calmed himself.

"Anything you want to add on that incident?"

"No, I don't think so. Just I was relieved to escape." Susan studied the notepad on her lap, she began tapping it with her pen. Without lifting her head, she continued.

"So, here's the problem. I have a very different account of all your statements. For much of it, it's her word against yours. But in the parking lot I have more to go on. Debbie had her job interview here on Tuesday, in the late afternoon. She parked her vehicle in our lot as she was instructed to do. After the interview, she went to the diner across the street to eat before heading home. As she reached her car, she states you walked into the lot. Surprised by the coincidence she decided to walk over to you to speak. Debbie said, you immediately became irate, shouting obscenities at her. She claimed you jumped in your car, started it, then accelerating hard, drove right at her. She says you knocked her down with your vehicle, turned around to shout more threats at her out of the car window, then just drove off.

"Ah, that's complete crap." Chris shouted, struggling to keep himself in check.

"Chris, it's very important you calm down, or I'm going to have to stop this."

"Sorry." Chris accepted. "It's just so frustrating how she is twisting the truth."

"Okay. We'll continue, but I ask you to remain calm and civil."

"Yes, okay." Chris agreed.

"We checked with Prestons, the diner across the street. They confirmed Debbie attended their premises on Tuesday. I also asked the repair garage opposite the parking lot entrance if they could check their CCTV. We don't have anything in the lot but their camera looking over the forecourt apparently also includes a view into the lot through the entrance. I'll read out what the business

97

owner replied to my email request." Susan pulled out her phone, opened the email and began to narrate the contents. "Hi Susan, No problem. I just checked the forecourt camera on Tuesday. About half-six, through the entrance you can just see a woman come into view, then immediately she is thrown up by a black vehicle striking her at speed. She is left lying on the floor in clear view of the camera. The vehicle spins around, draws alongside her. The driver can be seen shouting at her through the open window. Then as she staggers to her feet, he drives off at speed. I have saved the footage. If you want to contact the police, I will be happy to give this to them." She stopped. The room falling abruptly silent. A disconsolate tension endured. All in attendance could sense it.

"Look, yes. I clipped her with the car. It was an accident. She stood in front of me and would not let me drive home. As I tried to get away the car brushed her. She couldn't have been that badly hurt if she started work here today." Chris knew his reasoning was near futile at this point.

"So why did you not mention hitting her with the car before? That's a significant event, but you didn't even hint at offering it up until I revealed this to you."

"I didn't mention it because it makes me sound guilty when I'm not." Chris's voice was fraying more with every word.

"I have to say, it certainly does not paint a good picture for you right now, especially when you couple together today's threats of dragging Debbie down the stairs by her hair." As Susan finished her damning observation, Norman finally stirred from his inert posture. He sat up, looking Chris directly in the eyes.

"This is all very concerning Chris." He spoke softly, but with conviction. Acutely aware every word was being permanently documented on electronic file. "We want to believe you Chris, but there's so much of your story that frankly just doesn't stack up. I don't deny, it appears as if this woman has caused you some kind of friction. But the evidence and witness statements of your actions and reactions is just so far out of proportion. This is a very serious situation." Chris nodded his head. Scolded by the man at the top, he felt ashamed.

"Look Chris." Stepped in Susan. "These incidents are beyond what we can reasonably deal with as your employer. I will now pass this all on to the authorities, to properly investigate. In the meantime, I am going to have to suspend you, effective immediately. You will remain an employee and receive full pay until the outcome of the investigation. At that point we will decide on what sanctions, if any, we serve against you. Be aware the termination of your employment is one possible measure."

Chapter 13

Chris stepped into his apartment, his heart pounding. He was totally fucked. Debbie had done a real number on him. Flipped him from victim to attacker in one foul swoop. He slumped hazily into his couch, as his mind's eye pictured the scene. Cassey and Lucy approaching Susan in her office, recounting the horrific attack Chris had bestowed on poor innocent Debbie. Susan bringing the pair over to the couch, allowing them to tell their story of ignorance. Handing them both a tissue as they wept over the horrible scene they had witnessed. He could picture the whole affair as it had transpired, like some psychic voyeur in retrospect. He imagined Susan calling Debbie in to ask her what happened. This poor woman on her first day, suffering a venomous verbal attack. Debbie would lay it all on thick, no doubt. She had gone to a lot of trouble to set this all up and now she was going to milk it for all it was worth.

Almost certainly she would start off mute and defensive. Making Susan use all her tools to extract the testimony. Debbie would deliberately have held key information back, providing just enough to whet Susan's appetite, keeping her digging. Slowly stringing out every aspect, playing her like a fiddle. Allowing Susan to believe she was the one in the driving seat. Deploying all her skills and experience to unearth the facts out of the poor victim. Yet in reality, she was a patsy. Another utensil Debbie could manipulate into her web of obsession against him.

The corroborating CCTV could only have been a coincidence. Nevertheless, when you tell your lies well enough, to mirror the version that is true, a new reality is born. A parallel truth that tracks the actual facts. Just a smattering of minor details tweaked to provide a significantly different reality. The beauty of her lies, their close connection to the literal events, permitted Debbie to recall them honestly. Chris conversely, particularly with Katelyn, was trapped in a mesh of deceit, wrapping him up at every turn. When he looked back, what was his only crime? His single foul ball? Attempting to sneak out the following morning from her apartment. *Hardly grounds to bring out the electric chair.*

Regardless of truth or lies, at this point he was suspended. Potentially on a no return path to losing his job, his newfound relationship and if the police got involved; maybe more. Far more.

Sat on his couch, head in hands, Chris struggled to flesh out any possible room for maneuver. Unable to comprehend any realistic options to prevent the tidal wave of unjust scandal breaking on his shore. His attention was stunned back to the here and now. Someone knocked on his door.

For a second Chris stared without movement, endeavoring to evaluate who might be on the other side. Instantly his heart quickened. *Was it the police? To arrest him?* His mouth ran dry, his legs so weak he couldn't stand. In a conscious trance he just sat. The door knocked again. More forcefully. The effect of the reverberation jolted Chris back into reality. *Would the police really be here so quickly?* His alleged crime was hardly armed robbery. More likely, they would contact Chris by telephone and ask him to come in. Provide a statement of his own free will. On reconsideration he determined it must be Katelyn. Before leaving the employee parking lot, he had called her several times to no reply. He followed by leaving a text asking her to contact him as soon as possible. Most likely, she had driven over. Chris got up from the couch. He could only confess every detail, then hope and pray at least one person in this world would believe him.

Chris unlocked the door and swung it open. As he regarded the mystery visitor, his mouth fell silently open. It was not Katelyn, nor the authorities.

"Hi Sugar." Debbie greeted as she stepped in, totally uninvited.

Chapter 14

Completely sideswiped, it was the last person Chris expected to knock on his door. Yet at the same time he should have known this was coming. Debbie was on a mission to resurrect her imaginary relationship with Chris. Initially attempting to persuade him. Next endeavoring to seduce. When that approach failed, she advanced to harassing, quickly developing into outright stalking and intimidation. Now all those cards had been played, her subsequent act was manipulating the foundations of his entire life. To take away everything, job, freedom and Katelyn, unless he elected to play ball. Debbie had successfully racked the pins. Chris could only guess she had arrived to bowl her strike ball.

Debbie walked straight past Chris, stood utterly dumfound. As if it was her own apartment she strolled over to the couch and sat down. She looked up at Chris and patted the space next to her.

"Sugar, take a seat." Without a word Chris closed the door. As he did so, Chris's mind whirred for options. He had been naive for too long. He knew he must obtain some kind of evidence in his favor. Discreetly sliding out his cell from his pocket, he opened his office dictaphone app. Fumbling as he walked over, Chris set it to record without her knowledge. Electing to maintain some distance he opted not to sit in the indicated position next to her, instead selecting an adjacent armchair.

"Debbie, what are you doing here?" Chris placed his cellphone face down on the coffee table between them as he spoke, attempting to not attract attention to it.

"We need to talk. You're in trouble. I want to help you." She spoke with the sincerity of a close lifelong friend.

"Unless you're prepared to come clean, tell the truth to Susan and the police, you can't help me."

"Sugar, I've already told the truth. That's what has caused you all this bother. If you want me to lie to get you out of your troubles, then I will. I'll do anything you want." *Christ,* Chris thought to himself. *Does she actually believe what she's saying? Is she that crazy, her alternative reality is for all intents and purposes the truth in her twisted mind?*

"Debbie, I need you to listen and understand." Chris turned himself to fully face her, engaging directly in eye contact. "No matter what happens, whether I lose everything, go to jail, whatever. I want absolutely nothing to do with you. Ever." Chris spoke each word slowly and precisely in a vain attempt to reach her.

"Sugar, I know you're just trying to protect me from the trouble you're in, but really, there's no need. I'm here for you in good times and bad. I can help you, free you from the fix you've got into."

"You're the fix I'm in." Chris blasted back at her, all attempts to stay calm waning into nonexistence. "Why can't you just accept it and move on? We had one kiss. If we had sex, I can't even remember. It was meaningless." Chris immediately heeded his last remark had hit behind enemy lines. She did not react outwardly, but he could perceive an impact deep within her. She took a second before regaining her grip.

"Sugar, I love you. I know you love me. You can try to protect me all you like, but when you love someone, you share their pain. It's my pain as well. I can help you make this all go away. You must be brave enough to allow me."

"Do you really believe what you're saying?"

"Why wouldn't I?" Sincere candor lining the response. Chris jumped up from his seat and began pacing the living room. *How is it possible to debate and reason with someone this deluded?*

"I think this conversation is over."

"Okay Sugar, shall we go to bed instead?"

"Jesus Christ. Enough." Chris shouted. "I want you to leave. Right now."

"Sugar, please calm down." Debbie opened her arms, remaining seated. "You need a hug, poor thing." As previously, Chris's buttons were pushed to the point where control eluded him. He lurched forward, grabbing her upper arms. Forcing Debbie tersely to her feet. Realizing she could not prevent the motion, Debbie allowed him to achieve the maneuver. Once stood, she drove herself forward. Chris, not expecting the shift in weight, lost his grip. She clattered into him. Binding her arms around his upper body, planting her lips on his. In reaction Chris jolted his head back. The sudden movement and momentum caused Chris to lose balance. He staggered back, unable to regain control. His back crashed into his wall mounted television with a sickening crack.

The sudden stop in motion pressed Debbie hard against Chris. He pushed with all his might, but her arms were locked tight. Chris drove forward with his feet, thrusting her back until she lost balance. Still clenched to her cherished treasure for dear life, Debbie plummeted backwards, her legs giving way. Locked within her grapple, unable to stop the inevitable. Debbie, with all of Chris's weight on her, slammed onto the floor. The back of her head whacked the hardwood floor. In the same instant his forehead connected with her left eye, smacking into it with significant force. Chris without hesitation rolled off her, his head pounding.

Debbie lay deathly still for a few seconds. Chris gasped in fear. Before a cognitive thought formed, she began attempting to take sharp, shallow breaths. Completely winded, she lay paralyzed on the floor. Chris sat up dazed. For a period, he remained frozen, observing her fighting for breath. Blood began oozing out from behind her head. The manifestation slapped Chris back into reality. Without hesitation he jumped to his feet, running into the kitchen.

Returning seconds later with a first aid kit. Hurriedly he opened it, frantically snatching items out onto the floor. He sourced a large absorbent pad. Resorting to teeth, the sterile packaging ripped open. The pad fell to the ground. In crazed movements he grabbed it, all the while the appalling sound of Debbie frantically gasping for breath echoed around the apartment. Chris had to make a decision. A pool of blood had now formed behind her head, spreading out on the hardwood. He had to get the pad on the wound and apply pressure, necessitating lifting her head or turning Debbie on her side. If she had spinal injuries, moving her could mean paralysis.

"Debbie, Debbie, can you hear me?" She did not respond. Such was the extent of her chaotic fight for breath, Chris was unable to ascertain if she could not hear or just could not respond.

"Debbie, listen to me, can you move your legs?" Far from certain if this was the correct question to ask. Debbie noticeably moved one leg then the other. "That's good Deb's. I'm gonna roll you onto your side now. Chris recalled the recovery position from some distant first aid course. When he now needed it, his mind ran virtually blank. Attempting to get her over on her side, he clumsily accomplished the desired position revealing the gory wound. A horrifying spectacle of blood-soaked blond hair surrounding the noticeable injury. Chris placed the pad over the wound site, applying firm pressure. Debbie's breathing slowly but surely came back to her. Subconsciously he emitted calming shushing noises, as she gradually recovered from the initial trauma.

"Chris." She tenderly whispered.

"I need to get you to an emergency room." Chris softly instructed.

"No. Don't." She forced out. Her hand raised to his arm to signify her descent. Chris removed the pad briefly. The blood flow was slowing, allowing a hindered inspection of the injury. It was bad enough to require stitches, but not as severe as he first assumed. Already her impacted eye was swelling up, a reddish maroon was forming around the vicinity. It was going to be a nasty bruise. Chris folded the pad over between his fingers and applied a clean edge to the wound.

"We don't have a choice, Debbie. You need professional treatment. You have a nasty cut to the back of your head, and I'm sure a few broken ribs."

"No. It's gonna make it worse for you." She murmured. "It'll look really bad."

"It doesn't matter." Chris accepted. He knew the sight of her was a death nail in his coffin. No way he could come back from this. Certainly not professionally, but even the last thread of hope to convince Katelyn was now spent.

A sound in the apartment suddenly attracted Chris's attention. His cell was ringing. Surely it was Katelyn. Probably not the best time to take the call. He let it ring off as he kept pressure on the wound. He then remembered the whole incident had been recorded. A small sliver of restitution emerged. Eventually he moved the pad away. The bleeding had all but stopped.

"Debbie, I'm going to move over to the first aid box. Look for something to dress the wound."

"Okay." Debbie stayed in the position. Chris moved across, most of the contents were strewn across the floor from the initial panic. He found sterile wipes, adhesive sterile strips and a large, padded bandage. After cleaning the wound and her surrounding hair, the reduced severity was clear. Nowhere near the gaping wound Chris suspected. Suddenly the option of not attending the Emergency Room was valid.

"Do you think you can sit up so I can dress your head?" He asked.

"Yeah, just help me." Debbie wrapped her arm around Chris while he bought his arm around her back. Gently levering her up to sitting. Chris removed his support while Debbie clung on desperately attempting to maintain the physically close engagement. Too weak to resist, Chris successfully backed off. He cleaned the area again and applied the strips to prevent the gash from reopening. Finally, he applied the bandage. It appeared a touch excessive, but with thick hair surrounding the injury an adhesive band-aid would not be possible.

Once the amateur triage was completed, he slowly helped her onto the couch. Yet again, Chris could sense her taking more from the close physical contact than he was offering. What choice did he have but to aid her? She sat back uncomfortably, watching Chris intently. Chris squatted down to her eyeline.

"Do you want me to take you to the ER? It doesn't matter what trouble it causes. I don't mind."

"No. I don't need to go. Just let me stay here a while to recover." She pleaded weakly.

"Okay. How are your ribs? Do you think any are broken?"

"No. I don't think so. I was just winded." She responded.

"Okay. That's good. Let me get a bag of something frozen to put on that eye. Debbie nodded. Chris rose from his squatting position. As he moved across towards the kitchen, he inconspicuously swiped his cellphone off the table. Once out of sight the notifications confirmed a missed call and a text from Katelyn. He stopped the undisclosed recording, then opened the message.

Chris, what the hell is going on? You have a massive go at the new girl, then disappear. You don't answer your phone? Call me back.

Chris knew calling was currently not possible. Debbie either would eavesdrop on the whole conversation or worse make her presence known. Chris quickly replied.

Katelyn, something really bad is happening. I will call you as soon as I'm able but I can't right now. You have to trust me and I will explain as soon as I'm able. Whatever you hear about me isn't true. Please remember that. X

Chris selected the playback on his recording, placing the cell to his ear he prayed this would be the corroborating authentication of his version of events. Horror rose within him as he impatiently listened, there was nothing spoken to indicate to an independent audience the level of Debbie's delusion or culpability. Worse still the physical altercation, captured perfectly on the recording, provided the impression of Chris attacking Debbie, and seriously hurting her. There was nothing in this soundtrack to exonerate him, only to guild the noose already formed around his neck. Chris switched his cell to the do not disturb feature and placed it out of sight in the kitchen. After locating a bag of frozen corn and wrapping it in a

110

dish towel, he poured a glass of water. Ad hoc treatments in hand, he returned to care for his nemesis.

Chapter 15

Chris awoke, groggy. The effects of poor sleep enduring. Lying half upright, immediately he was aware of the figure pressed up against him. Her comatose breathing assured him Debbie was still alive. Chris's conscious thoughts gained traction promptly. What a disaster. How was he going to move forward from here? He had attempted to make a bed on the couch for Debbie. Sending her home just didn't appear an option. Dosed up on Advil she was unable to get comfortable. Somehow, she had manipulated Chris to shepherding her into his bed. While nothing improper had occurred, he had stayed with her.

Ambitions and goals at odds, this was all she ultimately desired. Chris knew, in her mind it was worth the injuries to gain this stronghold. For Chris himself, despite his predicament, forgoing all the possible ramifications, he could not be heartless. Whether her fault or his, she was genuinely hurt at his hand. His own moral compass compelled him to act with a standard of decency. To provide compassion, whether it was reciprocated or not.

Arms interwoven, as her perceived weakness prevented independent ability to make the journey, Chris rested her fully clothed on his bed. Once obtained, the physical bond had not been relinquished by Debbie. Virtually begging, she implored Chris to stay with her. Just a little while. Chris glanced at his alarm clock. It was gone four in the morning. The little while had become the best part of the night. His cell, unchecked for response from Katelyn, still discreetly placed in the kitchen.

Chris attempted to remove her arms off himself, but even in her state of pained slumber, Debbie still refused to relinquish her grip on him. Metaphorically and physically.

Chris opened his eyes. The scenario consistent, yet the parameters now different. Still interlocked with Debbie, she was now awake, observing her cherished treasure. Daylight was visible behind the blinds.

"Good morning." She whispered tenderly. Despite his transition into the conscious world, Chris detected the omittance of her pet name, Sugar.

"Hi." Chris attempted to reclaim his lost arm behind Debbie. Without protest Debbie lifted her torso to free the stricken limb. "How are you feeling?"

"Sore." She said as she stretched out, painful discomfort apparent in her action. Chris looked at her face, the bruising around her eye unambiguously apparent. The swelling however, successfully calmed by the now completely defrosted bag of corn. Left abandoned on the far nightstand. Regardless, there was no denying she had caught a firm blow. Combined with the gash on the back of her head, if she wanted to completely sink Chris, this was her coupon to success. With all the other circumstantial evidence, any attempt to account for the truth had crashed on the rocks, sinking with no survivors.

"What do you need?" Chris asked, preparing for a psycho edged retort.

"Painkillers." She answered, as if Chris was talking to a completely sane individual. The conventional response threw him completely and Chris just stared vacantly at Debbie. "Some Advil, anything." She added to confirm.

"Yeah." Chris got up from the bed, arm slightly numb, back aching from the awkward sleeping position. He collected the tablets left on the coffee table. Glancing up at his television, considering the substantial impact it had received during the brawl, it looked okay. An inconsequential relief, but still a reprieve of kind. He vacantly studied the blood pool, now fully dried on the surface of the hardwood floor. An amount surely penetrating the veneer to provide permanent staining.

Chris poured a glass of water from the faucet, seizing his phone in the process. Three missed calls from Katelyn. Chris quickly checked the log, one close to midnight last night and two this morning. He debated on sending her a courtesy text, but quickly decided against it. With the current unknowns entering into play, understanding his own footing was paramount before bringing her fully into this situation.

Sitting up, Debbie took the tablets. Her general persona appeared amiable. Chris decided to attempt to reason with her. Although all rationality pointed against any kind of positive progression, he did not possess much in the way of alternative options. Taking a seat lower down on the bed, he attempted to demonstrate willingness with a level of boundaries.

"Debbie, we're in a real mess here. What can we do to sort it out?" Again, Chris was surprised to observe her considering the question, rather than providing an instant prejudiced objective. He waited.

"Chris, you know how I feel about you." The continued notable absence of the Sugar reference provided Chris with optimism. He nodded but remained silent. "I love you completely, but I don't want to ruin your life. If you want me to lie to get you off the hook at work, then I will." The comment was as interesting as it was concerning. Debbie appeared to be demonstrating a genuine will to create a sensible dialogue, incorporating the potential to address the work situation. The point that stuck at the forefront of Chris's mind was the comment on being untruthful to achieve this. Even when calm and rational, her version of events remained the facts in her thinking. For this immediate conversation, Chris elected to overlook these noteworthy details.

"The problems at work are very serious. I really don't want the issues between you and me affecting my career."

"I understand it's really bad for you, I want to help and look after you." Debbie paused but evidently had more to add. Chris waited. "I love you Chris. I have to have you in my life. I can't go on without you. If I'm gonna get you out of this hole, you must meet me halfway. You can't expect me to get nothing back."

"Right?" A bewildered Chris responded. *So, we're part-way between bargaining and blackmail, are we?* He thought to himself. Chris knew it was important not to unnecessarily escalate the conversation so framed his reply in a measured fashion.

"The problem is Debs, you would always want more than I would give, even if I was prepared to entertain what you're proposing. As much as I want to sort this out, that is not something I can offer. I don't want to lead you on or give you false hope." He could see the hurt forming on her face, bracing himself for some kind of verbal or physical attack. Instead, she just sat there. Numerous individual tears ran down her cheeks. Eventually she gave a slight nod. *She's accepting it*, he thought.

"Chris, tell me. What is it about me you don't like? What did I do that was wrong?" Chris's mind engaged, fortunately his mouth didn't. *That you're a loony toon, totally deranged, living in some other reality, fanatically stalking someone you've known for five minutes.* The list could go on. The clearest answer would be to state he was already in love and was before they met. That would be poking the bear with a stick. Besides he had to keep Katelyn out of her mind and her sights.

"Look it's not that I don't like you and Friday night was fun, but I'm just not interested in starting a relationship right now, even a casual one. I'm sure you're a great catch for someone, but just not me. Don't waste your time on a dead end. Move on and find someone who can make you feel happy."

"No one has ever made me feel like you do. I won't ever find this again. I don't want to lose it. Lose you." *Shit, she's turning*, Chris panicked.

"Stay with me Debbie, please let's not get emotional or we're not going to sort this out."

"Can you just hold me for a bit?" Debbie pleaded, arms outstretching, a cascade of fresh tears running from her eyes.

"I'm not sure that's a good idea." Chris cautioned.

"Please, just for a bit." Not even sure why he relinquished, Chris slid up the bed. Sitting up against the headrest. Swinging his legs on, Chris allowed Debbie to bury her head into his chest. She wrapped her arms around him and wept.

Chapter 16

Officer James Rufus sipped his hot coffee. Only halfway through his shift, already utterly depleted. Triggering the familiar reverberating questioning of his choices in life. It was a major milestone to graduate as an officer of the law. Armed with strong principles and social ideals, he entered the world of the police patrol to make a positive difference. He imagined being regarded as a civic officer, working to bring trust of the police back to the street. To tackle racism within the community and his colleagues alike. He simply desired to contribute positively to his world.

Before his training was complete, the rose-tinted spectacles were already blurring. The heavy emphasis on firearm training was unmistakably the central focus. Time spent on de-escalation of situations almost felt like an afterthought. The disturbing overlying trend purposed Rufus and his fellow officers to resolve by exacting threat of maximum force, rather than refining ability to manage opportunities to defuse a situation.

Once on the streets it soon became apparent why so many officers become such authoritarian enforcers. Dealing with endless serious conflicts each and every day, under time pressure to resolve and move on to the next. The endless hostility coupled with general suspicion towards law enforcement, wearing down even the most composed individuals. Paperwork, red tape, and heightened threat of sanction encircled every infraction.

Each shift was a slog to the last, achieving only to fortify an underlying bitterness of society.

This was Rufus's hand. He had dealt it to himself, nobody else to blame. Sitting in the dull officer food hall, he took another sip. His radio crackled to life. The Incident Sergeant on duty requesting his presence. Finishing his coffee, Rufus stood up. Almost as bitter as the black liquid he gulped down. He allowed himself the pleasure of a brief stretch before making his way to the sergeant's office.

Rufus entered the incident room. A jumble of desks, seemingly placed at complete random granted the space an untidy, disorganized semblance. Throw in half a dozen officers all talking loudly on phones, mountains of paperwork, general clutter scattered across every surface. A perception accomplished of total chaos. He approached Sergeant Wilkins.

"Take a seat Rufus." The sergeant hastily instructed, quickly searching for the required document. Rufus did so. "I was given a report earlier regarding a workplace incident. An employee threatening another, including a vehicle hit and run. When I searched the names of the two involved it transpires one of them filed a report with you on Sunday about the other." Rufus looked at him blankly, waiting for more detail. Wilkins finally located the record amongst the stack before him.

"Chris Brooke and Deborah Green." He read off.

"Yes, I remember." Nodded Rufus. "Mr. Brooke came into the station, complaining she was constantly calling him. He'd had sexual relations with her on Friday night during a night out and she wouldn't leave him alone."

"Guess he was a good lay?" Wilkins joked. Rufus smiled without humor at the remark and continued.

"He showed me his cell, which was ringing, rang off then immediately rang again. I took the call. It was Ms. Green. I asked for her details, which she gave without protest. I then told her to stop calling him or I would arrest her."

"Hmmm, the report late yesterday came from the HR manager at Haskins & Wilcox. She states both parties are blaming each other, but the account of Ms. Green stacks up more than Mr. Brooke. The alleged hit and run incident, where Ms. Green was the reported victim, apparently was caught on CCTV by a neighboring business, Taylor's Auto Shop. If it wasn't for the hit and run, I'd have been happy to tear them both a new one over the phone and hope that put an end to it. As it stands, we're going to have to investigate." Wilkins sifted through the stack of reports on his desk. "Look, I'm backed right up here, I can't pass this onto the detectives. It's worse for them than me at the moment. I know you were due to go back out on patrol, but if you're up for it I can get you taken off so you can look into this."

"Yeah. Sure thing." Rufus returned enthusiastically.

"If it's straight forward, then use your best judgement. However, if this turns out to be more than what's at face value, come back to me." Wilkins handed over the report. Rufus flicked through as he rose from his seat.

"One question, you say Deborah is his colleague? It's strange he never mentioned that before."

"Yesterday was her first day at the company." Rufus nodded silently as he considered the fact with interest.

Rufus located an empty hot desk. The patrol officers did not qualify for their own desk, therefore sharing with fellow officers at the same level. He read the report, taking in all the details. Rufus had a choice to make on who to call first. Either Susan Roswell, the HR manager or one of the two suspects. He opted on Chris. The phone connected but rang off unanswered. It instantly occurred to him the phoneline out of the station automatically withheld the caller identity on cellphones. Chris probably would have suspected it was his assailant and not taken the call. He attempted Debbie.

Chris half lying, half sitting on the bed with Debbie's head on his chest was oblivious to the call. His cell was set on the do not disturb feature and left in the kitchen. Instead, filled with preoccupation on how to get this woman out of his bed, out of his apartment, out of his life. Both were startled by a buzzing between them. Debbie's cell was ringing in her pocket. She took it out, inspecting the notification. *No Caller ID* was displayed. With mild confusion forming on her face, she took the call. Although Debbie had been endlessly sobbing just a few seconds before, her voice sounded completely composed as she answered.

"Hello?"

"Hello, am I speaking with Ms. Green?"

"Yes, who is this."

"My name is Officer Rufus, from the Santa Rosa Police Department. You may recall we spoke on Sunday evening?"

"Yes, I do. Good morning officer." Chris tensed immediately. He threw a frightened look at Debbie. She instantly returned a silent gesture of reassurance back to him.

"Good morning. Is this a convenient time to talk?"

"Yes."

"A complaint has been made to us by your new employer, Haskins & Wilcox. Are you aware of this?"

"The HR manager informed me it was likely she would make a report but wanted to speak to the other party first. I was instructed to take today off while it was being addressed. I haven't spoken to her since and not checked my emails."

"Okay." Rufus paused briefly. "Now this situation appears to have developed somewhat since our last conversation. I'd really like to get your perspective on events to understand what Susan Roswell has reported to us. You agree Ms. Roswell is the HR manager?

"Yes, she is."

"Okay, good. Firstly, can I confirm yesterday was your first day of employment there?"

"That is correct officer."

"I'm interested why you would seek employment with the company Mr. Brooke is employed at?"

"It's a coincidence." She responded plainly.

"That's a pretty big coincidence."

"Is it? They're a substantial employer within Santa Rosa." While Debbie's tone was not impolite, it was direct.

"I think so. It's a consideration that is significant in my mind."

"Significant or not, I applied for the job on Thursday. I'm sure Chris has explained we met on Friday. You can check on my date of application to validate this." Chris silently eavesdropping to the side of the conversation audible, was taken aback. *Could this be true? Had she already applied before that fateful night?*

"I will check that, thank you Ms. Green. Let's move on for the moment. Mr. Brooke complained you were stalking him. He showed me his phone which was ringing with *No Caller ID*, as soon as the call went to voicemail, the caller redialed. I answered it and spoke to you, did I not?"

"Yes, that is correct."

"I took your details and warned you to stop contacting Mr. Brooke. You agreed."

"That is also true."

"So, before we consider the circumstances of further incidents, would you agree it is going to make validating other claims within this report difficult for you."

"It would, if I agreed with the report that has been submitted to you, but I am anticipating that to not be the case." Debbie returned confidently.

123

"Okay." Rufus pondered this with curiosity. "Just explain to me what happened."

"Well, yes. I was hounding Chris. When you answered the phone and took my details, I left it alone. It wasn't until I had my interview and noticed Chris in his office, that I appreciated he worked at Haskins & Wilcox. After the interview I decided it would be best to speak to Chris, to reassure him it was all a coincidence. I wanted to tell him I would leave him alone and not mention it to anyone there. I ate at the local diner across the street and waited for Chris to leave work. Lots of people left at five but Chris didn't. Eventually I gave up and returned to my vehicle in the staff parking lot. I decided to leave Chris a note instead on his windshield. As I was stood by his car, he happened to enter the lot. He assumed I was stalking him, got in his car quick and drove off. He knocked me with the vehicle by accident. He did check I was okay but once he knew that, he quickly left, I guess fearing I might do something."

"Uh huh." Rufus muttered as he took notes.

"Then when I started yesterday, he had a bit of a go at me. I tried to explain my innocence, but I guess he considered anything I said as suspect. Anyway, the argument was reported by someone else, Susan got involved and decided she knew the story. She didn't want to listen to my rationale. I asked her not to involve the police, but she was insistent." Rufus considered the testimony. Everything within her explanation appeared to be laced with deceit, yet it did fit well.

"So, if I were to phone Mr. Brooke, his version of events although skewed by the fact he believes your still stalking him, will fit with yours?"

"I'm confident his account of events will match. Look, for all the trouble this has caused I'm happy to leave my new job and find something else. I don't want his career marred by this. Susan needs to understand he hasn't done anything wrong."

Rufus continued to test her narrative with expansive questions. Debbie maintained a viable consistency in all her responses.

"Okay Ms. Green. I'm going to leave it there for now, but it's possible I will need to speak with you again. I may also request you to attend the station. Would this be acceptable to you, should it be necessary?"

"Of course."

"Thank you for your assistance, Ms. Green."

"No problem."

"Oh, just one more thing." Rufus did not intend the final question to sound so much like a Columbo impression, but all he was missing was the grey rain mac.

"Yes?"

"You say you were going to leave a note on Mr. Brooke's vehicle, by way of explanation?"

"That is correct?" Debbie responded confused.

"It's just I'm wondering." Rufus deliberately left a long hiatus. "How did you know which was his car?" The pause before Debbie answered was lengthy and her final response, far from comprehensive.

"I asked someone else entering the lot." Her tone tense, lacking the earlier composure.

"Ah, I see. That would make sense. Do you know who this person was?"

"No idea. Just some guy in a suit." Debbie's return dismissive, as poise restored to her voice. When the call ended, Debbie looked at Chris.

"You heard what I said, get your phone now. He's gonna phone you next. Tally your answers up with mine and it'll be case closed. Remember you still think I stalked you in the workplace." Chris nodded dumbly and rushed to the kitchen to find his cellphone. Walking back to the bedroom he observed three more missed calls from Katelyn and one from an unknown caller. Perplexed as to who the other caller was, he soon got his answer.

The phone set to do not disturb silently lit up without vibration as Rufus's call came in. The ever-familiar *No Caller ID* displayed, but as Chris was aware of the caller, he quickly deduced the origin of the previous call.

Chris was led through a near identical set of questions with the officer. He merged his answers to tally up with Debbie's, adding the slant of it was all due to the continued stalking. He confirmed the repeated calling had ceased since Rufus's prior intervention. He also neglected to mention the muffin basket. This aspect had not been discussed with Susan. Therefore, it was absent from her report. The details of all the activities matched up perfectly. Chris was sure this would at least remove the interest of the law and take him a large step towards redeeming his role and status at Haskins & Wilcox.

Rufus hung up the phone, comparing his notes. The two calls appeared to fit. The only real infringement, the fluke of Debbie taking a job at the same workplace as

Chris. Considering the substantial workload, it was more than acceptable to draw a case closed conclusion. Exonerate Chris with Susan and move on. Any other officer or detective in the department would have left it there. Yet all Rufus could consider was a niggle in his psyche, there was more at play here. Something was wrong. Both their answers matched too perfectly, almost as if they were reading from the same hymn sheet. Debbie had unambiguously lied about how she discovered which car in the lot belonged to Chris. Multiple points of concern revolved around his mind.

The unsettled officer made a decision. He sought to be different from his colleagues. Whether the police department's capacity to investigate existed or not, he elected to probe further. Obtaining the garage CCTV, the obvious next step. He also planned to confirm Debbie's date of application for the vacancy appointment. That would involve a call to Susan. Rufus nominated to postpone that conversation for the moment. He agreed with himself, if both aspects stacked up, he would have no choice but to give it up.

A quick call to Taylor's Auto repair produced an email containing the footage of the incident, plus a compressed file containing footage from the same camera, covering the whole afternoon. The clipped extract followed the incident as reported. It also married up with the verbal accounts. Frustratingly the aspects of the imparted narrative, possible to fabricate by either party were obscured from view as a result of the high walled frontage of the lot. Only events directly in front of the opening were viewable.

Rufus uncompressed the large file, then played the full footage. Commencing from exactly twelve noon, Rufus increased the spooling speed. At one, activity of people walking in and out of the lot increased. Lunchtime. After two all movement ceased beyond the entrance. He increased the spooling speed again, until at half-three a vehicle entered the lot. Rufus quickly returned to normal playback in time to watch a woman, identical to the figure being hit with the car in the extract, strolling out in the direction of the office. Due to distance and resolution, he was unable to make out her features. Yet her desirable womanly figure transmitted across without compromise. She encompassed a confident walk, head held high, as if she had already secured the job.

After further spooling the five PM rush whizzed by, a succession of stragglers trailed. Eventually by about half five the activity dropped down to virtually nothing. Then at close to six a familiar figure sped by. Rufus rewound slightly. Once playback was resumed the familiar woman strode back into the lot, self-assurance radiated in her saunter. Disappearing into the lot, Rufus increased the play speed to look for one particularly significant aspect. At just after half six, a man who clearly resembled Mr. Brooke hurried down the street. His composure far from secure, constantly looking over his shoulder. Despite the distance it was clear to see he was on the edge of running, watching for an anticipated attack. He too disappeared into the lot. It was not his body language that fascinated Rufus, or the clear smoldering panic in his movement. The confirmation he desired, provided. No other person entered the parking lot between the arrival of the two suspects. No mystery contender to inform Debbie which car belonged to Mr. Brooke. Confirming the lie Rufus already knew existed.

Rufus was ready to speak to Susan Roswell. Despite the time pressure to wrap this up he wanted to undertake this in person.

Chapter 17

"I think it's time I took you home." Chris ventured. Now midday, Debbie showing no signs of offering him a get out.

"I'm still pretty dizzy Sugar, I don't feel ready for those stairs." Chris inwardly groaned. It was plain she was not going anywhere without a battle. Reverting back to that nauseating pet name to boot. Chris was desperate to call Katelyn and confess all. He had hoped with Debbie aiding to calm down the situation with the law, she might be more complicit in leaving. Apparently not likely.

"I really need to use the bathroom though Sugar. Can you help me?"

"Yeah okay." Chris unenthusiastically agreed. Debbie slid her legs off the bed. Chris made his way around allowing her to place her arm across his shoulders. Unsteadily she made her way to her feet. Allowing Chris to take her weight, she shuffled in the direction of the bathroom. Chris could not determine how much of the performance was genuine. If any. Entombed within her charade, he lacked feasible options of escape.

Reaching the bathroom, Chris lowered her to sit on the edge of the bath.

"Can you help me with my jeans?" She asked.

"Can't you do it yourself?"

"I'm not sure. I'm not feeling very steady." Chris muttered something indeterminable under his breath. He lifted the toilet lid and avoiding all eye contact approached Debbie. Once assisted back up and maneuvered in front of the toilet he allowed Debbie to rest one hand on the top of the cistern and one on his shoulder. He undid her belt, jeans button and zip. The skinny fit jeans were tight over her womanly hips and rounded bottom. Getting some purchase over either hip, he pulled them down. To his surprise, although he knew he should have guessed, she was devoid of panties. Her perfectly trimmed womanly self was presented right before Chris. Quickly he bought himself back fully upright, pretending not to notice what Debbie clearly wanted him to observe.

As soon as she was sat steadily on the seat Chris backed right off, averting his gaze in an exaggerated manner.

"Call me when you're done." He said, turning for the door.

"You can stay if you want Sugar?"

"No thanks." Chris could not get out and shut the door quick enough. A limited imperfect window existed. Chris wasted no time in pulling his cell out to ring Katelyn. He walked into the kitchen, maximizing the space between him and his foe. Katelyn answered on the second ring.

"One second." She stated instantly. Chris guessed she was walking out of the goldfish bowl. "What the hell is going on Chris?" She blurted out, once out of ear shot.

"Look, I can't speak for long but the woman who started yesterday, Debbie, has been stalking me."

"Stalking you?" Katelyn returned, equal amounts of confusion and irritation in her voice.

"Yes. I met her on the Friday night out, for Sarah's leaving party. Since then, she has been hounding me nonstop."

"Why didn't you tell me before?"

"I wanted to." Chris eventually answered after a long pause.

"Was it her who trashed my car?" Questioned Katelyn, anger evident in her hushed tone.

"I believe so."

"Bitch." Katelyn snapped back. "Why didn't you say?" Katelyn thought for a second while Chris dithered over his words. "Did something happen between you two? On Friday?"

"Yes." Chris answered honestly. Enough lies. "When you didn't turn up, I guess I was just feeling rejected."

"I was watching my father die." Katelyn returned sharply.

"I know that now. At the time I thought you weren't bothered. I got really drunk and she approached me. I wasn't looking for anything, honestly. It just happened."

"Did you sleep with her?" Katelyn's tone was empty.

"No. Maybe. I was so drunk I can't even remember what happened. It was a big mistake. I regretted it the moment I woke up. I wanted nothing more to do with her. I'm so sorry for what I did."

Katelyn did not reply, the silence more painful than a scolding. Chris, aware that time was finite, pushed on. "She barraged me with endless phone calls, some texts, but mainly calls. I went to the police. They warned her to stop. That ended the phone calls. I thought it was over. She turned up at work and tried to attack me in the parking lot. Then your car was targeted. I didn't know what to do. When she turned up at work, I lost my shit. Now I'm suspended."

"You should have told me."

"I know it was wrong. I feel terrible, but I was scared it would ruin what we had before we even had the chance to get started."

"You should have told me." Katelyn repeated, almost to herself.

"Look, I'm trying to sort this out now. I'm not hiding anything from you anymore. But I have to go now. Can I meet you later so we can discuss this properly?"

"I don't know Chris. This is a lot to take in."

"If you don't want anything more to do with me afterwards, I'll understand, but please give me the chance to explain."

"Chris, I've got a lot of shit going on right now, they're not releasing my father's body for Christ's sake. They say the autopsy has raised concerns. They've requested additional lab tests. I don't know what's going on with him. The last thing I need is to be involved in something else so messy."

"Please just meet me. Please."

"I'll text you. I've gotta get back to work. Bye." Her words carried no emotion.

"Please text, bye." Chris squeezed in before she hung up. He stood vacantly, not certain what to feel. The news of Stan's body being detained was inescapably shocking. Beyond that consideration, he reflected on his inability to anticipate how the call would likely ensue. Failing to create a spin on his actions, the damage was absolute. He inwardly punished himself for being so stupid, how had he arrived at this point? If he had come clean earlier, would the fallout have been minimized? Was it even possible for him to fix this? A multitude of questions. An absence of answers.

Chris snapped back from his reflections. Debbie should have called out to him by now. He listened. Nothing. He walked hastily back to the bathroom door. No sound beyond. He gave the door a gentle tap. Still nothing.

"Debbie?" he called through the wooden blockade, knocking it again. Silence came back. He tried the door, it was locked.

Chapter 18

Annika buzzed through to Susan.

"Yes?" Susan replied.

"I have an Officer Rufus here. He would like to speak with you."

"Oh. Send him in, please." Annika motioned with her hand for the tall handsome officer to proceed. He stepped forward, giving the door a knock before entering. The office was surprisingly large, excessive vacant floor space a dominant feature. Paintings on the walls, two large couches creating a comfortable meeting area. If was a far cry from the setting he worked in, or even the most senior personnel back at the station. Clearly the private sector had considerably more fiscal comfort to lavish on its prominent employees.

Rufus could not help but seize a few seconds to take in the private workspace before addressing the woman stood before him.

"Ms. Roswell?"

"Susan, please." She greeted in a welcoming tone, striding around her desk, extending her hand. Rufus shook it.

"Officer Rufus of the Santa Rosa PD." He returned.

"Please take a seat officer." She motioned to the couches. "Can I get you a coffee or something?"

"No. Thank you." He replied as he sat. Susan took her usual place opposite.

"I guess you're here regarding Chris and Debbie?"

"That is correct. I spoke with both Ms. Green and Mr. Brooke over the phone before coming down here. I have to say, there are still some holes in the accounts. I am hoping you can clarify a few things for me?"

"Of course Officer, it's not a situation that is typical here. Hence why we wanted to pass this onto yourselves."

"The first aspect I would like clarity on, is the date Ms. Green applied for the vacant position."

"Hmmm. Yes, I can find that for you." Susan got back up and returned to her desk. Still standing she buzzed the intercom.

"Annika. Please can you confirm the date and time we received the application form for Deborah?"

"Yes certainly." Replied a raspy, intercom manipulated voice. After a brief pause Annika came back through. "It was two minutes past one on Thursday afternoon last week,"

"Thank you, Annika." The reply had been audible to all in the room, there was no requirement for Susan to repeat it. She returned to the couch. As she sat, mild puzzlement formed on her face. Rufus spotted the reaction immediately.

"What's wrong?" He enquired.

"Nothing, well its strange."

"What is?" He prompted.

"Well, it's just I remember releasing the job advert to go live on the recruitment platform at exactly one on the dot. It's not normally something I'd notice, but as it was exactly on the hour, it just stuck in my mind." Rufus waited as Susan was clearly speculating internally. "The application forms would take at least an hour to complete.

Possibly half an hour if you rushed them." Curious, thought Rufus.

"Could the forms be obtained beforehand?"

"Possibly. They are standard templates but bespoke to each department. We haven't released the admin role templates for at least a year."

"Could someone employed here have passed them on to her? Before the advert went live? He ventured.

"That is possible, but its only me, or Annika who has access to those documents." Before Rufus even had chance to consider his next question, Susan was back out of her seat. This time she didn't bother with the intercom, walking straight to her door. "Annika?" she called through the doorway as she opened it. "Did you send out the application forms to anyone before I released the advert?"

"No." Annika replied instantly. Although Rufus could not see her from his location he detected the slight confusion in her tone, enough to satisfy him it was an honest answer.

"You're sure?"

"Er, yes. Have I done something wrong?"

"No, nothing like that." Reassured Susan. "Never mind." Susan closed the door and retook her seat. "I'm sorry officer, I do not have an answer for you."

"The other aspect I want to explore is your impartiality when interviewing both individuals."

"Excuse me?" Susan moved sharply back into her seat. A look of disdain etched into her features.

"Don't get me wrong, but Ms. Green did suggest you had formed a picture in your mind from the account of the individuals who witnessed and reported the altercation in the kitchen. She felt you led her down the route of validating your own perspective of events." Susan shook her head, almost in disbelief.

"Officer Rufus. I have been the HR manager here for five years. I have headed up countless investigations. If there's one thing I know, there's always two sides to the story. In every conflict there is the face value event, but buried underneath are the root causes. It's my job to extract and understand them. Picking sides at the outset would not allow me to do this." Susan was stern in her response, she clearly did not take kindly to any accusation on her objectivity. Rufus was once again able to satisfy himself, this concern did not tally up.

"Okay, look. I do not have definitive proof, but I have been involved previously with these two on Sunday night. After speaking to them both today, Ms. Green's version of events had repositioned from the account she gave you. It was certainly more in line with Mr. Brooke's account. I'm going to recommend to him, he files for a civil restraining order against her. I did suggest this as a possible option on Sunday, but now I'm going to insist on it." Susan nodded pensively as she took in the information. "As for the hit and run, when entered into context, I'm inclined to believe it was a genuine accident. I know the footage alone, doesn't suggest that. With the subsequent information I've gathered, it stacks up.

"So will this be the end of the criminal investigation?"

"Yes, it will. There are still aspects that are perplexing, I haven't been able to fill in all the blanks. But there is nothing more that warrants my time here. My suggestion to you, is that in all likelihood Mr. Brooke is the innocent victim. I would recommend ending his suspension with immediate effect. As for Ms. Green, her behavior has been unacceptable towards Mr. Brooke. If you factor in the reliable prospect of a civil restraining order being served against her, it would be impossible to keep her employed in this office while Chris is here."

"I see." Susan confirmed.

"In short, I recommend dismissing Ms. Green."

"Okay. Thank you officer." Susan answered rising from her seat, shadowing Rufus's lead, who was already stood. Clearly the meeting was concluding. Following a handshake, and thanking her for her time, he left. Annika viewed his departure through her thick glasses. As soon as he had exited the corridor she got up, knocked on Susan's door and walked in.

Susan was just returning to her desk, appearing startled by the new intrusion.

"Yes, Annika?"

"Did I do something wrong? I didn't send anything out for the job." Susan took her seat before answering.

"Honestly Annika, no. It's just really strange."

"What is?"

"Deborah completed her application submission a couple of minutes after the job went live. I can't understand how that happened." Annika lowered her head, plainly considering the conundrum.

"That's bizarre." She muttered. Susan studied Annika, half expecting her to hastily recall sending something prior to the electronic advert going out, or at the very least offer some kind of explanation. She always considered Annika a little peculiar. Categorically proficient and dedicated in her professional role but in her personality something was absent. The same could be said about her appearance. Medium height, only slightly overweight, but amazingly curvy. The kind of figure that could be uniquely sexually alluring to any man with a pulse if only she bolstered it with confidence. Yet she was a wall flower, making herself almost invisible. Hiding behind those thick spectacles and a haircut which predated any fashion Susan could recall. All the potential existed for her to ignite the room, any room, all but the spark. That absent element stole her potential. Susan wondered if Annika was aware of the latent appeal she could exploit. She had never mentioned a boyfriend or even going on a date. She never made remarks about any desire, sexual or otherwise.

"I can't explain it." Annika finally conceded. "What did the officer say about Chris?" It surprised Susan, Annika actually asked something about the situation. She never pried, on any level. Sure, she had access to almost every confidential personnel file within the company, but it was her very reserved nature that made her perfect for the function she provided for Haskins & Wilcox.

"The officer recommended to end his suspension and move on."

"That's good news." Annika replied brightly, a small smile forming.

"Erm. Yes, it is." Susan agreed. Although her reaction was completely natural, Susan distinguished a discrepancy in Annika's typical impassive character. "Unfortunately, we are going to have to let Deborah go."

"Do you want me to print the standard template forms for an unsuccessful probation period for you to sign?" That characterized the traditional Annika. No personal opinion, no questions on why. Just clarifying what she was required to do.

"I think under the circumstances, I will tailor a letter. I'll send it across to you to both email and post to her."

"No problem. Do you want me to contact Chris to ask him to come back in?"

"Yes please. Ask him to report here to meet with me at nine am tomorrow. You can let him know the suspension will be lifted to stop him worrying, but no other details please."

"Yes, understood."

"I'd better go and see Norman to give him the latest."

Annika returned to her desk. As Susan left to update Norman, Annika pulled out her cell. She sent a quick text before continuing with her normal duties. Annika was just picking up the office phone to call Chris when an anxious Katelyn appeared walking down the corridor. She returned the handset to the cradle.

"Hi Katelyn."

"Hi, is Susan available?"

"Sorry she's in a meeting with Norman. I think it could be some time. Are you okay? You look a bit shaken."

"Not really." Katelyn returned. She offered a pretend smile. "Just life." Annika returned the smile.

"I'm so sorry about your father."

"Thanks."

"I've booked you off for the day you requested. The funeral I assume?"

"Yes. Thank you. Although it might have to change. We're still waiting on the pathologist to release his body."

"Oh. Anything wrong?" Annika's voice tightened as she spoke.

"I don't think so, just more tests to confirm the cause of death. I'm sure it's just the normal process."

Annika nodded distantly, before returning to Katelyn. "It will be given as compassionate leave, so won't come out of your annual vacation allowance. We can move the date if need be." Katelyn nodded. "Why don't you take a seat? I was just going to make myself a coffee, you could stay for one? Maybe Susan will return while you're still here."

"Okay." Katelyn said, less than sure. Annika had never said more than two words to her before. If anything, she got the impression of a mild hostility emitting from her whenever their paths crossed in the workplace. She could not help but feel Annika wanted her to stay for a reason.

Annika returned with two coffees, retaking her seat. Katelyn pulled across the chair left for waiting outside Susan's office and sat adjacent to Annika at the desk.

"So how are the funeral arrangements going?"

"It's all pretty much there, just this delay from the morgue. Mom has done loads. I think she wants the distraction. I worry how it will affect her after the formalities are complete."

"Yes, that's when the realization hits, I guess. It'll be important for you to support her through it."

"Not a pleasant prospect." Katelyn agreed. She took a sip of her drink. Annika never spoke like this, maybe she only showed character in moments of despair?"

"So, was it about the funeral arrangements why you wanted to speak to Susan?"

"No. It was something else."

"Oh, anything I can help you with?" Katelyn regarded Annika. She had arrived to attempt to ascertain further details relating to Chris's situation. She was not sure what Susan would divulge to her, but the need to keep up to date on proceedings had taken precedence. If Annika knew something, it was a possible avenue to explore.

"It's about Chris, and the incident yesterday."

"Hmmm. There's not much I can say about that." Annika confirmed, but her tone of voice suggested she was open to be tested on that point.

"It's just me and Chris started dating a few days ago. I don't know what the issue was with the new girl, but he says she was stalking him. I don't know what to think." Katelyn looked Annika square in the eyes, throwing a face of innocent pleading.

"Look, if I tell you a few things you have to keep it completely to yourself."

"Sure, of course." Agreed Katelyn, surprised Annika was prepared to disclose any information so easily.

"Chris is currently suspended, but he is about to learn the suspension is being lifted. That's not to say he hasn't done anything wrong, just nothing that can be proved. He's done some appalling things to Deborah and is going to get away with it. I can't go into specifics, but I strongly recommend you give him a completely wide birth. He comes across as a nice guy, but there's a dark side lurking underneath." Katelyn threw a stunned face.

"Whatever Chris has done. I assume it's bad if you feel compelled to break your confidentiality responsibilities and warn me." Katelyn responded. The insinuation that Annika was overstepping her boundaries reverberated loudly in her head.

"I haven't said anything I shouldn't. I'm just offering some friendly advice." The tone was somewhat less cordial than the content suggested. Katelyn quickly drank her coffee, stating she should get back to work. After thanking Annika, she hurried off. Annika watched her walk tensely down the corridor. A small grimace of indignation formed on her face.

"Overstepping my boundaries? Fuck you, bitch." She whispered to herself, before making the phone call to Chris.

Chapter 19

Chris squared up to the locked door. He took a few steps back to prepare himself before the attempt to break it open, confident Debbie had done something stupid the other side. Images of Glen Close in Fatal Attraction formed in his mind. He had to get in there. Now. Ready to propel himself forward, he took the first step as the lock clicked from the inside. Chris checked his run as the door swung open and Debbie stepped out, wrists completely intact. Chris felt foolish for the near dramatic rescue attempt.

"Why did you lock the door?" He queried.

"I needed to think." Debbie walked straight past him entirely normal. Suddenly there was no need for support. Ten minutes earlier she couldn't even pull down her jeans. "Come and sit." She instructed walking into the living room. Again, as if it was her apartment, Chris, the visitor. He followed her lead in bewildered obedience. Debbie helped herself to a seat, looking at the dried bloodstain on the floor. She patted the couch next to her. Chris took the seat as instructed.

"That's gonna be hard to get out." She commented, motioning with her eyes.

"Uh huh." Chris was not really listening. Something was completely different. The dynamic had changed. He could not comprehend it, although it was obvious. Debbie took her phone out and took a photo of the dark red stain. "What are you doing?" he challenged.

"I assume you want me out of your life? Forever?"

"Yes." Puzzlement lining the confirmation.

"That could happen, right now. But first there are things we need to agree on." Chris opened his mouth to speak. No words came. "Firstly, I know you've been doting on Katelyn for months. I also know you've recently got it together. After recent events she's probably going to be keeping a distance from you. Keep it that way. Completely cut it off with her."

"What? No, that's not going to happen."

"Yes, it will." She barked commandingly. "Listen good Chris. On top of all the evidence against you, I now have injuries and my blood soaked into your floor. I have a GPS app on my phone which will confirm I have been here since last night, even during my call from Officer Rufus. I come here, get beaten up, forced to stay against my will. Change my story under duress to match yours, exonerating you completely. If I went to the cops now and said you held me here after a vicious beating, forcing me to get you off the hook, what do you think might happen?"

"That's not what happened, and you know it. I'm not going to let you do this." Chris's words trailed off as the realization hit. He dropped his head into his hands, complete disbelief manifesting over every conscious thought. "But I'm innocent." He reasoned softly.

"Ha. Whatever. Your totally screwed Chris." Debbie allowed herself a moment of personal satisfaction. Once passed, She turned back towards Chris, her tone penetrating. "You will stay away from Katelyn. Forever. Or I will cripple you. Do as I say, and you'll never see me again."

146

"It won't work. I'll expose you."

"Chris, it will work and even if it doesn't, go near her again and I can promise you one thing. If I can't take you down, I will kill her." Chris stared angrily into her eyes. She met his gaze in composed dominance. "I wouldn't test the point." Chris broke off the visual standoff, jumping up from the couch. After pacing around, he turned back towards her.

"I don't get it, if I do this, you're going to disappear out of my life? That doesn't make sense, I thought you couldn't live without me?" Debbie roared with laughter.

"Oh Chris, I don't care about you. I've just been toying with you. It's all a game and you've been so predictable, a bit sad really."

"What?"

"Look, you're a good-looking guy, but I don't struggle in that department. If I'm honest, I prefer the single life. Do what I want, when I want. If I feel like getting laid, well it's not usually an issue."

"So why all the fucking charade?" He growled.

"You and Katelyn can never be. With this pretense not only are you tied into my will, but your stock has plummeted in Katelyn's eyes. Even if I allowed it, she wouldn't want to touch you with a stick."

"But why?" As Debbie opened her mouth to answer, Chris's cell rang out. Off the do not disturb function for the first time in days. The unexpected noise jolted Chris.

"You'd better get that Sugar." Debbie's directive infused with sarcasm. Chris could see it was Annika's direct line.

"Hello?" He answered warily.

"Hi Chris. I've got good news. Your suspension is being lifted." Annika announced excitedly. "Please can you report here at nine tomorrow?" Chris failed to share her joy, his head spinning.

"Yeah, okay." He muttered absently.

"You have to meet with Susan, and then you're back to work."

"Okay. Thanks."

"It'll be good to see you back." She offered sweetly.

"Thanks, I'll see you tomorrow." With that he ended the call. Looking back towards Debbie, he waited for the explanation. The context or content of the phone call failing to register in his mind.

"Was that Annika?" She asked.

"Yes."

"She's a sweet girl, don't you think?"

"Whatever. Tell me why."

"It's funny she should call at this moment." Chris threw Debbie a perplexed expression. "The second part of this deal I'm brokering with you involves her."

"Annika?"

"Yes. All you have to do to keep your ass out of the slammer and in your career is to stay away from Katelyn and start dating Annika." Chris could not help but scoff at the remark.

"What are you talking about?"

"It's pretty simple Chris. Annika has been obsessed with you since the day you joined the company. But she's so fucking timid with guys, she could never tell you. Then Katelyn enters the scene and you're like some lovesick puppy, chasing her round all day."

148

"Obsessed with me? She never made any indication."

"Yeah I know, but she's had a hard life. You don't know what she's been through. She deserves a little happiness, she deserves you." Debbie spoke with clear conviction. Chris finally retook his seat back on the couch. Rubbing his hands through his hair, he attempted to reset. Take some stock of this ridiculous state of affairs.

"You're saying you want me to start a fraudulent relationship with Annika?

"Yes, but you can bring her out of herself. It could be really good, for both of you." He shook his head, this was madness.

"Supposing I did, how long are you expecting me to uphold this farce?"

"If you end the relationship, I go to the cops. This kind of offence will stay convictable for years."

"You expect me to do this for years?"

"Yes." Debbie answered seriously. "You're trapped here Chris. This is not a bargaining situation. You need to accept your fate and work this to your advantage."

"To my advantage? What are you talking about?"

"Annika is a catch. Look beyond her glasses and shit haircut. She's a beautiful woman, both on the outside and within. You just need to develop her. Allow her to find herself. You could make it really good. One day you'll be glad I did this."

"Fucking hell Debbie, I already knew you were crazy, but this is beyond imagination. What is Annika to you? Why do you care so much to engineer this?"

"That's not your concern right now. Just know you don't have a choice. If you think I've been crazy so far, then that's nothing compared to what you'll witness if you fail me." Chris got back up again.

"Debbie I can't physically take any more right now. I need you to leave. Let me think about everything that has happened, everything you've just said to me." A desperation lined his plea. Debbie got up off the couch, brushing herself down. Her face indicated pain as her midriff straightened, clearly feeling the bruised ribs. Her eye half closed, deep purple coloring encompassing it. The bandage around her head, almost comical in appearance. Chris knew the wound beneath was far from a joke. She looked a mess, but it was an injury list bolstering her sick desires infinitely. Chris ushered her to the door, grateful she was finally departing, if only after the delivery of her fanatical stipulations.

As she stepped onto the outside staircase, Debbie turned to Chris to weight her commands one last time.

"Start a relationship with Annika. Don't fuck with me Chris. You can't win, and if you think your life is bad now, it's just the entrée to what I can deliver." Chris gave a short nod of recognition before slamming the door shut.

Hours later Chris drove up outside the formidable gates of Katelyn's driveway. The text to meet at hers came straight after she got off work. Katelyn was already outside waiting for him. As he pulled up, she jumped into the passenger seat.

"Shut the engine off." She instructed coldly. Chris complied.

"You don't want to go somewhere to talk?"

150

"Let's just stay here. I don't think this is going to take long." Shooting Chris an accusing look, Katelyn continued. "Tell me everything."

Chris went through every aspect with her, not pulling any punches. He talked about the drunken grope on Debbie's couch, passing out, the foiled escape in the morning. He went over the phone calls, the police involvement, the muffin basket. Explained the parking lot and workplace incidents. He even detailed the events of last night and this morning, admitting to the injuries he had caused to Debbie. He exposed her latest threats, if he continued his relationship with Katelyn. The desire to be completely truthful steeled within him, Chris even divulged Debbie's mandate regarding Annika.

"Chris this is hard to take in." Katelyn finally commented when he finished his full account.

"Tell me about it. I'm totally stuck, I don't know what to do."

"It's funny…" Katelyn said more to herself as she considered her thoughts.

"What is?"

"It's just, I went to see Susan earlier. She wasn't there but Annika wanted me to talk to her. Even made me a coffee. She warned me off you. It was really bizarre, she's barely said a word to me before, and then she's acting like my best friend."

"Sounds like she's aware of everything. Like she's actually involved in this sick plan." Chris slammed his hand on the steering wheel, jolting Katelyn out of her reflections.

"I'm not sure I can be mixed up in this at the moment. The whole atmosphere with the police has changed. I still don't know what happened to my father, but I know enough to understand the police are suspicious of his death. We're being treated as victims, but there's an underlying current. I think they are considering us suspects."

"That's ridiculous." Chris exclaimed.

"Maybe. Until they're satisfied there was no foul play, we're all under suspicion."

"Do you think it could be…" Chris did not want to say the "M" word "…foul play?"

"No. Of course not. Why would anyone do such a thing to my father? He never hurt anyone." I'm sure this will be cleared up soon, but until it's all resolved, I need to focus solely on my family."

"What are you saying?" He asked softly, turning to look her in the eyes. A single tear made its way down Katelyn's pale cheek.

"I can't be involved in this Chris, I'm sorry. I concede it's so weird, something is amiss. But whether you are innocent or not, all the lies and withholding you have undertaken is pretty hurtful. If things were better for me right now, maybe I could entertain considering my involvement. But with all this shit up in the air, I just can't." Chris grabbed her hand in desperation. Instantly Katelyn pulled it away, reestablishing her control of the discussion. "I've made my decision." With that she opened the car door and got out. Chris sat frozen, speechless. "Bye." She uttered with finality, firmly closing the door. Once she passed through the wrought iron gates

152

Katelyn pressed her fob, sending the gates on their journey to close. Chris watched her walk quickly up the driveway until she was out of sight. This time there was no look back, no wave, no bestowed smile.

Chapter 20

It was twenty minutes before Chris had to leave to make his nine meeting with Susan. The nature of atmosphere he would be walking into, beyond uncertain. Yet that consideration, a background element. He would pass Annika's desk to reach Susan. *What would he say? What would he do? Would Annika say something to him?* Question after question bulldozed through his mind, all of them bullying the others to take top spot in his consideration. Yet before all this was the dominating facet, he had lost Katelyn. His actions causing her so much pain. All while she was enclosed within her own grief.

Chris elected on another coffee as a substitute for the pitiful sleep. As he made his way into the kitchen, his cell rang. *No Caller ID.* Groaning, he took the call.

"Yes?" He barked.

"Good morning Mr. Brooke, this is Officer Rufus." Immediately Chris's persona lost its irritation.

"Hi." He softly offered.

"You thought I was Ms. Green?"

"Yes."

"Have your employers lifted the suspension?"

"I'm about to leave for a meeting with my HR manager. I'm informed it's to get me back to work."

"That's good news."

"Yes." Chris agreed.

"Your meeting is with Susan?"

"Yes?" Chris confirmed with surprise. Rufus was certainly on the ball.

"I met with her yesterday after we spoke on the phone." Rufus divulged, understanding the question Chris did not ask. There was a short pause. "Chris. Do you mind me calling you Chris?"

"Not at all."

"Good. Chris, have you completed the Civil Restraining Order forms?" Chris didn't answer immediately, knowing his answer might appear odd.

"No. I haven't."

"That surprises me Chris."

"It's just been so crazy. I'll get them done as soon as possible." Chris did not know whether the statement was a promise or an outright fabrication.

"Chris…" The shrewd officer hung the question out. He knew there was every logical reason to put this matter to bed. Acutely aware more pressing issues were occurring in Santa Rosa, demanding his attention. Yet he just could not throw this case from his mind. Rufus was compelled to cast the line out of the boat one more time, just to see if he got a nibble. "…what are you not telling me?"

"Nothing." Chris knew that was definitely a lie. So did Rufus. He waited silently. "I told you all I know yesterday. If you want more information, Debbie is the person to interrogate."

"You think I'm interrogating you?"

"No. I'm struggling to think clearly. I just need to get the meeting with Susan over with and then take stock of everything."

"Chris, whether you realize it or not, I'm here to help you. I can't do more without further information. There are aspects to this I have no knowledge of. If you let me in, I can work to get a resolution."

"I'm grateful for your help officer. I really am. But I'm so strung out right now. I just want to get on with my life." Chris could sense the desperation in his own voice.

"If you want that, let me in." Chris weighed up the pros and cons in his mind. By revealing all, he was leaving himself in a notably vulnerable position with an officer of the law. Yet unless he was prepared to go along with this ad hoc arranged relationship, indefinitely, the shit was going to hit the fan sooner or later. Having Rufus on his side might make the difference of walking away with his freedom, maybe his career and most importantly of all, salvaging his relationship with Katelyn. With this hasty consideration Chris played the only hand he could. He was going all in, and then some.

After Chris ended the call with Rufus, the officer remained at his hot desk. Running all the information through in his mind. Chris had disclosed every dot. It did not take a genius to connect them, but it still appeared a stretch.

During his interview with Susan, Annika had answered the question on sending out an application form prematurely. In the officer's mind, truthfully. Had he misjudged this? Annika was not in his thinking at that time. The tone of her reply, confusion, hesitation. Rufus originally considered the delivery laced with puzzlement. Fitting for a person asked such a random question out of the blue. Now though, with his metaphorical spotlight on it, the traits pointed towards a fictious answer.

Rufus glanced at the time, due in five to report for patrol. The complaint yesterday, submitted back to Wilkins as case closed. Rufus elected to go back to him. Ask for permission to open it back up.

To say Sargent Wilkins was less than interested in reopening such a trivial case was an understatement.

"Rufus, do you have any idea how much crap I took yesterday from the Patrol Sargent for commandeering you? It did not go down well; I can tell you. Now you want me to go back to him, asking for you again? To investigate the same complaint? That came to fuck all? It ain't gonna happen. Leave it alone and get back on with your job." Wilkin's voice was a mixture of shouting, berating, grumbling. Rufus already regretted making the request. About to turn on his heels and get out of there, Wilkins threw him a lifeline. "Give me one reason why I should override that jumped up prick and give you more time?"

"I think it's some kind of elaborate blackmailing plot. Ms. Green was engineering the potential collapse of this guy's life to force him into a relationship with another female colleague, Ms. Annika Smith. Ms. Green trashed his relationship with a woman called Ms. Fisher and is now forcing him to date Ms. Smith."

"Hmmm, that's interesting." Wilkins made exaggerated gestures as he considered the information. "Sorry. It's not enough, get back to work Rufus."

"Just one second." A voice interrupted from the side. Detective Hill put down the transcript he had been riffling through on a neighboring desk. "What's Fisher's first name?"

"Katelyn." Rufus responded, slightly off guard.

"Now that is genuinely interesting. Officer, you'd better come with me. Wilkins, can you inform the Patrol Sargent I'm taking Rufus? Don't know how long for."

"It'll piss him off." Wilkins warned jovially.

"Good, he's a prick."

Chapter 21

Embracing a sense of reprieve, Chris rode the elevator up to the top floor. Completing a frank and truthful conversation with Officer Rufus appeared a progressive move. A weight had been lifted. While the situation primarily stood as before, he had now put Katelyn fully in the picture. That was important. She deserved the truth if nothing else. His best chance to resurrect the phoenix of their relationship was to get every grubby little detail out in the open. Nothing more that could create further damage down the road, however this all played out. The latest move, fully involving Rufus, had to stack some of the odds in his favor. He materialized as a competent officer with a genuine will to do the right thing. He was one of the good guys, a powerful one at that. These actions ensured Chris was not alone, he had support.

Chris strode out of the elevator, down the secluded corridor. He purposed a walk of confidence. Yes, it was ninety percent pretense, but a sliver of authentic belief had now been forged. Chris held onto it. Appreciating it was necessary for what was to come.

Annika came into view. She spied him immediately, anticipating his arrival.

"Good morning Chris." She offered with a smile. Chris had to force himself not to greet her with total disdain. The effort in her appearance apparent. Hair, clean with a pleasant shine. Additional makeup than she usually sported, but not so much it detracted. The dress dominated his attention. A much lower cut than he had ever known her to attire. She certainly had ample cleavage. Chris wondered to himself, if she had been so desperate to attract his attention for all these years, why had she not made this effort before.

"Good morning Annika. You look nice today." Chris spoke fashioning the sincerest smile he could manage.

"Why thank you Chris." She replied, her cheeks instantly reddening at a rare male complement. She held the smile, but Chris could sense she was well out of her comfort zone. No doubt Debbie had been coaching her on being more extravert. *Full marks for effort, shame about the deceitful ruse to get to this point*. "You can go straight in." She eventually added. "Good luck."

"Thanks." Chris quickly continued on before his facade broke. Knocking on Susan's door he did not hesitate before entering. Susan looked up from her desk.

"Take a seat Chris."

Susan joined him on the green leather couches. A protracted, uncomfortable silence followed. Chris waited, wondering if he had got it all wrong. Was he about to be terminated? Eventually Susan gave a small reassuring smile. Not the same kind of gesture she had bestowed when they were colleagues on equal footing. Either way, it told Chris the worst possible outcome was not on the table today.

"Good morning Chris."

"Morning."

"Are you aware I was visited yesterday by an Officer Rufus?"

160

"Yes. I spoke to him this morning. He said he had been to see you."

"Good." Susan paused again. "Look Chris, this situation was not a good thing." He nodded. "I'm not really sure what happened, there are certainly some aspects which don't make sense to me. Officer Rufus explained he knew more about the circumstances than I had knowledge of. He was categorical that despite the incident in the kitchen and the car accident, no further action should be taken against you."

"Okay."

"Frankly, I would prefer some more context." Probed Susan. "In order to satisfy myself the decision is correct." Chris could not decide if it was requested for sincere perspective or blatant prying. Either way, his position was strengthened by the groundwork Rufus had already put in. He did not want to entertain Susan's curiosity unless it was absolutely necessary.

"Noted, but I really don't have any more to add from our last meeting."

"Okay. Understood." Susan knew better than to test the point. "Whether you are aware or not, word has got out amongst the workforce regarding the incident with Debbie in the kitchen. What are your thoughts on handling this?"

"What do you suggest?" Chris asked.

"I would recommend taking the fifth on it. Don't say anything at all. Any response you give will feed the gossiping, giving opportunity for those who revel in this kind of thing, the chance to twist and manipulate your reasons. I don't think there's anything you can say to pacify them."

"I would agree with that."

"Okay. I don't see any benefit in dragging this out any longer, you can consider yourself off suspension." Susan finished with another smile, of the variety Chris had been afforded when he was a trusted member of Susan's inner circle. Whatever she thought about the last two days, it appeared she was prepared to look past it. Chris returned the smile.

"That's good news Susan."

"Indeed." She agreed. Susan was about to get up when Chris motioned, he had something else to say.

"One question."

"Yes?"

"I assume Debbie is being terminated?"

"Ah. I'm glad you bought that up. Just so you're fully in the picture, that was the intention. I went to update Norman yesterday after speaking with Officer Rufus. Norman wanted to take another look at Debbie's work resume, to see if we could offer her a transfer to a different site within the organization. She previously completed data analysis for a pharmaceutical research company. I only scanned over the resume as Annika shortlists candidates. Turns out she has significant experience in pharmaceutical chemicals and drugs. She was certainly overqualified for the admin role here. Norman got in touch with our chemicals division based in Sacramento. They said they'd be happy to take her. We spoke to Debbie yesterday afternoon and offered her a position there. She agreed. She will work mostly remotely from home for four weeks while she arranges her relocation. It's at least a two hour commute each way, so not practical to stay here."

Chris considered this. While it was unsettling to think she was still a Wilcox & Haskins employee, it would get her out of Santa Rosa. Ultimately this might be a good thing. *Maybe Annika could go with her?*

"Okay." Chris responded.

"Nothing to add?" Susan enquired with interest, expecting a reaction to this news. Chris kept his thoughts to himself, giving a simple shake of the head to confirm. "It'll mean she's well out of your way." Susan could not help but add the obvious.

"Yes." Chris agreed, making no attempt to embellish his response. There was no need to comment further. He stood up, Susan followed his lead, also rising. She extended her hand, Chris shook it.

"I hope there is no lasting atmosphere between us." She added. "I had a job to do and based on the evidence in front of me there was no choice but to suspend you, pending further investigation."

"I understand. It's not a problem." Chris spoke reassuring words but without the conviction in his tone to back them up.

He left the office shutting the door behind him. He could almost sense Annika's eyes burning into his back. As he turned, sure enough she was poised at her desk, waiting for him to reappear.

"So, how did it go?" she asked expectantly.

"I'm off suspension." He modestly responded.

"Wow, that's great news. I'm so pleased." Annika was a different person. She never used words like "wow" or expressed any kind of emotion. Chris could only conclude Debbie had stipulated to Annika to make a

163

noticeable effort. To provide Chris with an opening to develop the, until now purely professional and largely nonexistent relationship. "You should do something to celebrate." She added less than naturally.

"I don't know if I feel like celebrating Annika, it's been a difficult time."

"Well, I think its super you're back in the team."

"Maybe I could go for a quiet drink with someone later to let off some steam." Chris knew he was laying the bait. Annika looked with all expectant eyes, noticeable even behind her lenses. "I'm not even sure who would want to join me." He teased. Annika opened her mouth, but no words came out. Clearly well beyond her comfort zone. Despite the circumstances of this abnormal matchmaking episode, Chris almost felt cruel to leave the emphasis on her to commit to asking the question. "Catch you later Annika." He closed as he began to walk away.

From the corner of his eye, he sensed Annika immediately panicking as her opportunity was disappearing. Chris continued to walk. Halfway down the corridor, before she finally found her flustered instruction.

"Chris, wait." Annika slid around the desk, quickly walking up to him, already halted in his tracks. Chris turned around to face her.

"Yes?" Annika stood before him. He naturally towered over her, at least a foot taller. She couldn't look him in the eyes, her head down, body tense, squeezing one hand in the other, she spoke with tentative words.

"I'd be happy to go for a drink with you. If you want?" Chris left her hanging. It was punishing, he knew her anxiety would be through the roof.

"Okay. Prestons at eight." He settled impassively. Without further word, Chris turned back towards the elevator and walked away.

Chapter 22

Detective Hill sat back in his chair digesting the full account of Officer Rufus. He had quietly listened with curiosity as the officer detailed every aspect from memory in a comprehensive timeline of events.

"That is very interesting Rufus. I don't suppose you're aware Katelyn's father died on the same Friday Chris hooked up with Debbie?"

"It's news to me. What was the cause of death?"

"That's the interesting part. Her father, Stan Fisher was epileptic. He was prone to rare but severe fits. On Friday he suffered a massive seizure and never recovered. The coroner attending was concerned. He ordered a full autopsy. We got the preliminary lab work back yesterday. The results are still inconclusive, but there's an indication some kind of toxin was ingested by Fisher. I requested pathology rush the remaining tests through. It all points to an unnatural death.

"Oh." Commented Rufus as he considered this fact. "It appears highly suspicious both these investigations are unconnected."

"Agreed. It might be just coincidence, but I doubt it."

"I don't do coincidence." Rufus returned flatly "So what is Stan's story?"

"He's a retired investment banker. One of those rich bastards we all love to hate. Relocated here eight months ago to enjoy life. Bought his wife and daughter with him."

"Any suspects?" The officer pushed, as his mind worked through the new information, looking for an association. Hill got up from the desk, walking around his small section of the office, pondering his response. Four detectives shared this one room, and it was still half the size of Susan's office. The desks constructed of the finest laminated chipboard. No expensive artwork littered these walls.

"As I say he's a guy we all love to hate, so there could be infinite possibilities. Naturally the wife and Katelyn. But from what I've seen so far there are no obvious motives or evidence connecting them. I could be wrong, but I don't think they are involved. Beyond that, it's early days. I haven't had chance to really dig into anything." Hill walked back to the desk, picking up his keys. "I was about to go over there and prepare for forensics when I overheard you and Wilkins. Fancy a ride along?"

"What about my patrol duties?" Rufus asked.

"Up to you. I could do with some help and the detectives are so stretched; I'll probably end up working alone. I just want a switched-on set of eyes and ears. As you've been investigating a possible connected case it makes sense to retain your services."

"Lead the way." Rufus did not require further persuasion.

Hill drove up to the colossal wrought iron gates. He pressed the intercom button.

"Yes?" A female voice returned after a lengthy pause.

"Detective Hill. I called earlier."

"Drive up detective." The gates began to slowly part, a motorized squeaking noise accompanied the movement. As soon as the opening became wide enough, Hill took his vehicle through, climbing up the long sweeping private road. Dense woodland encompassed the traversing cut through. For a short moment the impression was established of being situated in a remote woodland. Duly the trees receded into a wide parking area, seemingly too expansive to be considered a driveway. Beyond this sat a domineering edifice, constructed of glass and wood. Providing conflicting notes of contemporary and traditional. The size breathtaking, the architecture implicit.

"Jesus." Rufus exclaimed. Wonderment etched on his face. "That's a house?"

"He wasn't on a law enforcement salary." Quipped Hill as he pulled up near the entrance porch. "The wife is called Barbra, she's fifty-five, Katelyn is twenty-three years old."

Exiting the vehicle, Rufus scanned the surrounding area. The house was totally secluded by the dense woodland. It could not be seen from the road. He guessed the high walls surrounded the entire estate. Without a drone or helicopter the entrance gates were the only clue this place existed. Rufus, already speculating, could not help but contemplate the difficulty in gaining access to Stan once safely within the confines of his personal castle. Maybe Hill had been premature in not considering the immediate family as prime suspects. He joined Hill, who had already reached the grand, oversized entrance door.

A substantial locking mechanism shifting audibly, sounded, before the thick solid oak door slowly opened under manual effort. Before them stood a tall, weary appearing woman. Rufus could tell the type instantly, normally presented in thick expensive make up, designer clothing and immaculate hair. Those facades were currently abandoned. Dressed in sweats, hair ruffled, no attention to appearance whatsoever, she could have just as easily opened the door on her trailer park motorhome.

"Good morning Mrs. Fisher." Hill greeted.

"Good morning detective, I said before, call me Barbra."

"Barbra, this is Officer Rufus. He will be assisting me today." She shook both their hands before inviting them in. The grandeur continued inside. Rufus tried to not look as if he was totally astonished, but it was hard to disguise.

"This is an amazing house." He commented involuntarily, followed by mild embarrassment for talking out of turn. Hill was the lead detective. He was not far off a complete rookie. *Keep your eyes open and mouth shut*, he told himself.

"Thank you, Officer." Barbra answered lacking emotion. The superiority of her residence not a contemplation at present. Hill got straight to the point.

"As I discussed on the phone Barbra, I'm going to require Stan's computer, cell, any tablets or devices that may contain information."

"Of course. Do you know anything more yet?" She asked softly.

"Unfortunately not. At the moment the results are suspicious. It might turn out to be nothing untoward. But while we are in this interlude it's good practice to start preparing to investigate. I have requested the full lab work to be expedited. We won't get it all back at once, but it will be prioritized.

"Thank you Detective."

"Do you know any of Stan's passwords or security codes Barbra?"

"No. I'm sorry. He was very secretive on all that. I wouldn't know what to suggest."

"No problem. The cybercrime boys will sort that." Barbra gave a small nod.

"Would you both like a hot drink?" She asked.

"Actually Barbra, that brings me onto my next point. As we are possibly now heading into a full investigation, I've arranged for the forensic team to go over the house. Hopefully they should be here within the hour. I'm going to have to ask you to not touch anything and leave the house until this work is complete."

"Oh." Exclaimed Barbra, looking distressed at the request. "I wasn't expecting that. Couldn't you have warned me earlier?"

"Sorry, my bad. I should have said." Hill accepted. Rufus guessed Hill had deliberately neglected to notify Barbra. No warning. Just in case she had any potential evidence to conceal.

"Where is your daughter at present?"

"Katelyn is at work."

"Okay great. At this point I'm not going to request your or your daughter's cell phone, but I am going to ask you not to delete anything off, no matter how innocuous.

Anything deleted would still be recoverable, but it takes a lot longer. Can you pass this on to her?"

"Er, yes. I guess." Clearly Barbra was taken aback by the change in circumstances. "I'll just grab my car keys."

"Sorry, that's not a possibility either. We'll need to examine your vehicle as well. I have to arrange for Katelyn's vehicle to be impounded. Can you confirm it is parked at her primary place of employment?

"I guess so. I don't really follow her daily comings and goings detective." An audible tang of annoyance had entered into Barbra's voice as the idea bloomed in her mind, her relationship with Hill was now very different.

"Okay, no problem. Officer Rufus here can drive you to wherever you want to go." Rufus nodded at the unexpected task, as if he had already been briefed.

"And where am I supposed to go Detective?" Spikiness amplified each word.

"Sorry, I know it's an inconvenience, but we have to prepare for the worst. Is there any family close by?"

"I don't have any family here, as you well know. We only relocated to Santa Rosa eight months ago."

"It might have to be a hotel then, I'm afraid." Hill suggested.

"How long are we talking about?"

"I don't know at the moment. Hopefully it's a couple of days at most." The disgust on Barbra's face said a thousand words but she did not speak further.

"Where would you like me to take you?" Rufus asked, hoping to diffuse the rapidly escalating tension.

"I don't know. The nearest decent hotel." Barbra snapped. "Am I at least allowed to pack some clothes?"

"I'm afraid not at this point." With an audible huff, Barbra slammed her keys on the entrance bureau.

"This is ridiculous." She stormed out of the house. Hill threw his keys to Rufus. "Take her, but don't rush. I'm suddenly keen to seize Katelyn's vehicle before she gives her forewarning."

Chapter 23

Chris sat quietly at his desk. His office door shut. A magnitude of activity to catch up on. It was Friday. How his life had changed in one short week. Despite his concentration, Chris was aware of an array of glances from the goldfish bowl. All of them wondering, speculating, filling in the blanks for themselves. All except one. The only one he cared about. She did not look once in his direction. She knew the full account and yet she could not bring herself to even offer a momentary glance by way of absolution, or at the very least, a fleeting instant of compassion.

Not long before lunch he observed Carol, the receptionist appear in the bowl, walking straight up to Katelyn. She whispered discreetly in her ear, causing Katelyn to rise looking flustered and exit the room with her. *What could be happening now? Strange Carol actually came up and got her, rather than simply calling from the lobby.* Either way an issue was transpiring, but he had no right to involve himself. It was no longer his business.

Eventually she returned to the bowl, walking past Chris's office. Clearly distressed, Katelyn shot Chris a sideways look as she strode by. There was no attempt to enter, or even to gesture to him. He hoped it had nothing to do with Debbie or Annika. He conjectured it was more likely news about her late father.

As the working day officially ended, the near Friday stampede occurred. Within five minutes the office was virtually empty. The only souls remaining, Chris, Katelyn and two other personnel. Both typical unpunctual finishers. Chris quickly determined they were not hanging around in anticipation of a standoff between Katelyn and himself. He switched off his monitors, stepping out of the room. Awkwardly he made his way over to Katelyn's desk. Before he could find a sentence to string together, Katelyn let out a riled sigh.

"Chris." She whispered. "I don't want to do this."

"I'm not here to harass you. Are you okay?"

"Not really Chris. Please can you go?"

"What happened earlier, with Carol?"

"Nothing. It doesn't matter. Please go." Until now both had been discreetly muted. Katelyn raised the volume in her last comment, causing the other two to lift their heads.

"Okay. I'm going." Chris conceded. He turned, walking quickly out. Head low, avoiding the eyes of his other colleagues, he knew were watching his departure.

As Chris arrived at his car, his cell rang.

"Hello?"

"Did you make the arrangement as planned?"

"Yes. Eight at Prestons Bar."

"Good. See you later."

"Bye." Chris responded but the caller had already hung up. Chris got into his vehicle to go home and prepare for undoubtedly the most strenuous date of his life.

Hill parked his detective issued Sedan back at the station. Before they got out, he turned to Rufus.

"It's been a long day and we're far from finished, you okay to carry on?"

"I'm fine." The officer answered.

"Good. Make sure you log your overtime. I'll sign it off."

"Thanks." It had not even occurred to Rufus he would have finished hours ago if out on patrol. "Do you always work such long hours?"

"Sometimes. Well, more often than sometimes." Hill admitted.

"You don't get overtime though." Hill laughed at the observation.

"No, I don't. What can I say? Someone has to get the job done." Rufus nodded thoughtfully at the comment.

Once inside, back at his desk, Hill opened his emails.

"One has just come in from the lab." Hill commented, moving his screen round so Rufus could also observe. He opened the attached document. A report listing a range of chemicals found in Stan's corpse. One had been highlighted. "Tetrodotoxin." Hill read out loud. "What the fuck is that?" He scrolled to the bottom of the document where the lab technician had added a comment.

Stanley Fisher has substantial levels of tetrodotoxin in his system. I am unable to establish the point of entry. The pathologist should be able to determine

this once I have completed the full
testing. I do not wish to second guess his
conclusions, but I can confirm the levels
found are well beyond the threshold of a
lethal dose.

"Any idea what that is?"

"Nope." Confirmed Rufus. Immediately Hill opened Google and searched the word. Both read the highlighted results with much interest. Hill read one out loud.

"Tetrodotoxin is an extremely potent toxin found mainly in the liver and sex organs of puffer and blowfish."

"Fugu." Rufus replied, aware of the infamous Japanese delicacy.

"Any restaurants in Santa Rosa serve Fugu that you know about Rufus?"

"None I'm aware of." Hill continued to scroll through the numerous articles. "Some of the severe symptoms of tetrodotoxin poisoning are cardiac arrhythmias, muscle contraction and paralysis." He turned to look at Rufus. "Probably easily confused with an epileptic fit, in someone known to suffer with epilepsy."

"It all fits." Rufus agreed. Hill turned towards Rufus, both energized by this development.

"Okay, we don't have a lot of time. This new information is useful. We stick to the plan as agreed."

"Yep, I'm on it." Rufus replied as he got up.

"Log onto Hoskins's terminal." Offered Hill, motioning to the neighboring desk. "He's certainly done for the day."

"He won't mind?"

"Frankly I don't care if he does. Time is of the essence." Rufus wasted no further moments, jumping into Hoskins's seat.

Chapter 24

Chris entered Prestons twenty minutes early, aiming to arrive before Annika. He looked around anxiously. There was no sign of her. The establishment had a reasonable number of patrons. Some propped at the bar consuming a post-work Friday beer. There were a decent number of families at tables enjoying a meal out. A smattering of couples were also dining. Much to his relief, Chris could not see anybody from Haskins & Wilcox in attendance.

He walked over to the seating counter and waited for a staff member to notice him. Eventually a girl in her late teens approached, bestowing a halfhearted smile.

"Good evening. I'm Maxi, have you made a reservation?"

"Yes, it's under Brooke. I requested the booth in the bottom left corner." Maxi scanned the reservation list.

"Yep, got you. Follow me." As instructed, he walked after her to the prebooked booth. From this vantage point Chris was afforded an open view of the entrance but was also secluded from many of the fellow diners. He sat on the side enabling the desired outlook. Maxi handed him several menus.

"Can I get you something to drink?"

"Sam Adams please."

"Coming up." Maxi turned as she spoke and disappeared off. He hoped she would be quick with his beer. Tension was building up inside, a cold one, largely desirable at this moment.

Minutes before eight Annika strode into the diner. She looked as nervous as Chris. Scanning quickly around the seated tables for her new companion. Chris sighted her instantly as she entered, his eyes locked on the entrance from the moment he sat down. He could admit she looked good. A mile away from the Annika he knew. Under different circumstances he may well have been pleased with this evening's company. She moved her gaze in his direction, Chris raised his hand.

Spotting the motion, she formed a small smile of relief. Annika walked towards the booth. Chris involuntarily tensed his whole body. It was showtime. He moved his glance from the fast-approaching date to the patrons on the opposite side of the establishment, frequenting the bar. By the time he returned his gaze she had arrived and slid quickly onto the bench opposite him. Chris gestured for them both to slide across the benches to the secluded side of the booth. She followed his lead, taking them both completely out of sight of everyone else. Annika instantly appeared utterly embarrassed, she could only manage momentary glances at Chris, her eyes flicking all over. A nervous smile kept forming as she fought to keep herself in check.

"Good evening Annika." Chris offered.

"Hi." She replied as her personal battle continued.

"Would you like a drink?" He asked. His first beer, already finished. "Yes please. A large white wine." They both clearly required something to settle them, but for different reasons. Chris poked his head out from beyond the confines of the booth. He was relieved to see Maxi approaching.

Drinks ordered they were again alone. An awkward silence ensued. Annika's eyes were everywhere. Chris's mind blank as an empty piece of paper. Eventually it was Annika who rescued the sinking ship.

"I'm so glad you're back from suspension. That must have been awful." *You don't know the half of it*, Chris thought. He quickly reconsidered this. *Actually, you probably do.*

"Yeah, it was horrible. It was good to be back at work today."

"Did you catch up on your work?"

"Mostly. I'll have to get some stuff done over the weekend, but I should be back on track for Monday."

"That's good. We can celebrate tonight." Annika began to calm down a little. Her erratic eye movements dissipating. Chris almost felt sorry for her. Clearly this was a major moment in her life, she had no idea what was about to happen. Maxi broke Chris from the thought, arriving with their drinks. As soon as she departed, Annika held her glass up to Chris. He chinked his bottle against it.

"Cheers." They spoke in unison. Without further delay both took a welcome generous swig of their beverages.

"I'm really happy to be here with you." Annika blurted out sounding somewhat childlike. Chris was about to respond when two figures approached the booth.

"Mind if we join you?" Not waiting for a response, they took the empty seats on both benches, filling the booth. Annika sat open mouthed at the intrusion. Chris, waiting for it.

"Officer Rufus?" Annika exclaimed. Displeasure evident in her tone. The officer had taken the space next to Chris. Out of his uniform, dressed in civilian clothing.

"Good evening Annika. This is Detective Hill." He replied gesturing to the man sitting opposite him.

"What are you doing here?" She asked. The annoyance abundantly obvious, her highpoint moment was rapidly souring. Without waiting for an answer, she looked directly at Chris. "Did you know about this?" Chris did not respond.

"Annika, it's very important we talk." Hill instructed, taking control of the situation. "You are in a very serious situation." Annika took a consolation mouthful of her wine before gesturing she was prepared to listen. "Can you confirm you know Deborah Green?"

"Yes."

"Do you know her outside of her employment of Haskins & Wilcox?" Annika thought for a moment before responding.

"I think I need to leave." She said, although trapped in the confined dead-end booth by Hill.

"Annika. I strongly recommend you stay. As I said we're looking into a serious situation. What happens here could have a major bearing on your future."

"That's what I'm afraid of. I'd like to go now please."

"If you leave now it's going to be much more difficult for you." Rufus interjected. "Speak with us, we can help you.". His voice filled with sincerity. Annika gave a sigh.

"Yes, I know her outside of my employment." She finally admitted.

"Did you send her the admin position application forms before the job was officially advertised?" Hill asked sensitively.

"Yes, I did." She looked at Rufus. "I know I lied, when Susan asked me, but there's no crime, is there?"

"No, that's not a crime." Hill reassured. "Tell me how you know Debbie?"

"I just do."

"She only relocated to Santa Rosa recently. I'd like to know what your relationship is?"

"We're just acquaintances. I don't recall how it started. Don't you know people who live beyond here? Can you recite how you met each and every one of them?"

"Okay, let's stay calm. Describe your relationship now."

"We're just friends. She told me she was looking for work. I knew the position was coming up, so I forwarded her the application documents. I told her the job would go on about lunchtime, last Thursday. I didn't realize she would submit the moment it went live." Annika shot the detective an unimpressed look. "Is that it? Can I go?"

"So, are you on a date now with Chris?"

"It's not a date. Chris wanted to celebrate getting off his suspension. I offered to join him. For all I knew there could have been a load of people out with him."

"Hmmm, well its four now." Hill joked. Annika did not appreciate the humor. "Do you know why Chris was suspended?" Annika stared briefly at Chris. His eyes were fixed down on the table. He did not want to look at Annika.

"Of course I do. It's my job to know."

"Something that interests me. Debbie is your friend. You get her a job at Haskins & Wilcox. Then after her interview, Chris strikes her with his motor vehicle. On her first day he audibly threatens to drag her out of the office by her hair. Now you're out celebrating with him for getting off the hook. That seems strange to me, would you not agree?"

"Look detective, she's a friend. Nothing special to me. I know she's very possessive when it comes to men. If she was hassling him like that, I don't blame Chris for retaliating. She asked me for a favor to get the job. She asked, I helped. I don't hold some unwavering loyalty to her."

"She's only a friend, nothing more?"

"No." The response conveyed uncertainty, worry filled Annika where this might be leading.

"Interesting." Hill said more to himself. "What about Katelyn Fisher?" Annika noticeably flinched at the name.

"What about her?"

"Is she a friend?"

"No. Just a colleague. To be honest, I don't really know her." Maxi reappeared, somewhat startled by the two new gentlemen present at the table.

"Er, do you want more drinks? Are you ready to order?"

"Can you give us five hon?" Hill asked. Maxi looked at Annika, who was clearly distressed. Hill recognized the concern on the server's face. He pulled his badge out and flashed it to her.

"Don't worry, she's fine." He reassured. With a nod, Maxi scurried off.

"So, Katelyn is only a colleague? She is nothing more to you?"

"No."

"Where is your mother?" The randomness of the questions was really throwing Annika. Desperation to escape filled her.

"She's dead."

"I'm sorry to hear that. When did she die?"

"Fourteen months ago." Chris was surprised. He did not know anything about this, normally the office gossips wouldn't even allow you to have a bowel movement without everyone knowing about it.

"Do you mind me asking how she died?" Hill probed.

"Yes I do." After letting go a long sigh, Annika answered. "She committed suicide."

"That's awful. What about your father?"

"Never knew him. I've got no idea where he is now."

"What was the circumstances of your mother's suicide?"

"Jesus, I'm not getting into that now. She was depressed, got treated like shit by men and couldn't take it anymore. I want to change subject."

"Okay. Fair enough. Does Debbie know Katelyn's parents?"

"No. She's never mentioned them." The apparent unpredictability of what topic would be raised next was completely unsettling Annika. She considered jumping up on the table and making a run for it. But with the tight space and her heeled shoes, it did not lend itself to actually executing the scheme. Instead, she guzzled back her remaining glass of wine.

"Do you know Katelyn's parents?"

"No. Why would I? I know Katelyn's father died of an epileptic fit last Friday, but only because I work with her and organized her compassionate leave. I don't know anything beyond that."

"Just to update you, we are no longer treating her father's death as natural causes. It's now a homicide investigation." Annika's face visibly drained of all color. She said nothing. "When was the last time you saw Stan?" The pause was epic. Within the confines of the tiny booth time stopped.

"I've never met him." She eventually snapped.

"Interesting." Hill pondered thoughtfully. Annika's face was reddening, a mixture of intensifying stress and torment. Desperation to escape this ambush.

"Tell me about Debbie's time at Foundation Pharmaceutical." Hill continued the haphazard line of questioning.

"What? I don't know anything about that."

"Her previous employer."

"I don't know anything."

"So, you never visited her, when she worked there? In Fremont?

"No."

"You're saying when I check the visitor book, your name won't be in there?" There was a long pause before Annika answered.

"No."

"What did Debbie tell you she was working on there?"

"Nothing. I have no idea what she did there."

"She never mentioned her work on a new groundbreaking pain relief treatment for cerebral palsy?"

"No."

"Well. I find that bizarre." Hill shook his head in an exaggerated display of confusion. Annika opened her mouth to reply but stopped herself from engaging further. "This drug is said to be revolutionary, it's still out for FDA approval but the community of cerebral palsy sufferers are very excited about it. While Debbie is no scientist, she was heavily involved in its development. I can't believe she never spoke about it to you."

"She never mentioned it."

"Did your late mother know Stan?" Annika was now beyond her threshold. She had to get away. Right now.

"Am I under arrest or something? If not, I want to leave right now." She attempted to stand as best as the overhanging immovable table would allow. "Let me out please."

"I've only got a couple more questions." Hill protested.

"I don't care, I want to leave now." She demanded, her voice elevating. Desperation building. Hill raised both hands in the air in surrender. He slid his way along out of the seat. Annika desperately followed in an ungainly exit. As soon as she was out, Annika was gone. Hill slid back in and looked at Chris, who lifted his head for the first time since the pair of law enforcers arrived.

"I think your date is over."

Chapter 25

Chris returned from the restroom with his head spinning. His involvement in luring Annika into the trap was beyond distressing. It was torture to spectate at her shock demise, knowing she had expected this evening to be the night of her dreams. Whatever the circumstances and underhanded tactics that led to their date, Chris could not shake the feeling Annika was as much a participant as himself. Something dark and evil was at work here. Chris doubted the source was Annika. He had every reason to hate her, but all he felt was pity and compassion.

Chris rejoined the officer and detective who were deep in discussion. They quickly muted the topic as he approached.

"Thank you for your help on getting us access to Annika." Rufus offered as Chris sat down. "You okay?"

"Yeah." Chris said quietly. Both the law enforcement officers waited as Chris was clearly plucking up the courage to ask a question. "Judging by the questions you just asked, you both know more about my situation than I do. Care to fill me in?"

"We don't know as much as you think, but yes, today has been a very productive day. Unfortunately, every answer has led to a host of more questions." Hill was about to continue when Maxi tentatively returned.

"Sorry to interrupt. Do you need anything?" She kept a clear distance from the table but could not prevent herself from peering around Hill to see if Annika was still in attendance.

"You can get him another one of those." Hill said pointing to Chris's half-drunk beer. "Unfortunately, I'm still on duty, do you serve root beer?"

"Yes."

"Okay, I'll go for that."

"Same." Added Rufus. As soon as the server was out of earshot, Hill turned back to Chris.

"There's some stuff I can tell you, some I can't. I also have an important question for you." Chris nodded with apprehension. "I need to know more detail about your one-night stand with Debbie."

"Like what?"

"As I understand it, she bought you back to hers. She attempted to seduce you, but you didn't actively engage." Chris looking deeply self-conscious, nodded to indicate Hill was correct. He quickly took a draw from his beer on the go. It didn't remove the embarrassment. "Then you woke in her bed, naked, but without any recollection of undressing, getting into bed or any other activity that may or may not have transpired that evening.

"That is correct."

"You have absolutely no recollection of having any sexual relations with Debbie that night?"

"None whatsoever."

"Is that something that has ever happened to you before?"

"No, not really. I've forgotten innocuous events of an evening before when that drunk, but anything significant I'd always remember. There's no way I could have full

188

sex with a stranger and not remember." The further Chris allowed himself to consider this fact, the more dubious the apparent sequence of events became. "I can't believe I could get completely naked and in bed with her and not recall that either, yet I know that happened."

"Chris, did Debbie give you anything while you were in her apartment?"

"Like what?"

"Anything, a tablet, a drink, some food?" Chris thought back to the hazy rendezvous, an engagement he had been desperately attempting to disregard from his mind since it had ensued.

"Yes. She made me coffee. I remember now. After she had finished making her play on me, she offered me the coffee I originally came back for. I was desperate to leave but she was insistent. In the end I gave in and humored her."

"I think she drugged you." Chris was startled. He looked at Rufus for validation. The black officer nodded his head gravely.

"What? Like a date rape drug?

"Yes, I believe so. In Debbie's former employment she may well have worked with Rohypnol, better known as Roofies or Gamma-Hydroxybutyric Acid, more commonly referred to as GHB. Ketamine is another possibility. They are all classic date rape drugs. I suspect Debbie spiked your coffee with one or a mixture of these substances."

"That's crazy." Chris could not absorb this information. The table sat in a moment of silence while he attempted to process the severity of the situation.

Appropriately at this point, Maxi returned with the drinks. Looking as terrified as Annika had shortly before, she served the beverages hastily, eager to get away.

"Cheque please." Hill called as she made her retreat. With a small nod she was gone.

"I need you to come into the station after this drink. We'll drive you over. It's almost certainly too late for a urine or blood test to detect the presence of these drugs in your system, but a hair follicle test will confirm this suspicion. We can get this off to the lab tonight. We should get the preliminary ELISA test back by close of play tomorrow. The more accurate confirmation test to rule out false positives is three days."

"Yeah sure." If he was drugged, he wanted to know. "So, what was the rest of the questions about? You think they murdered Stan?" Hill and Rufus exchanged glances. Rufus gave a shrug.

"Chris, I can't tell you everything and what I do say now stays at this table. Understood?" Hill spoke in a muted tone, leaning forward on the table. His expression conveying, he was deadly serious.

"Of course."

"The Fishers relocated here from LA for Stan to retire." Chris nodded. "Do you have any idea why they chose Santa Rosa of all places to relocate?"

"Katelyn said Stan always loved this place. She told me roughly twenty-five years ago his plane from LA to San Francisco had to divert here when on a business trip. Technical difficulties or something. He had to spend the night and just fell in love with the place. He regularly visited between LA and Frisco. She said one day he

190

announced he was retiring and wanted them all to move here. I don't think it was a popular decision, but Katelyn soon settled in. I don't know about her mother."

"What do you think really grabbed him all those years ago on a one-night emergency layover?"

"I've no idea. It's not a bad place to live but hardly the city of dreams."

"What if I told you, on that chance night, it wasn't the architecture that moved him. Maybe something more organic?" Chris thought for a minute, trying to interpret the cryptic information.

"Stan met someone?"

"He did indeed. He spent the night with a woman he picked up in a bar."

"How do you know this?"

"I'd like to say I'm a good detective, but it's more luck. I happened to speak to the right person today who gave me a lot of background."

"He fell in love with this woman?"

"Kind of, but not from the one night of passion. He got her pregnant."

"Oh."

"Stan kept a secret double life. Rhonda gave birth to a daughter. He visited as often as he could, sent money, etcetera. It all ticked by for years, two or three visits a year. The daughter grew up and moved on with her life. Stan kept a relationship of sorts with the daughter, but once she had moved out, he cut it off completely with her mom. It's quite impressive he managed to maintain the charade for some twenty-three years. The mother took it pretty hard, became a depressed alcoholic. Pretty tragic. Last year she ended it all. Hung herself."

"Jesus." Chris exclaimed. Shortly afterwards the penny dropped. "Annika's mother?"

"Yes."

"Annika has a sister?"

"No Chris. Annika is the daughter." Hill gave Chris a few seconds to digest this before continuing. "It hit Annika pretty hard. Although she kept herself together at work, she was in a real mess. She kept constantly threatening to expose Stan if he didn't step up and support her. I guess Stan decided to take a massive risk, rather than coming clean to his family. He moved them all here so he could be more in Annika's life, keep her sweet and still try to live the double life."

"So where does Debbie fit into all this? Or me for that matter?"

"Well, that's the questions we are asking ourselves Chris. We don't have those pieces together yet."

"Do you think Annika killed Stan?"

"Again, we don't know. We need to fathom Debbie before we can understand and answer that question." Chris took a long drink of his beer. His head swimming with the information. "The other interesting case in point; If Stan had made so much effort into maintaining his double life, why would he let Katelyn work in the same office as his secret other daughter?"

Chapter 26

Another bright sunny morning commenced in Santa Rosa. The ambient temperature still far from peaking. The warmth currently at a comfortable level. Hill allowed himself the pleasure of just basking in the sunlight, lent against his police issued detective Sedan. The Fisher family had been given the green light to return home. Hill, already there waiting to greet them.

Continuing to commandeer the ever-willing Officer Rufus for the next two days, despite this being his rotated weekend off. Hill asked him to start late. Yesterday was a long day even by Hill's standards, he did not forecast that situation improving over the weekend so thought it better to allow his makeshift partner some rest.

Hill removed his sunglasses while unlocking his cellphone to check for fresh email activity. A recent couple from the forensic team detailing what was searched, tested and taken for further inspection. Another from the cyber nerds who were already combing through Stan's electronic devices. Hill previously outlining what would be of interest beyond the clearly illegal or clandestine. The department always performed to a prodigious standard, often central to cracking numerous cases over the years. Hill held full confidence, if there was something on Stan's hard drive to acquire, they would retrieve it.

No emails today from any of the labs dealing with the autopsy. The standard delay, a source of genuine frustration. Until gathered, the full homicide resources were unavailable. Instead he would have to rely on his savvy detecting ability. Hill locked the cell, closed his eyes while directing his face up to the warmth of the sun. The distant sound of an approaching car engine became audible down the driveway. Moments later a taxicab pulled up at the house. With a weary expression, Barbra and Katelyn departed. A spontaneous night in a hotel with no change of clothes had visibly burdened them further.

Katelyn looked over towards Hill while Barbra paid the fare. The taxi pulled away leaving them stood lost in fatigue. Hill hauled his frame off the side of the vehicle. Leisurely he approached them.

"Good morning." He greeted.

"We were told we can go back inside now." Barbra conveyed tensely. Fearful Hill was at hand to put a stop to their return.

"Yes, that's correct. You should have an email providing an inventory of the items we have removed. They will be returned to you as soon as is possible." Barbra gave a frosty nod but said nothing more. "Katelyn." Hill stepped closer. "Could I borrow you for a few minutes? I have a couple of questions." Before she could respond Barbra stepped forward.

"Detective, we haven't even stepped foot inside. Can this not wait? I'm sure Katelyn would at least like a shower and change her clothing."

"Appreciated, it won't take long." He reassured.

"I'm sorry but not without our lawyer present." Barbra stated firmly. I had a long conversation with him on the phone last night. He was explicit that we should not talk to the police without his presence."

Hill smiled to himself. "Yes, that's good advice, especially if I considered Katelyn a suspect. But here's the thing. Katelyn is not a suspect in my mind. However, I do have a couple of individuals, not in this family, who are of great interest to me. I believe Katelyn may know information that can assist me in developing them from persons of interest to firm suspects. I would sooner undertake this work now, so I can close the net on them before they disappear. If I have to wait for your lawyer, then…"

"Absolutely not." Barbra interrupted angrily.

"Don't I get a say in this?" Katelyn snapped. Barbra did not respond, looking at Hill with total mistrust. "I'll speak with you."

"Katelyn, that's not a good idea." Barbra warned.

"Mom, it's okay. I can look after myself." Barbra held the stare at Hill for a long period. Eventually she silently turned and disappeared inside the house.

"Thank you Katelyn." Hill said as soon as they were alone.

"Just find out what happened." She returned. "What do you want to know?"

"I believe Chris has told you the full story regarding Debbie and Annika?"

"He has. What does that have to do with my father?"

"How would you describe your relationship with Annika?"

"Pretty much nonexistent until Thursday. Then suddenly she was like my best friend, until I found out it was all a ruse to make a play for Chris."

"What about Debbie?"

"No relationship at all. I had never seen her before the day she started working at my office. I said good morning to her, but that was it. Then after it all kicked off with Chris, I never saw her again."

"Okay. Tell me about your father. Is there anything I should know about him you wouldn't want to say in front of your mother?"

"Like what?"

"Do you think he was ever unfaithful to her?"

"Daddy? No way." The question, clearly offensive.

"Look, I know this is a difficult subject, and not nice to even consider, but it is important. Think back. Could it be possible?" Katelyn stopped for a minute to consider the topic.

"I think you're way off detective. There's nothing I'm aware of to even suggest he would do anything like that."

"But he was away on business frequently, often for a week at a time."

"What does that prove?"

"Nothing." Conceded Hill, putting his hands up. "It's just it does give him the opportunity, could we agree on that."

"What's your theory? You need to be careful what you say without any evidence to back it up." Katelyn threw back. She did not like the insinuation one bit. Hill changed tact.

"When is the will being read?"

"As you well know detective. It has stopped due to the investigation." Hill gave Katelyn an impertinent glance.

"No chance, you could ask your mother to provide me with written permission to take a look?" Katelyn did not answer, rolling her eyes by way of response. "Tell me about the night your father died."

"I've already done that. Read the statement."

"I want you to tell me."

"I got home from work. I was supposed to be going out that night. I went straight to my room and got showered and changed. I didn't see any of the family. They were home but it's a big house. Before I dried my hair, I came down to fix myself some food. Daddy was in the kitchen. He didn't look very well. Before I had even asked him what was wrong, he collapsed on the floor and started having a seizure. I moved a couple of chairs near him out of the way, while shouting for mom. As she came into the room, my father stopped moving. I checked for signs of breathing." Katelyn had to pause her account as tears ran down her face. Hill allowed her a moment to collect herself. "I performed CPR while my mother called for an ambulance. I kept the CPR going until the ambulance arrived. We watched while they used a defib numerous times to start his heart. Then they said he was dead."

"Any visitors to the house that day, you know about?"

"None, but I was at work for most of the day."

"Tell me about the CCTV camera on the front gate."

"We've said all this. It broke about a week ago. Daddy never got around to fixing it."

"Don't you think that's a little strange?" Katelyn did not respond immediately. The question hung like a bad smell. She moodily kicked some gravel before looking back at the detective.

"Yes now, of course it looks strange. Now my father is dead, and our house has been combed over by a forensic team and I'm answering questions about his murder to a detective. Yes, it looks completely fucking suspect. But at the time it didn't. Daddy just complained that another crappy overpriced piece of technology had failed, and he would have to get it sorted out. At the time home security was just a deterrent. You don't actually expect to ever have to need it."

"Maybe. I don't know, it's possibly my line of work, but I see it differently. I observe firsthand the bad things people do. Kinda changes your perspective." Hill gave a small ironic smile. Katelyn did not return it.

"Anyone in the house ever lost their fob for the gates?" Hill watched Katelyn physically jolt as a revelation occurred in her mind."

"Yes." She whispered deep in thought.

"Who?"

"Me."

"Where and when?"

"A few weeks ago. I went to work, used the fob to exit. When I got home, I reached the gate, and it was gone. Holy shit. I thought at the time it had just broken off. I had a spare. I didn't tell anyone." Hill could see the stress building in the young lady as dark connections were being made into the scenario that now appeared to have played out.

"Where do you keep your keys when you are at work?"

"They are just placed on my desk, in plain sight."

"Can you remember if you left them unattended that day?"

"I can't say for certain, but I leave my desk all the time, meetings, going to speak to people in different departments out of my office. There would have been opportunity to take the fob." Hill took his cell out and started dialing.

"Can you remember what day? It's important." Katelyn thought for a moment.

"I can't remember. Damn it." She shouted angrily at herself.

"Anything memorable on that day? Anything we can use to pinpoint when the fob went missing?" Katelyn thought hard, she closed her eyes visualizing.

"Yes. It was the same day Sarah handed her notice in." As Katelyn made the connection, Rufus answered Hill's call.

"Rufus, where are you now?"

"I'm just about to reach the station."

"One sec. Katelyn do you know if there is CCTV in your office?"

"Yes, there is." She confirmed.

"Rufus, I need you to get hold of Susan Roswell. Find out what day Sarah..." Hill looked at Katelyn.

"DeAngelo" She confirmed.

"What day Sarah DeAngelo handed her notice in. Then check the CCTV on that day in Katelyn's office. You're looking for someone removing a fob from her keys on the desk. Move quick." Hill hung up and looked at Katelyn.

"One other question. What were the circumstances of your employment at Haskins & Wilcox?" Katelyn thought back.

"Now you ask that, it was slightly peculiar. A week before we relocated, I got an email advertising the position. I had joined a local recruitment agency to look for work, but the email wasn't from them. It was directly from Haskins & Wilcox. I wondered at the time if someone at the recruitment agency was selling details of good candidates on their books, kind of a black-market deal. As far as I can tell I was the only candidate so secured the position after a telephone interview with Susan the day before we flew out here. It didn't strike me as strange at the time, but now that I look back, it's odd."

"What was your father's reaction about your job."

"Again, it was really odd. He was always a stickler for me to earn my own way in the world. Not to rely on his money. But he was not pleased when I told him I had the job. I could never understand why. He kept saying there were other jobs, better jobs in Santa Rosa. He was quite forceful. It made me dig my heels in and refuse to go elsewhere." Katelyn paused, looking at the ground. She raised her gaze up to meet Hill's. "Was his issue something to do with Annika?"

"Quite possibly. I'm still trying to understand it myself."

"The key fob. It's going to be Annika." Katelyn stated knowingly.

"Yes, it would appear so."

Chapter 27

The mid-morning sun radiated through the curtains as Chris lay motionless in his bed. Wide awake and had been most of the night. Processing endless thoughts, not knowing where to start. His cell rang, bringing him back into the present. The caller identity withheld. Chris knew this could be Rufus or Hill. Just as likely it might be Debbie. There was no way to tell.

"Hello?"

"Chris, what the fuck happened last night?" It was Debbie and her tone indicated she was not amused at the proceedings of his date. "Annika said two cops interrupted you both, throwing loads of stupid questions at her."

"I had no idea that was going to happen." He lied. "They put the screws on me as well, after she left." Chris decided his best play for the short term was to appear completely ignorant. He prayed she would buy it.

"Annika said they asked questions about her mother and whether she knew Katelyn's father?"

"Yes, that's correct, they seemed to know the answers to the questions they were asking. One of them was Officer Rufus."

"Rufus? Shit, that guy is becoming a pain in the ass. What did you tell them?"

"Nothing I haven't said before, about you stalking me. That's it. What else do I know?"

"What about your date with Annika? Did you reveal the circumstance? My involvement?" Debbie sounded tense. She was used to being in control, even when her act was to portray the opposite. Now a joker card had been unexpectedly played, she was genuinely alarmed.

"Annika told them we had just met up to celebrate my return from suspension. She said she had no idea how many others were attending. I went with that. They didn't seem to be interested in that aspect." Chris, now the one to feed the alternative reality. She gave the impression she was buying it. How the tables had turned.

"Good. Let's keep it that way. What do they know about me?"

"Not a lot. They seemed to know loads about Annika but not you. I think they were hoping Annika would help them link you into it all. She didn't give them anything of use. I take it you know they are treating Stan's death as murder?"

"I am aware."

"Are you worried?"

"No. Why would I be? I had nothing to do with that man. I don't know him. My only interest was getting Katelyn's dirty claws off you."

"There's something I need to ask you." Chris solicited awkwardly. "It's not relevant to this, but I need to know all the same. That night, when I came back to yours, did we have sex?"

"What, don't you remember?" She belittled. Despite everything working against her, Debbie could not help but take a condescending tone.

"It's a simple question Debbie. Did we have sex or not?"

"Well apart from the fumble on the couch, you passed out pretty soon afterwards. So even if I wanted to, it wasn't going to happen. Besides Annika would have killed me. Look, I've got to go. Keep your mouth shut and stay out of the way. Whatever happens I can still bring you down any time I want."

Before Chris could protest, she hung up.

Hill returned to the station. The conversation with Katelyn proved fruitful in attempting to maximize time efficiency. Once the conclusive lab results came back and it was officially a homicide investigation, much more resource and labor would be at his disposal. For now, on the investigating side it was just him and his conscripted police officer.

He returned to his office. A conference call was set up with Foundation Pharmaceutical shortly, Debbie's previous employer. He was very interested in what they might be able to reveal. While waiting, Hill looked through his emails again. Still nothing from the police labs. The delay was intolerable. Eventually Hill logged onto the video calling platform early, unable to meaningfully engage in anything else.

The clock slowly ticked past eleven, the arranged start time. Suddenly the screen flickered, switching to reveal a grey-haired gentleman. Easily mid-fifties, a gaunt thin face, framed with wire rim glasses and a white lab coat. He looked every bit the stereotypical pharmaceutical scientist.

"Good morning." Hill welcomed.

"Good morning detective." The face on the screen returned with a strong English accent. "I am Dr. Brian Rose, the project lead for new drug developments. I believe you have some questions regarding Deborah Green?"

"Yes, that is correct doctor." The scientist pulled a face of modest embarrassment.

"Call me Brian, please." He offered informally.

"Thank you, Brian. I appreciate you speaking to me on a Saturday."

"Not a problem, I pretty much work every Saturday."

"I assume you worked with Debbie?"

"Yes, she was one of my lead technicians. We had a close working relationship."

"Can you briefly describe her role to me?"

"I guess I would describe it as a hybrid role. The scientists employed here are working to develop new drugs. We determine a disorder with inadequate treatments. Research and understand the condition to either progress a drug already in existence or go for an entirely new treatment. We conduct all the testing ourselves, including human trials. Once we get the patent and the FDA approval, we sell a license to whichever of the major drug companies is prepared to pay the asking price. Sometimes it's multiple licenses, sometimes an exclusive deal. Occasionally even the patent itself."

"Sounds like a lucrative business?"

"The upfront costs are massive and there is no guarantee we will get the FDA approval. It's a high stakes game, but yes, when it pays off, it really pays off. I'm not a shareholder but I very much wish I was. Anyway, back to Debbie. Her job was integral to supporting the developing scientists. We want those individuals to concentrate solely on the development task. The technicians organize the prep work, ready the necessary materials and equipment. They structure the results and data analysis. All the things we don't want the scientists to waste their time on. It's a very difficult position. While the pay is good, it doesn't scratch the surface of what the scientists cost us. The technical understanding and application of a lead technician is right up there. Not an easy buck to earn."

"How would you describe the competence of Debbie?"

"Professionally, very competent."

"What about outside of the professional confine?" Brian dropped his head with a self-reflective smile on his face. With a touch of humor galvanizing his words he responded.

"She was a bloody pain in the ass."

"How so?"

"She liked attention. Male attention. She seemed to like the married ones best. There's a number of married men here who I know had some sort of extra-curricular activity with Debbie. I'm sure there's plenty more I don't know about. Either way it was very disruptive to the working environment. Far from ideal."

"If you don't mind me asking, were you one of these men?" Brian gave a hearty English private school laugh.

"Lord no. I'd like to say I'm far too old, but I don't think that bothered her. I was more of a father figure to her, she certainly needed one in her life. I spent a lot of time trying to undo the fixes she got herself into. When the request came through for someone to speak to you about her, I was the natural choice. To be honest she got herself into a position where her employment became untenable. She left before the axe was swung. I assume she knew it was coming and wanted the end to be on her terms."

"Yes, that fits with the profile I'm establishing on her."

"Do you mind me asking what this is about? Is she in serious trouble?"

"I don't know at the moment. I can tell you this is a homicide investigation."

"Dear Lord." Brian exclaimed.

"I don't know what Debbie's involvement is at the moment, if anything. But she's certainly ranking as a suspect."

"That's very sad and disappointing news Detective."

"Indeed." Hill agreed. "Did Debbie have access to the drugs?"

"Yes she did, both the raw materials and the finished development products."

"Are these substances tightly controlled?"

"Yes very. To be honest the lead technicians have more access than the development scientists. Everything is recorded, closely measured, and audited. But there always a level of shrinkage that cannot be accounted for.

Not so much with the developed products, but the raw materials. Depending on the quantities used there is a formula for an acceptable level of this unaccounted shrinkage. Too high, or too frequently, it would be flagged and investigated."

"Was Debbie ever flagged and investigated in this nature?"

"You think she stole out of here?"

"I don't know. Possibly. Call it an educated hunch at this point in time." Hill answered honestly. He was concerned Brian may start to cover for Debbie if she was special to him. Hill could withhold a lot more if inclined, but decided if he was open and honest, Brian hopefully would reciprocate. It was all a judgment call. Most of his profession was centered around knowing who and when to reveal withheld information. Hill had a knack for it, assisting in making him a successful detective. Sure, he got it wrong sometimes, but to profit from others, occasionally you need to speculate to accumulate.

"Technically it would be possible if she was careful and didn't get too greedy. She would be looking to undertake this when the yield figures were reasonable and could only take so much as not to bring the wastage figure above the threshold of concern."

"If I name some random substances, will you be able to tell me if she had access to them?"

"Some, yes. There is a wide range of raw materials, so I might have to check."

"Fair enough. First up, Tetrodotoxin." Immediately Hill recognized the reaction of horror in Brian's face. Even through the electronic portal it was palpable.

"Oh my Lord." Brian finally stammered out. "We are in the latent stages of developing a drug to provide pain relief for cerebral palsy."

"I read this on your website. It listed the names of individuals key to its development. Debbie was named."

"That is correct." Brian confirmed shaking his head, displaying distress. "One of the active ingredients is Tetrodotoxin. There's a microscopic amount in each tablet. It's a highly toxic poison, a sodium channel blocker. In the quantity we use, it provides a mild paralysis of the muscles giving the patient the impression of their muscles relaxing. It also impairs signals to the brain, disrupting the pain sensors, masking their signals. Too much and the patient will lose the ability to control their breathing. They would asphyxiate fully conscious."

"Debbie had access to this?"

"She did. We pioneered our own, awaiting patent, technique for extracting the toxin of the ovaries of the Diodon Liturosus better known as the Puffer Fish. While we were perfecting the extraction technique the yields were all over the place. It's not the kind of substance you can easily buy in at pharmaceutical grade. We had to produce it ourselves. She would have had plenty of opportunity to pilfer a small quantity without anyone being any the wiser. Not that you would need much in any case. A twenty-five-microgram exposure would be lethal. To give you context, a cyanide exposure would require two hundred and fifty micrograms to be deadly, ten times as much."

"Okay, that's clear and concerning in equal measures. What about Ketamine?"

"Hmmm, it's not impossible. We do hold it here, but not something I recall her having direct access to. Probably a substance it would be easier for her to acquire on the street."

"What about Rohypnol or GHB?"

"Yes, both are ingredients in the cerebral palsy medication. Probably more problematic to remove in any great quantity undetected, but she certainly had frequent access."

"Okay that's very useful to know. Did she ever mention a woman called Annika to you?"

"Not that I can recall. That's quite a distinctive name. If she had mentioned her, I think I would remember."

"What about Santa Rosa? Did she ever mention here?" Brian thought for a while.

"No, I don't think so. Doesn't ring a bell."

"Stan Fisher?" As before, a noticeable reaction in Brian manifested.

"She never mentioned a Stan to me."

"You're sure?" Hill's sixth sense detected fabrication.

"Not that I can recall detective." Despite hill's suspicion he elected to leave it alone for now. Other thoughts were processing, taking precedence.

"Did she ever talk about her parents?" Brian hesitated a long time, clearly framing his answer.

"Towards the end, when all her misdemeanors were coming out, she got really emotional with me in my private office. She spoke about her father who had shunned her, her whole life. It was the only time she ever mentioned him, or any family member. I'm certain she never stated his name. She never spoke of her mother."

Hill had to fight to maintain an even complexion as the sideward concept developed within his focused mind. Was it possible she was also a daughter of Stan? Could his philandering have extended beyond Rhonda? Might Debbie be another half-sister? It would explain her affinity to Annika. If a total outcast by Stan, it might also account for her hatred towards Katelyn. This unsubstantiated speculation appeared to fit nicely into the missing part of the puzzle.

Chapter 28

Chris spent a few hours catching up on his work, preparing for Monday's management meeting. Far from enthusiastic about standing out in front of his peers, all attention focused on him. This during a period where he and his non-professional activities were of such interest.

Chris was nearing a respectable finishing point when his cell rang. Potentially a call from Hill or Rufus to enlighten him on the preliminary lab results. He viewed the notification bar to see a strange number rolling across the screen. It seemed a long time since anyone was happy to reveal their number to him.

"Hello?" He answered.

"Hi Chris, its Annika."

"Hi." His response was flat. *What now?*

"Sorry for just running out on you last night." She offered. Chris could not determine if she understood the dynamic. Did she comprehend he had been working with the two law enforcers or had she considered him as surprised as her, when they gatecrashed the party.

"That was awful, last night. I felt terrible for you." Chris tested the point. A long pause ensued. Annika was not ready to fill the gap. Chris had to improvise, sell his position to her. "They started on me after you left."

"Really? The assholes." She appeared to be buying it.

"Yeah. Assholes." Chris agreed.

"What did they ask you?"

"They asked what I knew about you, but mainly Debbie. They seemed to think I knew more than I did."

"It's so awful." Annika muted softly. "Look, with so much going on, I'm feeling really bad about you getting caught up in this. I think I need to fill you in a bit more. I don't want to ruin our friendship and I don't want you to think badly of me. I just need to be honest."

"It's okay Annika. You can talk to me."

"Look, if I tell you this, you need to keep what you know to yourself. You can't go running to Officer Rufus or that other one. Most of all, you can't tell Debbie what you know. If she finds out, she'll kill me." Chris failed to determine if the last remark was a figure of speech, or an actual prediction. Whether everything he would learn would be filtered to Hill and company, depended on the context. Better at this point to appear a team player.

"Okay Annika, you can trust me."

"Shit here goes. Stan. He's, my father."

"Oh."

"Yeah. I know. That makes Katelyn my half-sister. It's all a big secret. Stan visited me and mom regularly. We were his secret family, but he stuck by us. I appreciate it's a bizarre setup. I didn't know any different. It was normal to me when I was growing up. He loved me, made our time together as a family really special. I loved my dad. Everything worked, until…" An emotional pause followed. Chris could hear Annika breathing heavily as the weight of the confession bore its toll. "Until he broke it off with mom. Then everything went wrong. My mom became dramatically depressed overnight. Her decline was devastating. When she took her own life, I, I…" Annika

212

failed to finish. Completion was not required. The weight of the broken sentence as heavy as any combination of fitting vocabulary. Eventually, she continued. "He was there for me. He even relocated his other family here so we could be local to each other. I'm grieving for my mother, clouded in the shame of suicide and now my father, but nobody knows. I'm totally alone with it all."

"I'm so sorry Annika, that's awful."

"You have to know Chris, it's Debbie who killed him."

"Oh." Chris simply responded, distracted in the consideration of what Annika's part was in all the dark endeavors.

"I'm certain it was her. I'm also worried you might think I had something to do with it."

"I never said that." Chris replied awkwardly.

"It's okay. After what has been done to you, if I were you, I'd be thinking it. Honestly Chris, I really didn't have anything to do with it. The whole thing with Debbie, you and me. It was all her handywork. One night I confessed to her how much I loved you, for years, but never had the confidence to even hint. I couldn't even bring myself to provide you with some signals. I told her, you were completely oblivious. It was all fine until I told Debbie I knew you had fallen for Katelyn. She became really angry. I really don't understand why Debs cared about it so much. Just something I admitted in a drunk girly conversation after we shared a bottle of wine. Before I knew it, she strongarmed me, getting her a job at our workplace. Then she went out on that Friday to compromise you. It was all a setup, a trick. I had no idea

213

what she was up to. Saturday, she confessed what she had done. I couldn't believe it. The girl is a total psycho. She started telling me how she planned it all to play out, to eventually force you into a relationship with me. I was terrified. I wanted no part of it. But she's so crazy, I had to go with it, or I might end up her target. I felt awful." Annika's emotions boiled over during the admission, sobbing as she confessed.

"It's okay Annika." Chris responded soothingly.

"It's not okay. Even going out last night before the police ambush. I felt sick to my stomach. I wanted you, yes. But not through threat and intimidation. You have to understand how difficult this is for me to speak so candidly. I want you still, but only if you want me. Not forced or blackmailed into being with me. I was so scared. Terrified. I had to go along with it."

"Okay Annika, I believe you." Chris thought about his next question before throwing it out there. "Why are you telling me now? The threat of Debbie hasn't changed, has it?"

"No, that hasn't changed. The magnitude has though. I had no idea until last night, my father's death was murder. I loved him, aware of his epilepsy. It terrified me he might have such a terrible episode it permanently affected him. Might even kill him. When I learned he had died as a result of an extreme epileptic fit, I was devastated. My worst fears had come true. As scary as Debbie is, it did put her in the background. It was easier just to go along with her ruse and wait to sort it out as soon as possible. I did not want to go up against her while secretly grieving for my father. That was until last night, discovering he had been murdered. Chris, it could only have been her. I was following along with her plan, as some sort of ignorant accomplice. Now it's taken on a macabre persona. I spent all of last night thinking, what I could do to put it right. I just couldn't settle on what, other than come clean to you. I need your help Chris. What the hell are we going to do?"

"We could speak to Rufus, if you came clean about all this, it might help." Chris offered sincerely.

"No. It might completely backfire on us. Debbie can still push forward with her threats against you. If the cops fail to prove Debbie's involvement in my father's death, she could easily walk, regardless of whether they know it was her. I don't think it's a good idea to back that woman into a corner. She's unhinged, I don't even want to think about what she's capable of."

"I honestly don't know what else to suggest. I can't understand her interest. You say she's an acquaintance, just a friend. Why would she go to all these crazy lengths to get us together? What's in it for her? Even if she was intent on making it happen, why take such an extreme tactic? Above everything else, why kill Stan? How does that help her goals?" Chris identified there was more information available. If Annika legitimately wanted to partner up to protect them both, she had to provide all the context.

"I spent the whole night asking myself the same question. Why would she kill my father? There is no motive I can see. The only explanation that makes sense to me, is she went to the house to kill Katelyn."

215

A chill ran up his spine. "Kill Katelyn?" Chris's voice raised as anger intensified within. "Kill her? Just to enable us to be together? I don't buy it. It's too extreme."

"Well." Annika spoke softly, as if scared to admit it out loud. "That's what I kept thinking but look at the timeline. Thursday, she applies for the role at work, telling me to ensure she is the only candidate put forward for the position. Friday evening, she goes to remove the competition. Katelyn. I suspect if all had gone to plan, she would start working with us. You wouldn't know her from Adam, but without Katelyn in the game, she could manipulate both of us into getting together. I presume profiting from your grief. However, something went wrong, possibly my father discovered her in the house. He accosts her, so she kills him instead, getting out quick. She thinks on her feet, reconfiguring her plan and departs directly to the leaving party. She waits for an opportunity to make contact with you. Then, well, you know the rest."

Chris did not respond. He thought through the legitimacy of the scenario as Annika had comprehensively laid out. He could not deny there was a tangible logic to it. Even considering the obvious severe magnitude of the events.

"I don't know." Questioning his own judgements verbally.

"Chris, she's crazy. With what she's done to you alone. Is it really that hard to picture her taking it further?"

"Yeah, maybe. But it still doesn't answer why? Why do this for you? What is her loyalty to you?" Annika did not respond. Her long silence confirming to Chris there was an answer. She just did not want to admit it. "Annika, if you want my help you have to tell me, now."

"I saved her life." She blurted out. Chris waited for Annika to disclose the details. Annika continued to sob before elaborating.

"I've known her for a long time. Just a friend, but a better friend than I admitted last night. She just turned up months ago. She had fled Fremont, been sacked from her job. She was in a complete mess. I took her in, I didn't have a choice."

"She forced you?"

"No. A moral choice. I had to help her. Anyway, after about a week she was really blue, not crying or talking. Completely introverted, just a hollow shell. One morning, I was leaving for work. She kept asking what time I would be home. Similar odd questions. I got halfway to the office, but all I could think is she mirrored my mom the last time I left her, before she killed herself. I turned back, headed home. I found Debbie unconscious. She had taken an overdose. I called the paramedics and saved her."

"Shit." Chris whispered.

"She didn't talk about it for ages, not with me anyway. She got counseling and started improving. One night we got drunk together in my apartment. That's when I revealed my long-standing crush on you. Shortly afterward she acknowledged what happened that day. She kept talking about how I saved her life, and now she was going to sort out mine. I didn't think much of it, drunk rambling. However, it's developed into this. She's obsessed with making this happen. All the madness, it's all at her hand. It appears she has now killed for the cause.

217

Even if it wasn't her intended target. I had to go along with it out of fear of what she might do next. I didn't want any of this. Now things are starting to fall apart, who knows what she is going to do next."

Chris pondered the information, unsure what to say. His instinct was to go straight to Rufus and Hill, Annika in tow and divulge the whole dirty business. He also understood it was the last thing Annika wanted. She was scared and did not know who to trust, all apart from Chris.

Chapter 29

Hill ended the call with Rufus. As he did so, the lab preliminary test result came back on Chris's hair sample. GHB was present in his system. Another puzzle piece locked in. He had been drugged. Seemingly on the night, back at Debbie's flat.

Rufus's call confirming Annika had removed the fob from Katelyn's key as suspected. Hill sat back in his cheap fake leather desk chair. It was all coming together. He now had enough to credibly tie in both Debbie and Annika to Stan's murder. Plenty of factual substance to provide motive. Still required, was to understand who did what, and when. Clarify which party led and which enabled. On the face of it, Debbie stood strongly out as the pack leader, but years of experience told him not to jump to conclusions.

Hill summoned Rufus to return to the station. The next move would be to arrest Debbie. He was now ready to bring her in. Knowing enough to ask the right questions to fill in the blanks.

Hill debated on the pros and cons of letting Chris know the results of the drug test. Eventually electing to sit tight on this information for the time being. Once Chris learned this it might cause a reaction. Hill wanted to maintain the status quo until he had taken his turn with Debbie.

◆ ◆ ◆

Ninety minutes later Hill and Rufus entered the interview room. Hill cast his eyes upon Debbie for the first time, electing for a black and white to apprehend the suspect.

Hill sat directly opposite Debbie. Her left wrist cuffed to the table. Rufus parked himself on an adjacent table, leaving Hill to work his magic. A tense silence ensued. Debbie stared hatefully into Hill's blue eyes, a look that said a thousand words and then some. Hill held the psychological contest, ensuring he kept his face and posture as relaxed as possible.

She was certainly a pretty young lady. It did little to soften her hard edges. Just from visually regarding her, it was clear this girl could look after herself. Without preamble, still maintaining eye contact, Hill reached across to activate the recording device. He reported the date and time, who was present in the room, finally announcing Debbie had been arrested for the suspected homicide of Stanley Fisher.

"Miss Green, do you understand why you are here?" She nodded slowly, still holding the threatening gaze. "Please speak for the recording."

"Yes." She answered, her voice measured. Unphased.

"Can I call you Debbie?"

"Debs." she responded.

"Okay, Debs. Debs you have the right to a state appointed defense attorney. Do you want to exercise that right?"

"No, I'm happy to continue."

"You want to waver that right?"

"Correct."

"Debs, when was the last time you saw Stan Fisher?"

"I've never met him, that I'm aware of." Debbie broke her eye contact mid-answer.

"Okay, when was the last time you visited the Fisher's residence?"

"I've never been there. I don't know the man, let alone where he lives."

"So, you weren't there on the twelfth, last Friday?"

"No." Hill let out a surprised scoff.

"That is strange."

"What is?" She responded. Immediately cursing herself, appreciative he was baiting her.

"The CCTV in the house doesn't corroborate that fact."

"Really?"

"Debs you have to understand we have a clear picture of what happened that night in the house. I strongly recommend you start telling us the truth or you're going to make things worse for yourself."

"I've told you the truth."

"You're sticking to your story despite CCTV evidence against you?"

"Yes. I suggest you had better show me this evidence you refer to, or I shall assume you are trying to lead me with the threat of something that does not actually exist."

"You don't think it exists?"

"I know it doesn't. I wasn't at the house that night or have ever been, so how could it exist? The fact you are talking about it but not actually showing it to me does support that fact." Debbie stated with confidence. While Hill expressed no outward expression, internally he was taken aback. This lady was composed, aware and confident. Breaking her would not be straight forward.

"All in good time, Debs. For now, let's just stick to questions and honest answers. Did you find Stan's death upsetting?"

"Should I? I never knew the man. I'm only aware he is Katelyn's father and that was through Chris and Annika."

"What would you say if I revealed I knew he was your father?" It was Debbie's turn to scoff.

"I don't know what you think you know, but you're wrong. I never had a father. Whoever it was who knocked up my mom, it wasn't him."

"Interesting." Hill paused for effect. Debbie shot him a look, gesturing to get on with it. "Dr. Rose recalls you talking about your father Stan. He told me all about it." Once again Hill deliberately screwed the facts as reported to him. He knew fully, the admission from Dr. Rose recalling Debbie's conversation regarding her no good father never revealed a name. Brian had only provided the general context of the conversation. While Hill knew this, Debbie did not. He anticipated throwing his hunch at her would trigger a reaction, possibly substantiation. Debbie however, sat impassively under the weight of the embellished revelation. The only outward reaction, a flash in her eyes. Barely perceptible. Hill identified it. "Along with other evidence I have obtained," Hill invented. "I am confident he is your father, and you know it. The DNA swab you took when being processed into custody will prove it."

"Frankly, I do not have the first idea what you are talking about detective." Debbie responded in a matter-of-fact tone.

"Are you denying, you worked with Doctor Brian Rose at Foundation Pharmaceutical?"

"Obviously not. You found my previous employer? Good for you. Evidently, you're a top-notch detective if you found that out. I'm denying Stan is my father." Hill smiled to himself, looking up to the ceiling.

"Debs, this is ludicrous. The DNA match will prove what we both already know in a few days. Why keep lying to me? What is the point?" Debbie shrugged her shoulders but did not respond further.

"Okay. As you bought him up, let's talk about Chris. To save a bit of time, Officer Rufus here, has brought me up to speed on all the events that transpired since your original get together, two Fridays ago. Interestingly, the same date as Stan's murder. I am also aware it was a big charade to force Chris into a relationship with Annika."

"I have no idea what you're talking about."

"Come on Debs. You can't keep telling me black is white and expect me to buy it. We've spoken to both Chris and Annika. They revealed the whole shady scheme. All the details matched in their account. Annika is not going to uphold your lies, so you had better start getting with the program." Hill's temperament quickly altered, resolute firmness filled his words, like a schoolteacher addressing his naughty class. "Start telling me the truth or I'm charging you right now."

"It would appear you know more than I do detective."
Debbie remained completely unphased in her tone. "I have
no clue what you are talking about."

"This is not a clever tactic Debbie." Hill warned,
getting up from his seat and pacing away from the table.
Rufus took his cue.

"Deb's, you're in a bind right now." He spoke softly.
"Open up to us, we can help you. What's done is done.
Let's work together to minimize further pain and
suffering. Let us in." After a long pause Debbie used her
uncuffed hand to point to the visible bruising around her
eye.

"If you're interested in helping me, look at this."
After indicating to the eye injury, she turned her head.
Lifting her blond hair to reveal a healing wound. Finally,
she pulled her top up as best she could, exposing dark
yellowy bruising all around her midriff. "Are you even
interested in what has been done to me?"

"Chris has explained all that, no dice." Hill fired
angrily from across the room. Rufus cut him off.

"You're out of order Hill." He snapped firmly, before
turning back to Debbie. "That looks painful. Yes, we can
get the doctor to examine you and take a statement. We
have to finish this interview first. Let's work together to
get this done, then we can address your injuries."

"My god." Debbie laughed to herself. "You guys. Are
you trying to pull a good cop, bad cop routine on me?"
She continued to laugh. "Do I really look that stupid?"
Neither officer reacted or responded, but Debbie knew she
had called them out. Silly little games were not going to

fly with her. Eventually Hill retook his seat and looked Debbie square in the eye.

"Tell me about Annika? How did she feel about you murdering her father?" For the first time there was a clear reaction from Debbie. The smug grin was instantly wiped from her face, replaced by astonishment.

"What?"

"Annika's father. Stan. Does she know it was you who killed him?" Debbie sat in stunned silence, clearly reeling. Was it possible she did not realize Annika was Stan's daughter? If his theory panned out possibly Debbie's own half-sister? It did not fit, Hill hypothesized it was impossible for Debbie not to be acquainted with this critical aspect of the whole episode. Yet here before him, he witnessed her genuinely appear to learn this for the first time. Despite all her bravado and deception, this was a reaction she was unable to conceal. "Debbie?" Hill prompted. She sat in quiet rumination. Eventually her eyes raised to meet his.

"No comment." She flatly responded.

"Really there's nothing you want to say on this matter?"

"No comment."

"Well, that is interesting. It would appear you did not know Annika was your half-sister.

"No comment."

"Tell me why you left your position at Foundation Pharmaceutical?" Hill changed tact.

"No comment." Clearly Debbie was now rattled. She was no longer in control, not willing to play anymore. Despite her withdrawn engagement, Hill elected to fire a few more cannonballs her way. Just to cement his breech within her defenses.

"Do you want to know what the cause of death was?"

"No comment."

"Tetrodotoxin poisoning."

"No comment."

"What substance were you working with in your lab?"

"No comment."

"Tell me about the patented blowfish tetrodotoxin extraction technique you helped to develop there?"

"No comment."

"Did you know Chris had traces of GHB in his system? From the drug test we performed on him."

"No comment."

"I believe tetrodotoxin and GHB are both active ingredients in the cerebral palsy medication you helped to develop. Is that correct?"

"No comment." Debbie had shut down. Each time she repeated the monotonous phrase, she gave no emotion in her voice, no reaction in her body language. Hill knew though, behind the hard veneer she was breaking. "I want legal representation please."

"You want to stop this interview now, until you're appointed legal aid. Is that correct?"

"Yes."

"Interview terminated at twelve twenty-two." Hill stopped the recording but didn't get up. He held an abrasive glare at Debbie, which she failed to meet. "You're backed into a corner here Debs, you can give me the silent treatment all you like, but it ain't gonna get you out of this one." Hill sighed, relaxing his tense body position and purposeful stare in equal measures. "Is there anything you want to tell me off the record?" Rufus squirmed slightly, shifting awkwardly on his makeshift table seat. This was not following protocol. Hill should not be doing this. Rufus, still wet behind the ears, was a stickler for the rulebook. It appeared the detectives made their own rules.

"Like what detective?" Debbie sneered. "You've already made your mind up, so what's the point? I don't think the truth would stop you now."

"So, explain it to me, give me something to corroborate your innocence. You can appreciate from where I'm sat, it looks pretty damning for you."

"Despite how it looks, and everything I've done, I did not kill that man."

"Debbie, he died from tetrodotoxin poisoning. You're the only person who could possibly have access to that substance. If it wasn't you, how can you explain that."

"Just because…" Debbie started but stopped herself. "No comment."

"There's no recording Debs. Tell me."

"No comment. I want a lawyer." Debbie demanded with a finality in her voice.

"Rufus. Return her to her cell and let the custody sergeant know she wants legal representation. Could take a while on a Saturday afternoon Deb's. Hope you didn't have plans for tonight." Without further word Hill exited the room.

Chapter 30

Hill returned to his desk. A mixture of satisfaction and frustration consuming him. The advancement of the case over the last two days was nothing short of dramatic, yet at the critical point Debbie had adopted silence. With impending legal representation, he would be unlikely to get any more information directly from her. He checked his emails. Still no finalized autopsy from the coroner. There was an email from Foundation Pharmaceuticals. He clicked on it. A PDF file was attached.

Good afternoon Detective,

Thank you for your request. We would normally keep our visitor information completely confidential unless a warrant was issued for the information. However, as you have indicated the seriousness of the crime and that your investigation is time critical I will in this occasion make an exception. I have reviewed our electronic visitor's log. As this is an information restricted facility, all visitors must produce photographic ID to be processed and verified before admittance is accepted. It would be near impossible to enter under an alias. I cross referenced any visitor for

Deborah Green and found one visit from an Annika Walker a week before Debs left us. I presume this is the same Annika you mentioned you are interested in?

I then searched Annika Walker for any other visits. It appears she attended previously, visiting a current employee, Steve Lewis, two days beforehand. I have attached the visit logs and Steve's contact details as a PDF.

I hope this is of some help to you.

Regards
Greta Schmid
Chief Security Officer

Hill opened the attachment. It all seemed to check out. Where Debbie's involvement ended, and Annika's started was a complete mystery. It was clear Debbie was not going to be a fruitful source of information to clarify this. The primary option now, to bring in Annika.

Chris could feel his hand shaking listening to the ringing on his cell. He willed Katelyn to take the call.

"Hi Chris." The tone of her opening address amicable

"Hi Katelyn. I'm sorry for calling. I'm not trying to hassle you."

"It's okay. Sorry for being so stark in the office yesterday."

"How's things your end?" Chris delicately enquired.

"The same really. It's a full-on homicide investigation now. They have just returned my vehicle after forensic testing. I think they are still waiting on the full autopsy results, but they seem convinced."

"Is that involving a detective Hill?"

"Yes. How do you know that?"

"He's been questioning me about Debbie and Annika." Chris kept his answer short. He wasn't sure what Katelyn knew but didn't want to interfere with Hill's process.

"They are both suspects." Katelyn agreed. "I think Annika stole my key fob for the gates. The detective is checking that out on the office CCTV, but I haven't heard back yet. I'm certain it was Annika." Chris wavered on whether to divulge his latest theory. Ultimately electing on keeping himself open and honest. Withholding information had not been his friend where Katelyn was concerned.

"I'm not so sure. Yes, Annika appears to be heavily involved, but I don't think she is acting on freewill. Debbie is the one pulling the strings. I think she has coerced Annika, like she attempted with me."

"What makes you think that?"

"I don't have all the facts, but Annika is scared of Debbie. She didn't want the forced relationship with me.

230

She admitted she had liked me for years but only wanted it to be a natural relationship."

"You believe her after everything that has happened?"

"I do, there's a lot more to it than I believe you know. There's something else I need to tell you." A long pause followed.

"What?" Apprehension rendered her reply.

"I've just spoken to Hill on the phone. They performed a drug test on me last night. The results came back with a positive on GHB."

"GHB? What's that?"

"It's a date rape drug. Debbie gave me a coffee back at her apartment. Hill thinks she drugged me and set up the whole thing. Making me think something had happened, but it didn't. The last time I spoke to Debbie, on the phone. I asked straight out what happened between us. She admitted nothing went on."

"That still doesn't excuse your lying afterward."

"No, you're right, it doesn't. I made a mistake, under difficult circumstances. I'm so sorry. Please Katelyn."

"Okay, I get it." She sensitively conceded. "I just can't think about us right now."

"I'm not asking you to, but I had to tell you, so you know the facts."

"Understood. Look Chris, I'm prepared to look at us when this is over. Is that fair?"

"Yes." Chris could not contain his delight. "Thank you."

"What is the rest of the story then? That I don't know."

"I think it's better discussed in person, not over the phone."

"Can't you just tell me. Don't you think I have the right to know?"

"Yes, I completely agree. It's better discussed face to face. Can I come over to yours?"

"I don't think that's a good idea. My mom is on total high alert. If you turn up, she'll be asking lots of questions. Are you able to say your piece in front of her?"

"I think I'd feel more comfortable speaking to you alone for now."

"I could come to yours?"

"That's not a good idea either. I do not know what Debbie is planning next, but for all I know she could be hiding in the bushes outside. If you turn up, well, it wouldn't be good."

"Meet me at Riverfront Park. The spot you took me to, over Lake Wilson."

"Yeah, okay."

"Leave now. Let's both get there as soon as possible."

"Okay, see you shortly."

Hill remained at his desk. Rufus, accompanied by two fellow officers, left half an hour earlier to pick up Annika. To bring her in under police caution. The confirmation just coming back to Hill, she was not at her place of residence. Whereabouts unknown. Hill could not shake the feeling something bad was going to happen. With Debbie in custody the prominent unknown variable belonged to Annika.

232

He reread the email from Greta. Why had Annika visited Debbie's facility to meet a random employee before meeting Debbie herself? There was more to learn, it would seem. Hill dialed the number for the employee in question, Steve Lewis. The call was answered on the second ring.

"Hi. Steve Lewis speaking." A voice responded. In the background young children could be heard playing.

"Good afternoon, my name is Detective Hill, from the Santa Rosa Police Department." The phone stayed silent for some time, only the infant laughs and shrieks audible.

"How can I help you?" Steve finally responded uneasily. Hill then overheard an adult female voice in the background.

"Who is it Steve?"

"Just work." He hurriedly responded, clearly moving out of earshot of those in his present vicinity.

"Are you okay to talk?" Hill asked. There was an audible sound of a door shutting.

"Yes."

"Does the name Deborah Green mean anything to you?"

Hill heard Steve sigh down the phone. "Yes."

"How would you describe your relationship Mr. Lewis?"

"Nonexistent. We used to work together. She left months ago. I haven't heard from her since."

"What about when you did work together?"

"She was a colleague, that's it."

"I know there's more. Please elaborate or I'll have to subpoena you and get you on the next flight to Santa Rosa."

"Alright, Jesus. I had an affair with Debs. It lasted around six months. It was a massive mistake. I have a family, young children. I totally regret the whole thing. I broke it off with her and within a couple of weeks she quit her employment. I never saw her again."

"How would you describe Debbie?"

"Unstable. One minute coming across all confident and in control, the next she was completely vulnerable, afraid of her own shadow."

"Hmmm, would it be fair to say she was always vulnerable, the bravado a mask to conceal the real Debbie? Albeit very convincing as her true self?"

"Yes. I would say that's a pretty accurate description. What is this about detective?"

"A homicide investigation. Debbie is a suspect."

"Oh." Steve suddenly felt weak at the knees. He visually checked the location of his wife and kids through the closed glass patio doors. They were otherwise engaged, playing in the yard. He took a seat before his legs gave out.

"Tell me about your relationship."

"It was just a stupid fling. She was always flirting, constantly making sexual innuendos. Debs was a very touchy person. She would put her hands on me, on my back, my arm, sometimes my face. Anyway, one evening we were working late. The rest of the team had left for the day and one thing just led to another."

"Did you have sexual intercourse? At work?"

"Yes."

"Was that the only time, at work?"

"No." Steve lowered his voice. "We had sex multiple times there, more often back at her apartment after work. It was a short drive away."

"Do you think you were the only employee who engaged in sexual relations with Debbie during her employment?"

"No. I was pretty certain there were others during that time, but when it all blew up, it seemed she was screwing half the married men there. She had multiple partners on the go at the same time including me."

"When you say, it all blew up?"

"A complaint was made to Dr. Rose, the development lead. He began to investigate. We were all questioned, every member of the team. I kept my mouth shut, denied everything. I'm pretty certain everyone else did the same. It was just kind of blowing over when we attended a team meeting for the whole department, probably about seventy staff, when one guy just got up and announced he had been having an affair with Debbie. Admitting to incidents in the workplace. Then he started reeling off the names of numerous colleagues, explaining they all had done the same. Debbie just sat there, looking dismayed. He had to be forcibly escorted out of the meeting. It was horrendous. Then Debbie ran out. It ended up being the last day of her employment. She met with Doctor Rose and quit at the end of that shift. Everyone named, including myself, had families and wives. Doctor Rose did his best to cover up as much as possible. The guy who spilled the truth walked, but with so many people in the know the rumors just keep circulating. I think my wife is still unaware, but many of my fellow colleagues have seen their marriages fall apart. Loads more have left the company."

"You're still there?"

"Yes, I looked at leaving, believe me. We would have to relocate. I know my wife would not entertain that, so I'm stuck sitting on a ticking time bomb. I keep her away from any work functions, but it's only a matter of time."

"Who is Annika Walker?" Hill fired in, catching Steve off guard.

"Erm. I have no idea." His response less than convincing.

"Mr. Lewis, Steve. This is a time sensitive homicide investigation. I don't have time to fuck about. I'm not interested in hurting you and your family, but I need to know the truth, right now. Who is Annika to you? I know you know her. She visited you at Foundation Pharmaceuticals." There was a long pause while Steve readied himself with the explanation.

"She called me the day before she visited, posing as a pharmaceutical grade raw material supplier rep. I get them all the time. I tried to blow her off, but she was insistent on visiting. In the end I agreed just to shut her up. It was all a ruse. When she was alone with me in my office, Annika told me I had to come clean about my affair with Debs to everyone. Then name any other colleagues I knew about or even suspected was involved with her. She said if I didn't do it and undertake a good enough performance to make her job completely untenable, or if I warned Debs she would go straight to my wife and reveal all."

"Did she explain why she wanted you to do this?"

236

"No, I have no idea. To be honest I wasn't really asking a lot of questions at that point."

"So why didn't you go through with it and reveal all?"

"I was still plucking up the courage. It seemed pretty obvious by doing this my own job would be untenable as well. If that happened my wife would definitely hear about my affair, so I sat wavering. When Chucky gave his performance to the meeting, it occurred to me this woman had not put all her eggs in one basket. Clearly, she had targeted at least two of us, probably more. Chucky was just the first to crack."

"There's no record of Annika visiting anyone else onsite." Hill observed.

"Annika mentioned she had struggled to get hold of me outside of work, so had set up the fake rep routine to achieve contact. I guess she managed to get to Chucky and anyone else, outside of work."

"Annika visited Debbie two days after your meeting. Do you know anything about that?"

"No, not a clue."

"You're sure? It won't help you to hide anything from me at this point." Hill warned.

"Completely sure. The fake meeting, and the call to set it up was the only time I ever heard from or about Annika."

"Is there anything else you want to tell me? Or anything relevant I haven't asked you about?"

"No, I don't think so." Hill waited, just to be sure. "Oh, it might be nothing."

"What?"

"Doctor Rose. More of an observation than fact. He had a really close relationship with Debbie. As far as I can tell nothing improper, but as the rumors circulated following Chuck's announcement his name kept coming up. Stories about employees he had sacked to protect Debs. I don't know if any of it is true, but there's something between them that doesn't sit right with me. I just can't put my finger on it."

"Okay Mr. Lewis, I'll bear that in mind. I may need to contact you again. Thank you for your help, I know this is a difficult subject. I'll do my best to keep your name out of the investigations."

After completing the call Hill sat staring into infinity for a few minutes, his brain whirring. Eventually he picked up the phone and called the Cybercrime department.

"How's the Fisher examination going?" He asked the department sergeant.

"Only one aspect of note currently. We've discovered an odd large financial transaction prior to his death. Three million dollars going into what appears to be a phantom account. Still looking into it, I'll let you know when we've put it together. Otherwise looks reasonably clean so far."

"That is interesting. Keep me posted on that. There are some new aspects I'm interested in. Firstly, are there any records of an investment in a company called Foundation Pharmaceuticals? Secondly some more target names, Annika Walker, Rhonda Walker, Dr. Brian Rose and Steve Lewis. If you get a hit on any of those I need to know immediately. Might be connected to the abnormal transaction."

"Sure thing, I'll get the team straight on it."

Chapter 31

Hill and Rufus sat in the police chief's office. Rufus had never been invited into his office previously. He considered the size and eminence of the private sector office of Susan Roswell. Impressive in its own right, the chief's workplace sat mediocre in comparison.

"Okay, Hill. Break it down for me. What have you got?" Chief Lance asked. Hill finally obtaining the coroner's report confirming what was already known. The difference now, providing Hill the green light to commandeer a task force of detectives and officers to aid him in the investigation.

"Stanley Fisher, a wealthy investment banker who relocated to Santa Rosa eight months ago was murdered in his home on Friday twelfth. The autopsy report has just been submitted by the coroner confirming the cause of death was an intravenous injection of Tetrodotoxin."

"Tetrodotoxin?"

"It's the lethal substance found in the ovaries of puffer or blow fish. You may know it as Fugu?" The commanding officer nodded slowly. "A twenty-five-microgram exposure is fatal. Its estimated Stan was injected with nearly two hundred micrograms."

"Okay, that's clearly enough to do the job. What's the circumstance"

"Stan has a wife, Barbra and an adult daughter, Katelyn. I can't rule out their involvement yet, but they are not on my radar. Stan had a second, secret family here in

Santa Rosa, with a partner, Rhonda and another adult daughter, Annika. The partner committed suicide fourteen months ago. It would appear Stan broke it off with Rhonda after Annika moved out of the family home. I don't have many details on why she ended her life, but I think Stan was a major contributing factor. Interestingly when the Fisher's relocated to Santa Rosa, Katelyn took a job at the same workplace as Annika, although I'm reasonably certain that Katelyn knew nothing about her secret half-sister. We have CCTV evidence of Annika stealing Katelyn's security fob to allow her access into the Fisher's estate.

"So, Annika is the prime suspect? You put the employment aspect down to what, coincidence?"

"No coincidence." Rufus spoke quietly, shaking his head.

"We are pretty certain Annika sent Katelyn an email containing an application for a position at Haskin & Wilcox." Hill elaborated. "I don't have the electronic paper trail yet, but we should be able to find it." He sat forward. "There is another prominent aspect. A young lady named Deborah. She, as far as we can tell, is yet another secret daughter. I currently have her in custody. She's not talking until she has a lawyer, but she is heavily involved and a suspect of equal prominence. Both Annika and Deborah have been working together on this, causing a lot of hassle for Katelyn's would be boyfriend, Chris who is another employee in the same firm. She had access to the Tetrodotoxin and was likely the supplier and possibly the administer."

"Sounds complex."

"It's getting more and more perplexing. For both suspects there's a face value aspect of motive. Revenge or anger against the father, but I don't think that is the whole story. There is more going on, for it all to make sense. The other crucial aspect is establishing who did what and when. With Deborah in custody, hopefully I can get some answers. A warrant is out for the arrest of Annika, but her location is currently unknown."

"You think she's on the lam?"

"I don't know. But I'm concerned."

"Okay. So, what now?"

"I need bodies, some more detectives and officers to help with the investigating."

Lance paused for a long time, seemingly weighing up his decision. He flicked his pen between two fingers, back and forth, tapping the end loudly on a notepad.

"I think we need to consider making this a federal case and get the FBI in to take over." The police chief spoke firmly but without conviction.

"What? No way. Absolutely not. There's no jurisdiction to warrant turning it over to the Feds. I just need some willing labor." Hill barked back.

"Okay, here's the thing. I just don't have anyone to give you."

"Jesus Christ, Lance." Hill responded. His voice bathed in anger.

"Look, I've had your sergeant up my ass." He fired back looking at Officer Rufus. "He's throwing his toys out of the pram about your retention. Personally, I can't stand the prick, so Hill if you really want to keep the case, you can keep Rufus for as long as you need. You're already

242

tying up half the Cybercrime department. I'll permit that to continue until all the electronic information has been extracted, but I can't offer you anything else at the moment. It's not personal. I can't give what I don't have."

"Okay sir, understood." Hill jumped up from his seat, quickly leaving the office before he said something he would later regret. Rufus politely nodding to the police chief, followed him out.

Hill slumped back in his chair. Rufus skulked around awkwardly in the doorway. It was late Saturday afternoon, the other detectives were not present, off enjoying their weekend. The office was theirs alone.

"What?" Hill fired at Rufus.

"You've still got me." He offered, a tinge of humor in his response attempting to lighten the mood. For a few seconds Hill just stared back at him. Eventually he broke into a half smile, rolling his eyes.

"Maybe that's what pissed me off." The short-lived tension dispersed. "You okay to carry on Rufus? Do you want to take a break?" Before Rufus could answer, Hill's desk phone rang. Hill noted it was the Cybercrime sergeant and quickly answered.

"Hill."

"I've got something that might be very interesting to you."

"Good, let me have it." Rufus watched Hill's face as he listened, anxious lines of concentration contorted, but quickly relaxed as the valuable information was delivered. Hill broke into a smile, sitting forward in his seat. "Nice.

Good work Sergeant. Let me know when you find anything else." He put the receiver down, looking up at the young officer. Rufus arched his eyebrows waiting for an explanation.

"How long until Debbie gets legal aid? I think I have some interesting questions to ask her."

"What?" Rufus asked impatiently. Hill opened his mouth to speak, but before the explanation was provided, Hill was interrupted by another call. Hill did not recognize the number.

"Detective Hill."

"Good afternoon detective. My Name is Arlen Jackson. I am a TSA officer based at San Francisco Airport. I've just had a hit on a name you submitted on our database. A Doctor Brian Rose."

"Thank you Arlen. Where is he now?"

"He's just entered departures. We got the hit as he passed through security."

"Does he know you're on him?"

"No. I wanted to check with you first."

"Good. Where is he travelling?"

"Sonoma County Airport." Santa Rosa's local airport.

"Hmmm, that is interesting. Okay Arlen, let him travel. Don't give him any indication there is an issue. Give me the flight number. I want to track him when he lands."

Chris arrived at the same parking expanse used previously with Katelyn. Instantly spotting her beat-up car, already parked up. Chris hurried over to the vehicle, discovering it empty. Tension or expectation was building within him. Unsure which, he broke into a jog. Hustling up the hill to the arranged meeting point. Negotiating the tight squeeze through the overgrown entrance, penetrating into the solitude of the undisclosed beauty spot. Chris hurriedly broke through to the other side of the wooded perimeter, expecting to find Katelyn waiting on the bench. It was empty. She was nowhere to be seen. Chris looked hastily across the dense tree line, but to no avail. Katelyn was not here. Quickly pulling out his cell, he rang her. The ringing continued on and on. Each repetition amplified the tenseness, until eventually the voicemail kicked in. Chris left a brief message confirming his arrival. He ended the call and made his way back out of the small clearing. *Did she get lost? Maybe Katelyn had gone the wrong way out of the parking area?* Chris asked himself all the logical questions but could not shake the sensation something was wrong. Very wrong.

Chapter 32

Officer Rufus parked up at Charles M. Schulz Sonoma County Airport, located on the outskirts of Santa Rosa. Named after the famed cartoonist of the Peanuts comic strip. The airport logo depicting Snoopy with full flying hat, scarf and goggles attire. Flying atop of his kennel. The image bought a touch of nostalgia to Rufus. Childhood memories when the world seemed a nicer place.

He quickly shook off the sentiment. He was here on a mission, way outside the scope of basic officer training. His objective, to tail Dr. Rose. Not get spotted, not alert the mysterious visitor, and establish why he had elected to update his status from incidental witness to a possible contributor, collaborator, or even suspect.

Rufus was thankful it was a small airport, making his role much easier. After parking Hill's Sedan in a primary spot to tail a taxicab or anyone who might be meeting Dr. Rose, he made his way inside. Sculptures, renditions and wall-based illustrations of all the key Peanuts characters littered the airport giving it a unique character. Rufus promptly made his way to the TSA office.

Soon after, Rufus, located just out of sight of the arrival's security check point, lingered with purpose. A solitary station opened for the travelers from San Francisco, controlling the flow of the arrivals. Rufus, unsure what the doctor looked like, other than a description from Hill, arranged for a signal to alert him when Dr. Rose passed through. He would then filter into other arriving passengers to anonymously track the doctor. He could feel his breathing intensifying with the anticipation. Rufus calmed himself. A cool head was required here.

All that went out of the window when the initial speedy travelers broke through from the arrival gate to the desk. The individuals in a rush to get through and be released into the freedom of the world beyond airport security. The pace picked up as these sharply focused individuals comprehended only a single station was operational. A heavyset female TSA officer stood authoritatively directly behind the booth. Before long the bottleneck formed a line of irritated passengers. A trickle of released individuals passed through, then all too soon for Rufus, the officer behind the booth glanced briefly in his direction, before returning her gaze back into the booth. This was the signal. A second after, a distinguished grey-haired gentleman strolled out, heading at pace for the arrivals lobby.

Rufus gave chase, keeping his distance as far as he dared. Always fixing his gaze away from the route of his target, he focused his peripheral vision to track his movements. Rufus was not sure if this was how the professionals followed someone, but it seemed the obvious tactic to take. The doctor headed directly for the exit, occasionally looking around, as if to confirm nobody was following him. On a couple of instances, the doctor looked in Rufus's direction. The officer in civilian clothes maintained his course and eyeline, knowing an attempt to turn away with head or feet would make him visible to the doctor.

Brian hit the exit door leaving the air-conditioned sanctuary, instantly swamped by the heat of the late afternoon sun. Rufus maintained the gap, watching him continue down the tiled concourse. Towards the end of the walkway Rufus closed the gap between them, knowing he was entering the most probable phase while on foot to lose contact with the target. As expected, Rose turned towards the taxi rank, car hire and pick up area. Rufus did not know which his lead would choose, but he had to break away to retrieve his own vehicle. While still on foot, it would be irrelevant which the doctor selected, if he could not continue to give chase.

Rufus made a run for his car, tearing away in the opposite direction, he made record time to his vehicle, stowed in short term parking. As soon as the engine started, he raced out driving in the opposite direction of the one-way system to filter into the lane for prebooked taxis and collections. Reaching the queue of taxis, he slowed back to an appropriate speed, searching desperately to reacquire the doctor. Quickly relieved to spot him, the doctor passed by the prearranged taxis, now heading towards the unchartered taxis queue situated back in the short stay parking lot Rufus had just sped out of. The officer was stuck in the terminal looping roadway with no choice but to continue around until he could reenter the lot. Once back and reacquired with visuals of his target, Rufus maintained a sensible distance and calmed himself. He watched Dr. Rose jump in the back of a taxicab. Without delay the cab sped off, Rufus in discreet pursuit.

Chris, now beyond anxious, had scouted out a large area of the beauty spot, around the parking area and the agreed meeting place. All the time continually calling Katelyn's cell. Nothing. The only evidence of her possible presence was her vehicle. All possibility of her wandering about looking for the location, explored by Chris and ruled out. Something had happened to her. Without further delay he dialed Officer Rufus. The phone rang until the voicemail eventually kicked in. Frustration welled inside him as he tried Detective Hill.

"Hill." His voice responded upon answer. Chris experienced a minor reprieve as someone had actually taken his call.

"Hi, its Chris."

"What's up?"

"It's Katelyn. I agreed to meet her at Riverfront Park, to talk. But she's gone missing. Her car is here, but there's no sign of her."

"It's a big park Chris." Hill challenged.

"We agreed on a meeting point, she knew the spot and there's no sign of her. She's not answering her cell either. I've spent half an hour here looking for her."

"She's not answering her phone? Did you leave it on amicable terms last time you spoke?"

"Yes, she suggested we meet here. I think something is wrong. I'm worried Debbie might have done something."

"I have Debbie in custody. She's been here since midday. What about Annika? Do you know where she is?"

"No. She called me this morning. She told me she was certain Debbie killed Stan and was worried for her and my safety."

"She told you it was Debbie? As in she knew for certain?"

"Not really a statement of fact, more of a strong suspicion. She seemed pretty sure."

"Did she say where she was, or where she was going after the call?"

"No." Chris recalled the conversation, but with so much going on, his memory was hazy. "I don't think so."

"I currently have an APB out on Annika. I need to locate her immediately. Do you think she could be with Katelyn?"

"No."

"Why are you so sure?"

"I'm not a detective, but I don't think Annika is involved in the way you think. Anything she has done was under coercion from Debbie."

"Sorry Chris but I'm not buying it. Annika is not the innocent victim you think she is. Do you think there's any possibility Katelyn would go off with her of her own freewill."

"I don't think so. Not without meeting me, or at least calling."

"Do you think it's possible Annika has kidnapped Katelyn?" Chris stopped dead in his tracks as the prospect penetrated his rationale.

"There's no way she could know where we were going to meet."

"Maybe she followed you?"

"No, she was missing before I arrived here."

"Okay, maybe she tailed Katelyn. What is the state of affairs near where her car is parked? Are there people about." Chris looked around the clearing where their cars were located. The fear already manifesting from within, now compelling to overwhelm him.

"There's a couple of other cars, but it's completely deserted. Nobody in sight."

"Chris I'm going to try and get a couple of black and whites over to the area. I need you to keep looking. Check her car for any signs of a struggle, but don't touch it. Call me immediately if anything changes."

"Okay." Chris agreed less than confidently.

Despite the stress of every intersection creating an opportunity to lose sight of the fast-moving taxi, its vivid turquoise livery categorically assisted the large SUV to stand out of the crowd. Rufus growing in confidence kept a healthy distance. While the driver would not be looking for a tail, it was possible the doctor could be keeping an eye out.

The beige detective issued sedan was as plain as it was possible for a vehicle to be. Unless the strobe emergency lighting was activated for all intents and purposes it was an almost invisible vehicle of the road.

It soon became clear to Rufus, Dr. Rose was heading for Debbie's apartment, as they made their way into the heart of Santa Rosa. His taxi pulled up outside the decaying building, in a less than prestigious part of the city. Rufus pulled up on the opposite side of the street some distance shy of the cab. Rufus could just make out the doctor paying the fare. As he exited, he issued an instruction to the driver and hurried his way to the entrance foyer door.

Brian reached the door pressing the buzzer to Debbie's apartment. Anxiously waiting, he scanned the surroundings for any signs of unwanted attention. After satisfying himself, he brought his focus back to the buzzer, impatiently pressing it again. No answer. Brian elected to attempt Debbie's cell. Already calling her numerous times since landing. Each time to no avail. *Why would she not answer?*

Rufus watched invisibly from the low sun shadows blanketing his vehicle, waiting to see how it played out. He correctly guessed his mark was calling Debbie, knowing full well she would not be answering either the door or his cell. Not from her incarceration. The taxi had not pulled away. Again, Rufus could deduce it had been instructed to wait until its last fare disappeared inside the building. The Doctor eventually gave up and returned to the cab. Rufus continued his pursuit as it pulled away.

Away from the main link roads, other traffic to blend into was generally sporadic. Frequent opportunities for the cab to simply turn off and disappear out of sight existed, leaving Rufus with a conundrum. Stay close and risk being completely obvious or drop back and increase the threat of losing contact. For the short term he played safe and kept the tailing distance to a minimum. Before long Rufus could make an educated guess on the new destination. He elected to gamble on dropping back, trusting his hunch was on the money.

Rounding the corner onto the street where Annika's small two up, two down was situated, his instincts did not let him down. Sure enough the cab had pulled up outside. Rufus failed to locate a suitable inconspicuous spot to pull into. Thinking quickly, he elected to continue just as the doctor departed the taxi. To his relief passing directly by, unnoticed. The doctor was preoccupied with ensuring he identified the correct house. Once further up the road, Rufus found a gap in the parked cars lining both sides of the street. Swinging in he killed the lights and engine quickly before the doctor once again assessed for possible threat.

It was swiftly apparent to the officer, the doctor had lost interest in verifying this element. He was pacing up and down looking at house numbers. Clearly, he knew Annika's address but had never been to the property before. Once he discerned which of the small but pleasant houses was Annika's, he walked up to knock on the door. Rufus studied the actions with vested interest. The APB on Annika had been live since midday. If she answered he might be able to kill two birds with one stone.

Unfortunately for both Brian and Rufus she was still not at home. Despite the distance and Rufus's reflected viewing portal, clearly the doctor was not amused at this outcome. His body language, his movements, a tapestry of frustration and anger. The cab, once again instructed to sit and wait, emitted a low rumbling noise as the engine ticked over. Dr. Rose gave up and got back in the idling vehicle. Rufus scootched down in his seat as it passed by. The moment the cab hung a left, he started after the newest player in the suspect list.

By the time the uniformed officers had arrived at Riverfront Reginal Park, Chris was almost beside himself. Katelyn was nowhere. Whatever had become of her, he knew it was not good. The officers briefed by Hill did not require persuasion to share Chris's concern. While one spent time with Chris, examining Katelyn's parked vehicle and the arranged meeting spot, the other four wasted no time in splitting up to start the search.

Chris was pleased to have support, and their collective urgency. Equally disturbed, they conveyed serious unease at the fate of the young lady. After a short while, the lead officer, still with Chris, radioed back to Hill.

"We need to get the chopper out here. It's going to take forever to conduct a proper search. We've got less than ninety minutes of useable daylight." He barked to the detective.

"Already requested." Hill replied, his voice familiar to Chris through the static crackle distortion of the two-way communication device.

"And?" The officer impatiently replied.

"They're working on it."

"Copy." The officer rolled his eyes at Chris. "They better get their ass in gear." He muttered. Chris wasn't sure if the comment was directed at him or not. He gave a small nod anyway.

"What now?" He asked, already guessing the answer.

"We search on foot until we hear otherwise. Stick with me. I'll call the others in a sec so we can agree on search zones. I don't suppose you have a set of keys for her car, do you?"

"No. Why?"

"I'd like to rule out her being in the trunk." Chris looked twice at the officer, before the full depth of the statement hit home.

"Can't you break in? Hit the trunk release?" Chris heatedly posed.

"Nope. Not without a warrant, or proof of immediate threat to life."

"If she's in there, she could be hurt or unconscious."

"There's nothing to indicate that. I'd just prefer to rule it out."

"But you won't?"

"I can't. Its more than my job's worth." For a few seconds the two men just looked at each other. Chris's mind working overtime.

"You can't, but I could."

"I didn't say that." Chris understood simply by the tone of the officer's response, he could not do it himself. Nor could he request Chris to do it. But by raising the subject he was requesting. Asking, without asking. Chris did not hesitate further, turning round he located a sizeable rock on the ground. Picking it up and using his best pitcher's throw, launched the rock through the driver's side window. The reinforced glass was no match for the impact, instantly splintering with a loud shattering crash. Chris reached his arm carefully through the jagged hole, just able to reach the lever down to the left of the driver's seat. The trunk popped open obediently. Chris quickly ran round to join the officer. For a brief second both stood looking in surprise at the sight that met them.

"Is that Katelyn?" The cop asked quietly, before approaching the woman lying deathly still, in the rear luggage compartment. He checked for a pulse while Chris just stood frozen to the spot. Satisfying himself she was still alive, he began to gently shake her. "Katelyn? Katelyn? Can you hear me?" Still Chris remained planted to the spot, his brain not able to take in the event as it was transpiring. Finally, he found a shaky weakened voice.

"That's not Katelyn. It's Annika."

Chapter 33

Dr. Rose departed the taxicab for a third time, shrouded in an orangey dull haze from the setting sun. The merciless Californian heat promptly receding. He paid his final fare to the thankful driver and sent him on his way. Brian looked up at the beleaguered dilapidated building. After travelling around Santa Rosa for nearly two hours, he still had no idea where the current state of affairs resided. All he did know, currently he was massively out of pocket. The cost of the flight and three taxi fares, small potatoes compared to the nest egg he was so close to receiving. Yet as close as that money was, not a dime was currently within his grasp.

He returned to the entrance door of Debbie's apartment pressing the buzzer as he had done earlier, but now without any hope of a response. His efforts remaining unanswered, the doctor walked away. Crossing the street to take a seat on a seemingly random bench that sat opposite the apartment. What choice did he have now but to wait it out? Sit and hope by some miracle Debbie would innocently stroll by, on her way home.

Rufus continued to observe the man of interest as he rested apprehensively on the wooden seat. Ending his call with Hill, Rufus was up to date with the discovery at Riverfront Park. Medics now in attendance. Nothing was yet known about the circumstances that led to Annika residing within the trunk of Katelyn's car. Or about the current whereabouts of the vehicle's owner. Hill agreed with Rufus, there was not much more to gain by tailing Dr. Rose. Clearly, he was intent on making contact with either Debbie or Annika. Neither of which would be possible until Hill had obtained clarity of what their, or the doctor's involvement in the death of Stanley Fisher was.

Rufus departed his sedan, walking slowly towards Dr. Rose. As he ambled along the sidewalk, the doctor turned to look at the approaching pedestrian. Rufus kept his gaze nonchalant, not appearing to be looking at anything while surveying everything. Eventually Rose returned his gaze to the door of the apartment block, regarding the slow-moving walker of no direct threat. That Changed as Rufus drew alongside him.

"Dr. Brian Rose?" Rufus asked out of procedure.

"Yes?" The startled doctor returned.

"Dr. Rose. I am arresting you on the suspicion of being an accessory to the homicide of Stanley Fisher." The Doctor's head dropped at the weight of the words spoken. He continued to listen impassively as his rights were read to him while handcuffs were simultaneously applied.

The ambulance pulled out of the rural parking area. Onboard an incoherent Annika accompanied by a single officer. Riverfront Reginal Park was now littered with cops. The helicopter swooped by overhead scanning with its thermal imaging camera for any sign of Katelyn. It struck Chris as bizarre, one minute it was stretching the district law enforcers capability to get a few officers out looking, but then when an obvious serious crime had been committed, leaving Katelyn either a fellow victim or the suspect, out of the woodwork springs an army of labor.

Either way Chris was thankful for the effort to locate her. Annika's condition had been reported as conscious but not lucid. Unable to communicate at all, let alone provide an explanation of the sequence of events which led to her incarceration in the trunk. Or more importantly to Chris, the fate of the girl he knew he loved.

Rufus, stepped into Hill's office. The detective looked like he desperately needed sleep. Probably a beer first, but it was obvious to the young protégé officer, his mentor was exhausted.

"Dr. Rose has been processed. He hasn't been allocated a cell yet. I wasn't sure if you wanted to get him straight into an interrogation room."

"Has he requested legal representation?"

"No. he's not said much. Looks like he's about to cry."

"Okay let's give him a go while he's feeling emotional. It might be our best chance to get some information. Debbie's legal aid has just arrived so hopefully we can continue with her straight afterwards."

"Sounds like a plan." Rufus agreed.

Hill and Rufus returned to the room they had previously interrogated Debbie in. Before them, restrained to the table sat the forlorn figure of Doctor Rose. Both resumed their established positions, Hill directly opposite the scientist.

Rufus off to the side, half sat on a table edge. Hill quickly completed the formalities of introducing the recording.

"Good evening Doctor." Hill began

"Evening."

"Do you need anything? A drink of water?"

"No. I'm good."

"I must say, I'm surprised to see you here, in Santa Rosa." The statement hung heavily in the air. Rose did not attempt to respond, sitting motionless, head low. Eyes fixed somberly to a single mark on the tabletop before him. "Would you care to enlighten me on the nature of your visit?"

"After your video call, I was worried about Debbie. I still care deeply for her. She wasn't answering her phone. I decided to travel over here to check on her."

"That is very thoughtful of you. You must really care for this young woman." Hill intentionally left a note of skepticism in his tone. The doctor tentatively lifted his gaze up to meet the detective.

"As I told you previously, I became a father figure to her. She doesn't have anyone looking out for her. I'm just trying to help her." Hill studied the Doctor's eye movement and body language. He considered the answer had a strong element of truth to it. Now to study his expression when lying.

"How many employees did you sack unfairly to keep Debbie's antics quiet?"

"None. Absolutely none. I was the person who led the investigation when her improper behavior came to light, leading to the termination of Debbie's employment."

"So before it all blew up with Chuck's big announcement, you didn't sack individuals off to keep her under the radar?

"I said no. I didn't do that. I presume you've spoken to someone else at Foundation then?" Hill had satisfied himself. He could now visually detect a truth or a lie.

"Yes. I interviewed Steve Lewis. He told me about the big revelation. Let's go back to her actual father. We discussed this previously. Now I happen to know she discussed this with you in far more detail than you led me to believe."

"No, you're wrong. It was only the once and she quickly changed subject. I told you all I know." *It was a lie.*

"Doctor, I know you know who he is."

"No. I don't. And call me Brian."

"Brian, you know full well Debbie's father is Stan Fisher, the man who's murder you are arrested for."

"I don't know this man. I'd never heard his name before your partner read me my rights. Especially not from Debs."

"Well, that is very interesting." Hill got up from his seat and began his habitual pacing action. "Very, very interesting." Brian waited for the inevitable point to be made. "When we spoke previously, we talked about the fantastic amount of money Foundation Pharmaceuticals could make."

"What of it? I already explained I am solely an employee. I don't see any real reward for my effort and sacrifice."

261

"That is very true. As you said, it's those lucky shareholders who enjoy that particular privilege." Hill agreed.

"And the risk." Brian added.

"Quite, but on the whole, it's a profitable investment, yes?"

"Yes."

"Do you know any of the shareholders?"

"Yes, a few of them." Suddenly Brian's tone became uptight, uncomfortable where this was leading.

"Did you know Stanley was a shareholder? A recent acquisition, just as he relocated and retired, but a substantial one all the same." Brian sat quietly for a moment.

"I didn't know that."

"You didn't? How bizarre. We have been sifting through all of Stan's emails, both live and deleted. One was found in his sent box, addressed to Richard Fuller, your CEO. Thanking him for the site tour while he was a perspective investor. He paid particular mention to a Dr. Brian Rose who kindly spent a full afternoon with him explaining how the operation worked in actuality. The reality behind the glossy business model perspective." Although Brian was sat listening hanging his head low, the mention of the email caused him to slump forward, further reducing his presence. "It's time to start talking Brian."

"Okay. Okay." He finally conceded. "Yes, I knew Stan." The doctor gave a lengthy pause. "I was aware Debs was his daughter."

"Thank you, Brian. Was Stanley aware Debbie worked at the facility he was investing so heavily in?"

"No, he had no idea."

"So how come, of all the companies in the USA and beyond, he elected to invest so much into this particular one."

"Annika. She is also an estranged daughter of Stan."

"Yes, we are aware of her, go on."

"She spoke to Stan, all about us. Told him to check it out. Said he could double, even triple his money. I believe that was all he needed to whet his appetite and begin his own examination of us."

"Why was Annika so interested in Stan investing in the company?"

"I'm not totally sure. I presumed she was hoping for a taste of the profits. A kind of finder's fee?" Hill could tell the last answer was again lacking truth. He left it alone for the minute.

"Do you think Annika could have killed Stan for the inheritance? Or Debbie for that matter?"

"No. He never wanted anything to do with Debbie. I strongly doubt that he would include her in his will. The same goes for Annika. Although I believe he had a relationship with her, leaving her a tidy sum of inheritance would only lead to questions when the will was read. As far as I understand detective, he went to great lengths to keep Annika secret from his immediate family. I can't imagine he wanted to change that in his death and trash his legacy. Maybe he had a secret pot put aside for her?"

For the first time since entering the room Rufus spoke. "That's a very considered and rounded answer. It sounded to me like it's something you've been speculating on for some time."

"That would be correct. Since the video call with Detective Hill, I have been racking my brains to try and make sense of it."

Rufus flashed his eyes at Hill, who gave a small nod. Continue. "How well do you know Annika?" The officer probed.

"Not particularly well. She came to stay with Debs, near the end of her employment. I met her a couple of times. Very quiet and reserved."

"Were you aware she visited Debbie at work, at Foundation Pharmaceuticals?" Rufus enquired.

"No." The doctor answered very quickly. Hill recognized truth in his response. Rufus continued. "What about Steve Lewis?"

"Steve? What about him?"

"Annika visited Steve at work, posing as a sales rep."

"What? That can't be right."

"Well, it is. We've spoken with Mr. Lewis who told us all about it."

"That doesn't make sense. I can't understand it."

"Dr. Rose, I would like you to think back to the meeting where Chucky divulged to everyone what was going on with Debbie. Do you know what instigated him to do it. In such a public and damaging way?"

"No. I never understood why. He wouldn't tell me." Once again Rufus visually checked with Hill that he wasn't overstepping. Hill repeated the faint nod to continue.

"Annika was contacting the various employees engaged in a covert relationship with Debbie. Secretly threatening to expose them to their families unless they did what you witnessed Chuck do. I think most refused realizing the threat was at least as damaging as being exposed by Annika. Eventually Chuck was the first to crack." Rose lowered his head into his one free hand, shaking his head as truths he did not know were revealed to him.

"But why? Why would she do that? What is the gain?" He asked through his cradling fingers.

"I think Annika wanted to get Debbie sacked from her job. I think she wanted to ensure Debbie was so disgraced she couldn't even stay in Fremont, so she would have no choice but to run away." Rufus paused to let the theory sink in. "Where would Debbie go? She had no family, no friends. All except for one person, her estranged half-sister in Santa Rosa." Silence fell upon the room. No one spoke. Finally, the doctor raised his head to look at Rufus.

"I don't know what to say about that, other than I honestly had no knowledge of this." It didn't take a highly experienced detective to determine the statement was true.

"It's okay." Rufus reassured. "I can see you were unaware of this." His voice soft, compassionate. Rufus gave a fleeting look towards Hill, his signal to come back in. Hill took the baton without delay.

"So now you understand there is much you don't know, you'd better start talking about what you do know." Hill was loud, harsh in tone. Deliberately separating his approach from Rufus. He quickly approached the table, placing both hands flat on the surface, leaning his head in close to the doctor. "Understand this, Brian. What you say in the next few minutes will determine whether you serve three years or thirty." Hill was domineering, overbearing. "Who has the money?"

"What money?" Brian whimpered, almost too afraid to ask. Hill snapped back upright and slammed his fist down on the desk.

"I warned you, don't play games with me. Don't you dare lie to my face. Who has the three million dollars?" Hill immediately witnessed the harrowed appearance of recognition form on the doctor's face. The moment of comprehension. He, Doctor Brian Rose was not walking away free from this encounter. Hill stood over his pray with menace, threatening, lingering.

"Back off Detective." Rufus came in, gently pushing Hill away. Hill eventually turned and restarted his pacing at the far end of the room. Rufus took the seat opposite from Rose. He continued to speak gently. "Look, we know about the blackmailing. We know all about the money. We also know you don't have a cent of it. The reality right now and all you need to worry about is you could be an accessory to a premeditated homicide. You are potentially looking at an aiding and abetting charge. In Californian law that offence carries the same penalty as the actual killer will receive. Do you understand what I'm saying?"

"Yes." Rose whispered quietly.

"Do yourself a big favor and tell us everything from your point of view. We have enough to know exactly what happened, we just need the confirmation. There's no point in covering up now." Rose started to gently weep, he understood there was no escape.

"Oh lord help me." He uttered with acceptance. "I was getting increasingly frustrated with Foundation

Pharmaceuticals. They headhunted me from the UK nearly a decade ago. I was freshly divorced, two kids ten and eight. They promised me with hard work and good results within five years I would be rewarded with shares of my own. Making my sacrifice worthwhile. I worked day and night, six to seven days a week. I led the breakthrough projects. I made them very, very rich. What do I have for my efforts? Not a single share in the company. I accepted on good faith, and they ripped me off.

"I'm sure that made you very annoyed." Rufus agreed.

"When I looked at the hours I was working for my salary, the rate per hour was comical." The doctor sat upright for the first time. His mindset altered. No longer covering, hiding. This was now a confession. "Debs understood, she sympathized. Or at least I thought she did. In hindsight, I think she was just playing me, using me for her own gain. When Stan made the arrangements to visit, Debs informed me about who he was to her and about Annika. The next thing I knew Annika had travelled over and they revealed an elaborate plan to blackmail him. Once he had invested all his eggs in this one basket, they would jointly approach him. They proposed asking him for three million dollars or they would reveal who they were to his wife and kids. Simultaneously Debs and I would distort the lab results of the cerebral palsy medication to sabotage it. So much of the company's and Stan's capital was staked on its success, a possible failure would crash the stock price along with Stan's personal fortune. He would be staring down the barrel of a massive financial loss, plus a likely divorce, stripping any wealth remaining. Beyond the loss of status and family, it was a pretty scary fate."

"Why three million dollars?" Rufus asked.

"An even split, one million apiece. That was what we agreed. There was no point in demanding more than Stan could realistically get his hands on."

"So, where is that money now?"

"I don't have any of it." Rose said firmly.

Hill from the back of the room, obstinately commented.

"Is that why you came here? To stake your claim on the money."

"I'm embarrassed to say you are correct detective. It's not like Stan could withdraw three million in cash, so we needed an account for him to make the transfer into. Annika revealed her late mother had an account set up decades ago under a false identity. I believe she flirted with criminal activity from time to time. Annika said she had not closed it after her mother's death and had access to use it."

"Do you actually trust her?" Rufus delved.

"Not at all. But what choice did I have? The plan was to transfer the whole lot into the bogus account. Initially she would withdraw her ATM cash daily allowance each day, give Debbie her share and FedEx my cut to me at the end of each week. We thought once everything had died down, we could then risk transferring the rest of the money between us."

"When did Stan transfer the money?"

"A month ago. I haven't seen a single cent of it. Then you contact me to ask about Debbie's possible link to a murder. The murder of Stan. That was never part of the plan. I certainly would never entertain being part of a murder plot. I was horrified."

"Not horrified enough to come clean at the time though, eh doctor?" Hill quipped from the back of the room. "You knew the jig was up for Debs and Annika. You wanted to get in and claim your piece of the pie before the shit hit the fan. Is that not correct?"

"You are correct Detective. I wanted my money, but you must believe me, I did not want to be involved in this."

Chapter 34

After a short break, Hill and Rufus returned Debbie to the interview room. The time spent with Dr. Brian Rose, certainly prosperous. Many blanks were now filled, although key questions remained. Primarily, who actually delivered the killer blow to Stan.

A quick check on the latest from Annika informed them she was retained in the Emergency Room undergoing tests, not able to answer any questions. All the time Katelyn was missing, vanished without trace. The clock ticking remorselessly. A full-on man hunt in progress at Riverfront Regional Park without a lead to go on. All bar the fact Annika had been discovered in Katelyn's trunk. Was there a fourth player in this mix of deception?

Debbie sat with an emotionless expression on her hardened face. Her legal representative sat shotgun to her. Young, keen, hungry, inexperienced. Almost certainly she had never previously represented someone on a homicide charge.

Hill decided on an aggressive tactic. Following the normal process would result in a continuation of the no comment responses. He needed to rattle Debbie.

"Good evening Deborah. I trust your stay in the cells was a pleasant experience?" Debbie looked at him maintaining the bare expression. She said nothing.

"A lot has happened since we last spoke. Earlier we arrested Dr. Rose, here in Santa Rosa." Hill caught the flicker in her eyes. As much as Debbie attempted to disguise it, she could not prevent the subtle reaction. "He was outside of your apartment waiting for you to return. He offered a lot of information without protest, backing up what we've already learned and deduced. Primarily the fact you, Annika and he were embarking on an extortion racket against Stanley Fisher to keep his secret life under wraps. Three million dollars to split evenly between the three of you. Does that sound familiar?" Hill did not wait for Debbie to comment or refuse to answer his semi-rhetorical question. "He was horrified by the lengths you have gone to keep this dark scheme from coming back to bite you. Primarily killing your victim after you had received payment in full. Dr Rose has provided irrefutable evidence of your theft of tetrodotoxin from Foundation Pharmaceuticals which you used to kill him. We have all the information we need to put you away for the rest of your life. I really don't require you to comment further on this."

Hill got up from his chair to undertake some theatrical pacing, leaving Debbie to stew on the information. Rufus glanced at Hill, unsure if this was a hiatus for him to step into. Hill gave a subtle signal to sit tight. The Officer complied. After the silence had served its purpose, Hill reengaged.

"At this point in time I only have one concern. Something very important. It is time critical. We have Annika but she is currently in the Emergency Room so we can't question her for now. We also have Katelyn Fisher missing. I am very concerned for her wellbeing, and I need you to help. There is no time for games, the part where we dance around each other and jab is over. What has Annika done with Katelyn?" A strong projection of authority lined the last question, signaling he wanted an answer. Debbie whispered briefly into her aids ear. The young lawyer nodded before addressing Hill.

"My client is unable to provide you with information on Katelyn Fisher's whereabouts, but she is able to throw more light on what actually happened to Stanley Fisher and what Annika Smith's involvement is. She may be able to assist in building a picture to help you locate Katelyn."

"Really? Let's hear it then."

"Before she provides more detail, she is requesting immunity from prosecution on the blackmail charges that will be leveled against her."

"That's nice." Sneered Hill. "A young lady is missing and possibly dying as we speak. You can help her, right now. But you are going to delay proceedings while I get an agreement written up and notarized to save your own skin. Not good enough. You need to help me now. Once we find Katelyn, we can look at a deal. Until then it's not possible."

Debbie and the Lawyer whispered back and forth a few times.

"My client is holding firm. She will provide all the information you need as soon as the agreement is in place and signed off. There can be no exceptions." Hill slammed his palm on the tabletop, creating a loud audible bang. The young lawyer jumped in surprise, Debbie did not even flinch.

"You had better hope she is okay when we find her." Hill turned to the lawyer. "This is not a federal case so I

272

can't offer a federal letter of immunity. The best I can do is offer a proffer letter." The legal representative nodded to confirm she understood the difference. "Is she willing to continue on that basis?"

"She is."

"Very well. Interview terminated at nineteen-fifty-five." Hill stopped the recording. "Sit tight. I'm going to attempt to get this rushed through." The detective and officer left the room, placing a fellow officer on the door to keep watch. Both men hurried back to Hill's office.

"I'm going to try and reach the district attorney to see what can be done. I don't think she'll be too excited at this time on a Saturday, but you never know."

"Okay, I just want to check something quick." Muttered Rufus, clearly preoccupied by a thought in his head. He jumped on the neighboring console. Hill attempted to call the DA emergency contact number, but with no success. As he ended the call Rufus motioned for Hill's attention. The detective got up and walked over to the screen displaying a map of Santa Rosa.

"We know Katelyn left her residence in her vehicle at roughly the same time as Chris." As Rufus spoke his finger illustrated the point on the screen. "Chris's journey to the park is about ten minutes longer than Katelyn's. There is only a narrow margin of time for something to happen. Chris arrives at the park to discover Katelyn's vehicle has already arrived. We can't be certain, but it would appear Annika was in the trunk at that time. If Katelyn is not at the park right now there's one location that connects them all directly on her route to the park." Rufus traced his finger from Katelyn's family home on the logical route to the park. His finger stopped along a third of the route, directly over the location of Haskins & Wilcox.

"Interesting." Hill agreed. "See if you can get hold of Susan to get access to the building. Also pull some of the search team off the park to join you there. It's worth a roll of the dice. I'll keep trying to obtain a letter of immunity for Debbie.

Chapter 35

"We want to perform a CAT scan on Annika. We can fit her in now." The nurse informed the single officer who accompanied her to the Santa Rosa Emergency Room. "She can't wear the handcuffs for this. You are going to have to remove them."

"Okay, but I really need to use the bathroom first. I've been holding on, but I just can't wait anymore." Officer Daniels replied. "Can you get the hospital security to watch over her for a minute?"

"Sorry officer, the operator of the CT scanner was supposed to finish two hours ago. He's pretty pissed Annika has also been squeezed in. If we don't do it now, it'll have to wait until nine tomorrow morning when he returns for his next shift." The officer looked down at the silent, but conscious patient. Not moving, failing to communicate, like a cardboard cutout of a person.

The officer suspected confidently; she was faking. Despite this, the prospect of discharge into police custody was on hiatus until the doctors were conclusive on her health condition.

"Okay let's go." He agreed, his bladder ready to explode. The nurse and a porter waiting by the gurney transported Annika out of the room and into the elevator. Accompanied by Daniels, the sudden elevation increased the urgency within him. Reaching the room where the CT scan would be performed, the nurse turned to the officer.

"You can't go in there, I'm afraid."

"I've been instructed to stay with her at all times."

"Look, this is the only door in or out of the room. She cannot escape. There are no windows, she has to come back this way." The officer stared at the nurse for a while. Sensing her exhibit a degree of superiority over him. Why she felt the need, the officer could not be sure. But it was there and had been throughout the evening.

"Whatever." He simply replied shrugging his shoulders.

"The handcuffs, please." After another short pause the officer lent over the motionless young lady and released the cuffs.

"How long?"

"About ten to fifteen minutes." The nurse replied resolutely. "Probably closer to ten, he doesn't want to hang around." With that Annika was wheeled into a low-lit room. The large scanner, a dominant feature central before him. The officer watched her journey towards the apparatus until the solid laminated door closed shut.

Now stood in an austere clinical corridor Daniels was alone. His indignant bladder and thoughts for company. Right opposite as luck would have it, a bathroom. The officer knew he should not leave his post, but desperation integrated with unexpected opportunity commanded his thoughts. Wasting no further time and the decision made, he hit the door and much awaited alleviation.

Inside the CT scanner control booth, the frustrated operator's mood was not improving.

"God damn it." He crossly muttered so brashly to himself the whole room could hear it.

"Everything okay?" The nurse enquired.

"No. I was supposed to be at a family birthday meal right now, but I'm still here and the control panel now has an alarm message that I can't clear. I won't be able to perform the scan until its cleared."

"Oh." She replied, not really sure what she could say.

"I'm going to have to perform a full system reset and hope that works or there'll be no more scans until we can get an engineer to look at it. The reset is going to take a good ten minutes. You can keep her here while I try to sort it, otherwise it's not running until tomorrow, at least."

"Can I go?" The porter asked the nurse, already edging towards the door.

"Yes. Just let the officer know it's going to take a bit longer than expected." He gave a short nod as he turned, opening the door. The porter held it open as he glanced up and down the corridor.

"He's not here. Guess he took that bathroom break after all." The porter shuffled off allowing the door to close itself. The nurse watched the door slowly glide shut before glancing back at the operator in his booth, furiously pressing buttons while he audibly cursed under his breath. Eventually she turned her attention back to Annika lying directly down below her. Momentarily viewing a fist, before it slammed hard into her face. Startled, the nurse staggered backward in a daze, failing to witness anything of the second impact. Knocking her clean to the floor, rendered in a state of unconsciousness.

♦ ♦ ♦

Hill placed his head in his free hand. Unable to believe the information received.

"I'm so sorry." Officer Daniels pleaded.

"What do you mean, she's gone? Tell me what happened." He angrily demanded.

"I accompanied her back in the ambulance alone. She was completely unresponsive. At the ER, they started performing tests. It was taking so long. I was desperate to use the bathroom. They sent her for a CAT scan. The nurse insisted I had to remove the cuffs and was forced to wait outside the room. There was a john right outside and the nurse told me Annika would be in there for at least ten minutes. I know it was wrong, but I left my post to use the facilities. When I returned, she had suddenly flipped out, overpowered them, and made a run for it. I'm so sorry."

"Why did you choose to do it when she wasn't cuffed?"

"I know, I know. Sorry."

"Forget it now. Get searching for her. I'll try and divert some help across." Hill ended the call. "Fuck." He screamed in frustration. Fatigue biting badly now. New complications were unwelcome additions to the mix. A large Seven and Seven, quickly followed by a bed would be exceptionally welcome at this point. Instead. he made the call to divert yet more of the search team at Riverfront Reginal Park to the hospital, with one to stakeout her house. Knowing most of the team were now on overtime, there would be tough questions on Monday about the

278

massive use of resources. Especially if their collective efforts failed to reach a successful conclusion.

Chapter 36

Hill returned to the interview room holding Debbie and her unimpressed looking lawyer. Without an update from Rufus, Hill could not allow the situation to extend further. He needed to find Katelyn and at this moment Debbie was his only solid avenue.

Hill handed the document to the lawyer to peruse. She took her time checking each detail. Hill impatiently stood in the corner. Arms folded, tapping his foot, checking his watch every thirty seconds. Eventually the legal aid remarked to Debbie she was happy. She could sign if she wanted to commit to this route. Debbie signed without reading it, again looking totally relaxed and back in control.

Hill returned to the seat and resumed the recording.

"Okay Debbie, tell me where Katelyn is."

"I can't just give you that answer. I don't know that. I've been in here all day." Hill muttered something inaudible under his breath. Debbie continued. "I can give you the full honest story."

"Go from the start." Hill said in a softer tone, keeping both his exasperation and weariness in check.

"I was working at Foundation Pharmaceuticals as you know. I was aware Stan was my father. I had tried to previously reach out to him when I was a teenager. He'd not had any involvement in my life. My mother always trash talked him from as young as I can remember. I believed it back then, up until I was about fifteen. The desire to find out for myself was festering inside me. I eventually elected to contact him. He wasn't pleased to hear from me. Made it abundantly clear, he wanted nothing to do with me. That's pretty painful." Debbie paused for a short sigh, then resumed. "I grew up, got on with my life. Worked shit jobs to fund my own higher education. When I got the job at Foundation, I thought that's it. I've really achieved, now I'll be happy. I soon realized nothing had changed. The all-consuming hole he left inside me sucked up any joy or success.

After a lot of thought, I decided to have one more go at establishing contact. Being more mature I hoped if I could convey to him, I did not want his wealth or to destroy his family. I just wanted to get to know him. Just a little. I said everything would be on his terms." Debbie began to weep. These were not her typical performance tears. The delivery evidently authentic.

"He didn't give anything back, instead shouting down the phone at me to stop harassing him and stay out of his life. It kinda sent me over the edge. I began sleeping with married men I worked with. It didn't change anything. I just felt worthless. A doormat. That was until I started to get close to Dr. Rose. We never had a sexual relationship, he never tried anything on. He became like a father to me. He was mostly unaware of my multiple affairs. A couple came to light, but he hushed it up. Got rid of the employees and protected me."

"Did you not feel bad for the employees who were pushed out of their jobs? Their livelihoods?"

"I know I should, but no. I didn't. The sensation of a man protecting me was such a warm comforting feeling.

Something I hadn't known before. He treated me like a father should treat his daughter. Or so I guess. I'm not really an expert on gauging such a relationship." Debbie took a moment of quiet rumination.

"Go on." Hill gently prompted.

"Then I met Annika. I remember it well. I was sat in a coffeeshop all alone. Stood up by one of my lovers who hadn't been able to escape his wife for the night. So I went there instead, just to be surrounded by other people."

"You were lonely?"

"Yes. Terribly. I sat there nursing a coffee, in my own little world, when suddenly Annika appeared. She asked if she could join me. I can still remember looking around and viewing numerous tables free. She followed my eyes, quickly explaining she just didn't want to sit alone. I invited her to take a seat and we instantly hit it off. Talking for hours, like we'd always been friends. She told me her father had never wanted to be a part of her life, and with that in common we found an immediate connection. I had absolutely no idea her father was my father. That we were sisters."

"Until I dropped the bombshell?"

"Yes." The emotion built again, but Debbie kept a lid on it. "I only saw her on weekends. I didn't realize at that point she lived in Santa Rosa, not Fremont. We would get drunk together and just be stupid. It was nice just to be normal. When she finally revealed where she lived and had been traveling down every weekend, I should have realized something was wrong. Not only strange to put so much into a distance friendship, but also the fact she lived in the same city as my estranged father. Annika kept telling me how she had never had a friend like me before, it was worth the constant travelling. I guess it mirrored my feelings towards her, so I didn't question it. I blinded myself to the coincidence of Santa Rosa and Stan.

"I can understand that." Hill agreed, rapidly coming across as good cop in the absence of Rufus.

"Then one weekend, Annika drove straight from work on the Friday. As soon as she's through my door she's informing me she was inputting the details for a new employee that afternoon. When she was entering the emergency contact details, Annika realized the new girl's father was Stanley Fisher, my father. I had told her all about him. Well, all I knew anyway. I couldn't believe it. It was so weird, but time passed by. I introduced Annika to Brian, and we all got on fine. She didn't really mention Katelyn, so she kinda fell off my radar. It changed after a time, one weekend she revealed Katelyn had told her, Stan was looking to invest in Foundation Pharmaceuticals. I was speechless, trying to decipher what this news actually meant to me." Debbie looked Hill in the eyes. "When you interviewed me earlier, after revealing our shared bloodline, you said Annika tipped Stan about Foundation. That's why he invested in the company. It struck me then just how wrong I had understood the situation. Back at the time I thought he had chosen my employer because I worked there. Like he was trying to involve himself in my life, no matter how abstractly. Now I realize, he didn't even know I was employed there."

"You interpreted events from what you knew. From what made sense from your perspective?" Hill clarified.

"Yes. Exactly. I made a third attempt to contact him, reacting to the signal I thought he had given me. I didn't get a sentence out on the phone before he exploded. He told me if I called his number again, he would kill me, hanging up straight after. I was devastated, but it soon changed to anger. One evening both Brian and Annika were at my apartment. I was ranting on about how I wanted to teach him a lesson. It was that night Brian first mentioned we could blackmail him. Foundation Pharmaceuticals is not operated as a single organization. There are variants under slightly different names for the large investment products. I think it's an accounting ploy but also provides investors options to put their money into one single project or spread it across all operations. Go for one and the risk is higher, but also the reward. Stan had put all his capital into the cerebral palsy treatment. Brian suggested we could threaten him with burying the real test results in favor of doctored ones to trash the product. Plus reveal me, the secret daughter, to his family. I thought he was joking, but it soon became apparent he was serious. Drunk and angry, I was all for it. Annika willingly agreed, so we started planning it."

"The next day once I had sobered up, I dismissed the whole thing assuming the others would feel the same, just a drunk rant. Despite clear heads, they were both completely steadfast on the plan."

"Who was leading it?" Hill asked.

"Definitely Annika. I tried to reason with them both about forgetting the whole thing, but they didn't want to know. In the end I told them straight I was not up for it. I was backing out. They were not pleased to say the least. It was just too extreme, I couldn't do it, despite how I felt about that man."

"Okay, so what changed?"

"A short time afterwards, with our relationships still frosty, Brian asked me to sneak out some tetrodotoxin. I was totally shocked. He wouldn't explain what he wanted it for but attempted to make out it was no big deal. You have to believe me; I had no idea it was intended for use on Stan. I tried to get out of it, arguing the figures wouldn't stack up. He was totally dismissive, telling me when the unaccounted shrinkage was highlighted, the report would come to him. He could just sign it off and there would be no risk. I kept refusing, which caused more friction. It's not like he was asking me to swipe a pack of photocopier paper."

"Why didn't he just steal the stuff himself?"

"He didn't have legitimate access to it. Yes, he could easily get hold of it and remove some, but he could not do that without leaving an electronic trail. When we were next audited, the question would flag straight away. Why did someone without a work-related reason access a highly toxic, precious substance? If the quantity was also short, it would lead to harsh questions. He would be signing off the unaccounted shrinkage on a substance he had accessed himself. The auditors would be all over it. In short, if he wanted the damn stuff, he needed me to take it."

"So, you did. In the end?"

"Yes. Annika came to visit me at work. She had never done that before. She had no reason to. I collected her from the security station, immediately realizing the situation was getting out of control. I took her somewhere private. She was really horrible, domineering. She had a massive go at me, trying to force me to take it. Until then I hadn't even realized she was aware of Brian's request to me. I'm sure you can imagine numerous alarm bells were ringing in my head. She threatened our friendship. I'd never seen this side of her before. It was frankly scary. She told me straight, unless I got hold of the tetrodotoxin, we were done. Our friendship over forever. My relationship with Brian was already crumbling. I felt like my whole world was falling apart, but still I refused." Debbie adjusted her cuffed wrist trying to get it comfortable. Without word, Hill reached into his pocket and retrieved his keys. He unlocked the imprisoned wrist allowing Debbie respite. More good cop. Appreciating the gesture, she rubbed the reddened area, chafed by the constraining cuff.

"Two days after Annika visited you, she returned to Foundation to visit Steve Lewis. Are you aware of this?"

"What? No. I had no idea. Why?" Debbie looked back stunned.

"I think I can help you make sense of that. Let's move to the meeting where Chucky made his damning revelation." Debbie cradled her head in her hands, painful memories surfacing, taking bites from her dwindling resolve.

"It was horrendous. I had no idea it was coming. Just a typical team meeting. Progress updates, that sort of thing. Suddenly Chucky stood up and announced to the whole team he had been having an affair with me. I just sat there, stunned. Everyone looking at me. Then he started naming others I had been sleeping with. It was awful. Eventually I got up and ran out. I went to Brian's office to hide. It felt like forever before he returned. I was devastated."

"It must have been horrible. Do you know what caused Chucky to make such a public announcement?"

"No. I've never understood what triggered it and I haven't seen or heard from him since." Debbie looked up at Hill. "So why did Annika visit Steve Lewis?"

"For the same reason she visited Chucky and God knows who else out of your list of lovers. She was threatening them, to either make the announcement Chucky did, or she would go straight to their families and tell them everything." Debbie sat still for a few moments computing the information. Hill continued. "That's why Chucky did what he did. He was just the first one to cave in."

"I can't believe it. Why would she do it? Why do it to me?"

"I suspect I can help you to answer that question yourself. Tell me about the fallout of the situation following Chucky's big announcement."

"I was taking shelter in Brian's office. When he eventually returned. He kept saying there was no way back for me. I had to leave, restart somewhere else, making out it was in my interest, but also forceful. Repeating over and over, we needed to go forward with the plan to give me the capital to start again. He painted a picture of how bad it could be for me if I had to start again with nothing. He insisted I take the tetrodotoxin that day, then he would help me to secure my future finances. I was frightened and short of options. I understand it sounds a poor reason in the cold light of day, but at the time I was clinging onto the only hope in my lonely life. Yes, the money would be useful, but it wasn't about that. I needed to hold onto my relationship with Annika and Brian, to go through with it was the only option. I reluctantly agreed. I stole four hundred micrograms, ended my shift and never returned. Later that evening I gave it to Brian. He split the tetrodotoxin into two vials. He kept one and instructed me to pass the other to Annika. He didn't explain why, putting me on a flight to Santa Rosa to stay with Annika the next day. Alongside the tetrodotoxin he gave me some GHB, saying it might come in useful during the execution of the plan. I wasn't really sure why he gave it to me, but I was shellshocked. Not really thinking anything through. I passed the tetrodotoxin onto Annika and retained the GHB. You know what GHB is?"

"Yes, I'm well aware. I know you used it on Chris to set up his little scenario. I have to say I'm interested in what the point in all that was."

"That was for Annika. Although I didn't know then she was my half-sister, we developed a tight bond while I lived with her. I soon realized she was totally in love with Chris. Despite her sociopathic tendencies, she is truly shy with men. Especially if she is attracted to them. It gutted Annika that Chris was falling for my half-sister Katelyn. Of all the women in the world?"

"Indeed. Her half-sister as well." Hill pointed out.

"Yes, it would appear so. I hated Katelyn for taking all my father's love, while I had nothing. I guess jealousy motivated me. I can admit, in the spirit of this confession, all of the charade surrounding Chris was driven by me.

While Annika was aware and consenting, she was more focused on the money and Stan." For the first time Debbie's lawyer interrupted.

"Debbie, I just want to remind you what you have signed will exonerate you from the blackmail scheme and any accessory actions towards the death of Stan. It will not protect you from other offences, whether related or unrelated." She stated in a protective, yet professional tone.

Debbie nodded. "It's okay. I understand that." She returned.

"It seems a bit extreme, to go to the lengths you did?" Hill questioned to keep Debbie on her tracks.

"Detective, when I arrived in Santa Rosa, I was a complete mess. After a couple of weeks with Annika, I decided to end it all. I attempted to commit suicide. Annika saved me. On that day and mentally afterwards." Debbie drew in a deep breath, as more tears rolled down her cheeks. "I owe her my life and I hated Katelyn so much. I couldn't stop myself."

Hill silently pondered what he was hearing. Something in all this did not fit. If Debbie was indebted to Annika for her life, why was she so willing to sign a piece of paper to absolve herself and sell Annika down the river? Hill kept it to himself for now, but a large red flag was planted in his mind.

"Okay, let's look at how Katelyn came to work at Haskins & Wilcox. Please don't tell me it's a coincidence. I'm not going to buy that." For the first time since the interview began, Debbie threw a smile. A genuine one for good measure.

"If I'm honest, I'm now seeing this from a different perspective. Annika always told me she started checking Katelyn out after she realized Chris was falling for her. Although we knew about my connection to her, it was later where she discovered Stan's significant wealth. I always thought Annika and I met by chance and just hit it off. As I discovered Stan was investing in Foundation, I took this as a sign he wanted somehow to be closer to me. I wanted that so much, I ignored all the correlations. As I gathered it wasn't an attempt to connect, I remained in denial. The fact Annika worked with his daughter in a completely different city is too bizarre to consider a coincidence. I guess I was so blinded by my need for a friend, I didn't allow myself to question it. There was no relationship between Stan and Annika that I was aware of." Debbie ruffled her blond hair as she thought through her next question. "Did Annika and Stan have a relationship?"

"Yes. They did indeed. He kept her secret, but he was a father to her." Hill candidly answered. "He relocated to Santa Rosa to secretly look after Annika after her mother took her own life.

"Then she always knew about his wealth. I guess she must have engineered Katelyn to end up working at Haskins & Wilcox somehow?"

"That's what I'm thinking." Hill agreed.

"I suppose you have a theory about how I've been drawn into this. Please tell me what you're thinking." Debbie sounded almost childlike. As if frightened to put the pieces together herself.

Hill stood up to pace as he indulged himself in the question. He spoke with a soft caring voice.

"Annika sorts all the recruitment for Haskins & Wilcox. She probably knew what Katelyn did for a living. When she established, they were all moving to Santa Rosa, she could have targeted Katelyn with an email job advert for her specific role, knowing she would be looking for work. Once Stan got wind of who Katelyn was working with, no doubt he would have been as mad as hell. However, what could he say to Katelyn? He could hardly refuse to allow her to take the job without an explanation. I think it was a calculated trap. Annika possibly had been planning to exploit her father for a long time. At that point, maybe she didn't have a plan of attack, so like a chess player she started moving her pieces into threatening positions without striking. Having Katelyn in her grasp at work was one move. Seeking you out in Fremont was obviously another."

"She was just using me? There never was an amazing friendship that started by chance. I was targeted and conned." Debbie spoke softly, but an underlying anger resonated.

"I can't speak for the relationship, maybe you did have a real connection. You are half-sisters, after all. But there's no way your meeting was a chance event. She knew exactly who you were and came to find you."

Hill declined to add out loud, this sequence of events was one possible theory. There were others. This account, from a single perspective, fitted the timeline well. But the key question remained. Debbie was ready to sell Annika out before she had even pieced all this together. When she thought she owed Annika her life. When she was prepared to undertake and execute a crazy plan to coerce Chris into a relationship with Annika. It niggled at him, not going away.

"Tell me about the murder." He sternly fired out.

"I had no idea whatsoever. The first time I realized I had a connection, was when you asked me about the Tetrodotoxin. Until then I thought I was the victim of extremely bad timing. The money had been paid shortly before, so if I'm honest I was kind of pleased. He was never a father to me. He didn't want anything to do with me. When I learned he had died from an epileptic seizure, my first thought was there could be no comeback on the money we had taken. I know that sounds harsh, but if I'm truthful, it was the reality."

"How was the money paid?" Hill asked.

"Annika's deceased mother was no angel, or so I'm told. She ran a few black-market schemes in her time. When Brian first suggested the blackmail idea, Annika revealed her mother had an account under a false identity. She told us she opened it in the nineties, when forging a false identity was much easier to do. Annika closed all her accounts after her death but kept this one open, just in case it proved useful. As it turns out, it was perfect for a blackmail transfer of three million dollars. The single issue, which soon materialized, only Annika has access to that account. Brian and I were relying on Annika to transfer our cut. As soon as Stan died, she immediately became insistent on waiting, stating it was not a good idea to move such large amounts of money around until after the dust had settled. I wasn't particularly happy about it,

292

and I'm positive Brian wasn't. What could we do though?"

"So, you've not seen any of it yet?"

"Not a dime. It wasn't so much of a concern until you began conveying the truth about Annika. I'm kinda thinking I was never going to see any of the money." Hill considered this. Maybe she did have a good reason to stitch up Annika after all? For the first time Hill genuinely considered the legitimacy of the facts in this account.

"Let's go back to Stan's murder. You are telling me, you have no knowledge at all?"

"Detective, I promise you. For all the bad I've done. For all the deception and criminal acts. I had absolutely no idea. I can't even tell you who out of the two could be responsible. It's one or possibly both, but it wasn't me." Hill watched her carefully. Debbie was an enigma. Very difficult to read. Unlike Brian her telltale signs were masked, no clear indication of either a truth or a lie. Hill suspected she had trained herself to believe whatever she was saying, making a new truth to her own mind, allowing her to speak untruths and not react in the usual manner. She appeared completely honest, but he just could not be sure.

"Okay. Where were you at the time of Stan's murder?"

"That was the night where I met Chris. What time was he actually killed?"

"The 911 call came in at five past seven. The poison must have been administered within thirty minutes of that time."

"I was home alone at that time." Debbie thought back. "I left around, maybe seven thirty, it might have been earlier, walked into the city center and got a burger at McDonalds. There must be CCTV of me?"

"I'll check that. I'm not necessarily accusing you, but the timing does provide you a window. I can't categorically rule you out."

"Yes." Debbie weakly agreed.

"Look, we're trying to locate Katelyn. She left her house earlier to meet Chris at Riverfront Park. When Chris arrived, her car was there but Katelyn was not. Annika was locked in the trunk."

"So ask her, for Christ's sake." Debbie exclaimed.

"She's not talking." Hill answered. It wasn't a lie, but he felt it best at this point not to reveal she had absconded to an unknown location. "What do think that is about?"

"I have no idea." Debbie took a moment to consider this. Hill detected a new anxiety in her persona, but could not be certain he was reading it correctly. "Maybe she kidnapped Katelyn, arrived at the park and shut herself in the trunk, to try and look innocent?" Hill smiled to himself, breathing a laugh out of his nose.

"That's very good Debbie. You might have made a good detective in another life. It's the same theory we were looking at, however there are two glaring issues. Annika's time frame to kidnap Katelyn and hide her somewhere were a few minutes at best to arrive at the park ahead of Chris, so where is she? The other is if she is guilty and knows the net is closing in around her, why lock herself in the trunk? She's basically giving herself on a plate to us. She must understand the act of locking herself in the trunk to attempt to fool us is not going to outweigh the damning evidence against her. So, why do it?" Debbie thought hard.

"I'm sorry detective. I agree that doesn't make sense. I don't think I can help you any more than I have."

Chapter 37

Rufus stepped out of the Haskins & Wilcox building. A rising frustration that his hunch had not paid off. There was no sign of Katelyn or any kind of disturbance. Rufus reached Susan on her cellphone before leaving the station. She had in turn contacted the site security who rushed over to allow Rufus and the joining officers full access to search the building.

The shrewd officer even took the opportunity to quickly scan Annika's desk and drawers in the hope of finding something concrete. Not really sure what he expected to find, *a blackmail note? Three million dollars? A bottle with a skull and cross bones on it, marked poison?* There was nothing of interest.

Back outside in the sticky evening air, he repeatedly asked himself the same question. Now Annika had escaped, where would she go? Probably wherever she left Katelyn. As he reached his car the same questions rolled and rolled over in his mind. The timing was so tight, whatever Annika had done, she had executed it quickly and efficiently. Surely that narrowed the variables in their favor. It had to.

He sat in his car, considering what was certain. The last time Katelyn had been in known contact with anyone was the call to Chris to arrange the rendezvous at the park. Chris had stated she was at home, but how could he be sure? Was it possible Katelyn was not there? Maybe taking the call under threat and duress from Annika's hand. Rufus had to explore this thought. He dialed Barbra.

"Katelyn?" A panicked female voice answered after the first ring.

"No this is officer Rufus."

"Have you found her?" She fired out, talking over Rufus.

"No, not yet. I'm trying to clarify a couple of details."

"Okay." Disappointment lacing her consent.

"You are aware Katelyn discussed the meet with Chris on the phone?"

"Yes."

"Did you witness the call?"

"No. I didn't."

"Did Katelyn tell you where she was going and who she was meeting?"

"No, not really. I was in my bedroom with the door closed. She called through the closed door saying she was popping out for a short while. I called back asking where she was going, but she had already gone. She didn't hear me."

"But she was definitely at home?"

"Yes, what is this about?"

"Just wanting to check what is definite. Did you actually see Katelyn leave the house?

"No. I was still in the bedroom, with the door closed. I heard the entrance door close, then Katelyn's car start up. But I didn't watch her."

"Is there an officer there with you now?" He asked a touch impatiently.

"Yes, Officer Roscoe. He's sat opposite me." Rufus once again considered what was confirmed and verified. It would appear Katelyn did make the call from her home. There was no proof, she was the person leaving the house. No corroboration Katelyn, herself drove off in the car.

"Put Roscoe on please." He instructed.

"Hello?"

"Hi. This is Officer Rufus. It's an outside chance but Katelyn might still be at the house. Let Barbra know, but I want you to sweep the entire house, garages, outbuildings and finally the grounds. I have a few officers here, we're going to come over and join you now, just make a start."

"Okay, will do."

Rufus started his car, pulling away at speed. On the move, he radioed to the other cars to immediately head over to the new location. Finally, he called Hill to update him on his latest hypothesis.

Hill took the call moments after stepping out from Debbie's interrogation. His head swimming with all the possibilities of each aspect of this case. Fatigue all-consuming now, he really needed to sleep. Any opportunity, far out of reach.

Returning to his desk, Hill checked for any email updates. A series sat in his inbox all from the cybercrime sergeant. He opened the first with the title, "Who's the extra girl?" It revealed a succession of electronic images. Family photos by all appearances. The father, clearly a younger Stan. The mother promptly recognizable as

Barbra. With them were two girls, roughly about five or six in age. One possibly Katelyn, who was the second girl?

Hill scrolled down through the photos. A few taken in the yard, some clearly at Christmas and then on vacation. The mix showed the same two girls at varying ages. Starting roughly at five plus, up to mid-teens. Most photos missing one or the other parent. Hill guessed to take the photo. However, every photo had the two girls in. With close inspection Hill confidently identified Katelyn in each. He could not put his finger on the other child but regarded a familiarity in her face.

Opening the following emails, each came without text, just photos shot in various locations. The defining feature connecting each, the duo in unison. Happy, close, genuine. How a family should look in the perfect world. Hill considered the possibility it might be a best friend. One who probably had a crap life at home, so hung out with their friend and family, perpetually for escape. Possible, but the consideration did not really fit. *Would a friend join them on every vacation, every Christmas day? Every single backyard barbeque? No.* He continued to the last email where Katelyn was now aged mid-to-late teens. The later photos all shared one major difference with the previous sets. The other girl was gone. Not in any of the photos, as if she never existed. The composure of Katelyn, not as relaxed as previously. A falseness behind the smiles. Possibly just teenage angst. Maybe something more.

Hill returned to the earlier images, studying the mystery girl intently. Could it be? It certainly looked like her. Just like Debbie.

Chapter 38

"You released her? Why would you do that?" Rufus complained to Hill down the phone. Arriving at the Fisher estate an hour previously, to lead the team of officers in an exhaustive search of the property, outbuildings, and grounds. Quickly proving as futile as the Haskins & Wilcox site. No sign of Katelyn, or any indication of wrongdoing.

"I've got a theory." Hill replied in a calm discerning tenor.

"Another one?" It was Rufus's turn to permit fatigue and frustration to manifest in shortened patience. "You'd better fill me in then, cos I'm getting nowhere fast here."

"I'm tailing Debbie right now. If I can stay inconspicuous, I think she may lead me straight to Katelyn."

"Katelyn? Don't you mean Annika?"

"Possibly her as well, but I think her first meet up is with Katelyn." Hill confirmed. Rufus thought about it for a moment, before shaking his head to the cellphone.

"Why would Debbie know where Annika has hidden Katelyn? She was in custody when she disappeared. Have they got a mutual hideout or something?"

"Not exactly. I'm taking an educated guess here, but I don't think Katelyn is completely innocent to all these activities."

"She's involved?"

"Maybe. Look I've got to concentrate on not getting detected. When you've finished up there, you can call it a night or if you still have some energy, we can go over my thoughts. Preferably at a location with a liquor license."

"Sounds like a plan. Keep me posted."

Debbie's taxi, now on Highway Twelve, was heading out of the city towards Sebastopol. Hill expertly maintained his distance from the lead vehicle. This was no learning on the job amateur hour, like Rufus. Hill had been tailing vehicles inconspicuously for many years. He knew his trade well.

As the cab reached North Main Street it turned off, onto the suburban roads. It reached the Center for the Arts, stopping near the entrance. Hill looked around as he approached, observing an immediate turning to the right, just past the taxi. A slight hill elevated the area, providing an advantageous viewing platform. Chain link fences surrounded the building's rear parking lot, permitting unhampered observation within. *Ideal*, he thought to himself, carrying on past the stationary cab. Prior to Debbie exiting the vehicle, Hill killed his lights before swiftly pulling into a gap between other parked vehicles on the adjacent road. Only the building itself could obscure his line of sight.

As Debbie got out, the taxi swiftly pulled away and disappeared into the night. She looked around a few times. Hesitantly she ventured into the parking area which wrapped around the arts center, marked with a single row of angled spaces running parallel to each side of the building. Debbie cautiously continued towards the rear area behind the facility. A parked vehicle flashed its lights a single time. Debbie without further hesitation headed swiftly towards it and got in.

"Bingo." Hill whispered to himself, while quickly considering his options. Either race around to reach the vehicle before it pulled away to box it in with his own car or continue the inconspicuous tail. Pros and cons existed to both alternatives. If he jumped in with both feet now, the opportunity to gather more evidence on his latest hunch was squandered. Continuing the observation from a distance might prove fruitful. While on his own though, the risk of losing the car was high.

With no time to weigh it up, Hill elected to play safe. Restarting his vehicle and rapidly pulling away to complete an instant one-eighty turn, back on himself. The streets were quiet, no other moving vehicles to contend with. He hung a hard left at the small intersection before even hitting the headlights. The entrance to the parking lot approached quickly. Tires squealed loudly as he expertly forced the unmarked police vehicle around into the looped roadway. Racing down the side of the building, Hill observed the glow of newly ignited headlights appear around the back of the building. Rounding the last corner, the target vehicle was now in his line of sight, lights on and just beginning to roll away. Hill could not tell if Debbie and the other occupant were reacting to his appearance or were just pulling away of their own accord, but his window to box them in was rapidly disappearing. The rear tires failed to align with the front, suffering a pendulum effect from the previous tight turn. Close to straightening up, he slammed the accelerator to the floor, racing forward while the rear continued to fishtail.

Moments before reaching the front of the target vehicle, Hill violently switched to braking, further affecting the stability. Forcefully he adjusted his steering to avoid slamming directly into the other automobile.

The screeching of rubber on tarmac, all consuming, as the sedan finally anchored up. Tire smoke poured through the headlights as the vehicle finally came to rest, cutting off any chance of forward progression for the suspects. Hill hit the under-grill concealed strobe lights, bathing the immediate area in a blue and red smoky hazed glow. The final position, far from perfect as the other vehicle sat half out of the space, already angled towards the exit of the site. He knew if the driver was willing to force their way out, they could probably make it.

Fumbling quickly for his firearm, his worst fear materialized. Setting full lock on the steering, the confined automobile lurched forward, aggressively impacting into the police vehicle. Audibly raucous revving accompanied sounds of scraping metal while the assailants fought to free themselves from the makeshift obstacle. Hill's attempt to draw his firearm, totally hampered by the buffeting of the continuous impacts. With spinning wheels and multiple collisions into Hill's vehicle plus the neighboring car to boot, the detained automobile finally achieved its aim, breaking free and speeding out towards the exit. Hill slammed his car into drive, identifying the escaping vehicle as Annika's Hyundai. The governing darkness, coupled with the piercing dazzle of the headlights before the breakout, had prevented any chance of a positive identification. Even so, Hill was certain the person at the wheel was not Annika. His car accelerated forward, promptly he appreciated all was not well. Lurching sharply to the left, Hill counter steered hard to the right. It pulled left, followed by a lurch to the right. The course far from controllable as the ferocious motions continued nearly slamming him into the building itself. The right-angle turn approached, Hill gave it his best shot, but the maneuver was not achievable. Forced to concede defeat. He was going nowhere, the lead vehicle now fully out of sight. He smashed his hand down hard on the steering wheel, letting go a roar of pure anger.

Annika approached an inconspicuous ATM machine on the outskirts of the city center. Crouching low behind a parked car, she nervously surveyed the scene before her. Nobody in sight, all quiet. The street light illumination permitted a systematic scan through the lines of parked cars. All unoccupied as far as she could determine.

Annika fumbled her hand into her jeans back pocket, fishing out a bankcard. All other possessions were taken, her purse, keys and cell now gone. A secondary duplicate cash machine card, missed during the assault, remained concealed in her pocket. Something purposely undertaken for personal insurance.

Backup card in hand, she scurried across the street, inserting it into the machine. A seeming eternity passed before the screen updated to indicate the recognition of a card insertion and permit a personal identification number entry. The primary card, located in her purse and her phone set up with internet banking now gone. She understood the prize the attacker sort was access to the account. She silently prayed as she pressed the account balance option. The screen informed her the information was being retrieved, thanking her for her nonexistent patience. While waiting she considered her options to protect the three-million-dollar nest egg. Without a cell or access to her laptop inconveniently located at home, plus the addition of a fugitive status, her options were narrow to say the least.

Seconds later, it was immaterial. Annika's mouth fell open, the balance of the fraudulent account displayed on the screen. Forty-five cents, the current total.

Chapter 39

Hill was awake before first light. Gaining significant benefit from the handful of hours sleep procured. Now reenergized and ready to go again. A heightened APB was out on Annika's vehicle, Annika, Debbie and Katelyn. Hill had bullied to secure resources to work through the night, keeping a watch on Debbie's apartment, Annika's house and the Fisher estate. He had also managed to pull together a team to scrutinize the citywide CCTV systems to check Debbie's timings into the city on the night of the murder. The journey Katelyn supposably took from her house to the park yesterday afternoon and the movements of Annika's vehicle from the Art Center, both before and after. Multiple haystacks, but there were several needles to find.

Hill was also acutely aware the wrath of Chief Lance was waiting for him on Monday morning. All this labor and resource came at a cost. If you blew budgets the only reprieve was firm results. Hill speculated to accumulate and now had twenty-four hours to make it pay off, before that difficult conversation took place. He elected not to give it further thought, instead rushing to get ready and into the station.

"Do we have anything?" Hill asked the room as he entered the CCTV review department. Four operators who had given up their Saturday night and effectively ruined their Sunday all glanced up at him. Officer Matt Walsh, the department lead beckoned him over.

"Yes, I think so. We've got a few things which may be important to you." Hill took a seat next to Matt and waited as the saved footage was brought up on the monitor. "So, the emergency call from Barbra Fisher came in at five past seven. We're working on a thirty-minute window beforehand for the toxin to be administered but more likely within ten to fifteen." Matt introduced, bringing up fixed camera footage of a street. "This is the first camera Debbie would pass on her logical route to McDonalds." The footage began to play. Debbie could clearly be seen ambling down the road. The time on the overlay read eleven minutes past seven.

"Hmmm, she estimated she left her apartment at half seven." Hill observed.

"Even if she drove from the murder scene directly to this street at a crazy pace to get out and walk past the camera, I estimate she must have left the Fisher residence at ten to seven at the latest. I've checked the traffic cams for any erratic driving between the two locations. There is nothing that stands out to me." Matt advised.

"Okay, although that doesn't categorically rule her out, it's highly unlikely Debbie administered the poison. What about her movements from there?"

"Everything stacks up with her account from where we pick her up. She gets a burger, makes contact with Chris, hangs around and then intercepts him as he leaves for the night. Eventually takes him back in the direction of her apartment." Matt concluded. Hill let out a sigh.

"Okay, What about the journey of Katelyn from her home to Riverfront Park?"

"Yeah, we tracked that pretty well on the traffic cams. It's only ever a single driver in the car. On a couple of shots, you can actually see the driver's face. It's not clear enough, even enhanced, to state it is Katelyn beyond doubt, but it looks a lot like her. It isn't Annika. I'm pretty sure on that, do you want me to bring those up for you to see?"

"Leave it for now, I'll trust your judgement. Is it possible the car stopped off at any point?"

"I don't think so. There's a bit of time from where the car leaves the Fisher's residence before it's picked up on the cam network. Also, the final part of the journey is not covered, but along the majority of the route we have tracked the vehicle. There is nothing untoward to report I'm afraid. Working on the timings I'd say she drove from her house straight there. If anything, she did seem in a rush, regularly exceeding speed limits, but nothing too extreme."

"Okay, Thanks Walsh. Let's move onto Annika's vehicle from last night."

"We spotted this vehicle moving around for some time before you attempted to detain it and for a good while after. I've tracked its route on an electronic map with timings." The officer pulled up the image on the screen, proud of his workmanship. Hill studied it for a few seconds, nodding approval.

"Good work, can you email that to me?" Matt clicked his mouse a few times.

"Done. If they have left the city, I'm confident they didn't do it in this vehicle unless they used back roads. We've tracked every route out with cams and not pulled up any hits as of yet. We have software to do that for us and it's reliable. Either they switched transport or they're still local."

"I truly hope so."

"There's something else. I was able to get a few shots of the occupants. It's dark and as before the images are not particularly clear. I ran it through our enhancing software. It's brightened them up and improved the resolution." As Officer Walsh spoke, he put up the clearest snapshot taken. "You can see Debbie in the passenger seat and I don't know what you think, but I'd say that is Katelyn driving." Hill allowed himself time to study the image. A wry smile formed on his face.

"That is very interesting. I agree, that looks like Katelyn."

Detective Hill & Officer Rufus took the couch opposite Barbra. The woman looked at them in despair, fearing only bad news would be delivered sitting down.

"We are still unaware of the whereabouts of Katelyn." Hill fired straight off the bat. Barbra physically slumped her posture. The brace for the ultimate bad news postponed, for now. "The investigation however is throwing up some interesting aspects. If you are able to provide some context to these, it may help us to locate your daughter."

"Whatever you need detective." She offered. The frostiness of their last encounter gone. Just a mother, absent of her daughter. Pain and fear corroding her soul.

"Time is a paramount factor here, so honest answers provide the best chance of a successful outcome."

"I understand, just ask detective."

"We found years of family photos, many with another girl beside Katelyn. Who is the second girl?"

"Debbie. Debs." She answered as if waiting for the question.

"Deborah Green?"

"Yes. You know her?"

"Yes. She has been helping us with our enquiries." Barbra opened her mouth, hesitating before stumbling out her words.

"Did she kill Stan?"

"At this point, I'm pretty certain she didn't. That's not to say she didn't have some involvement. Can you explain to me why she is in your family albums?" Barbra let go a long sigh, preparing herself to go back there.

"Debs is Stanley's daughter." Hill nodded but did not interrupt. "He had an affair with some god forsaken piece of trash woman. She ended up pregnant with Debs. I found out fairly soon after she was born. It was horrendous. I was pregnant myself with Katelyn, weeks from giving birth. When I found out I thought my whole life was crashing to the ground. Stanley begged for forgiveness. I can't say I ever forgave him, but I put Katelyn first. She needed a father. Leaving Stan might have been better for me, but not for her. I sacrificed the decision I wanted, for her."

"That's understandable." Hill supported. "So how did Debbie come to live with you?"

"Debs did not have a good homelife with that woman. She was a mother only in legal status. She was neglectful, drunk most of the time and eventually a drug habit became an outright addiction. The Child Services got involved and eventually took Debs away. They contacted Stan to see if he wanted to take temporary custody of Debs before they put her into the foster care program." Barbra wiped a tear away from her eye. "We took her in, what else could we do? I didn't feel any malice towards Debs. It wasn't her fault. Anyway, temporary turned into permanent and she became Katelyn's sister in the full sense of the word. We tried to adopt her, change her name from Green to Fisher, but her mother always blocked it."

Inwardly Hill cussed himself. He should have spent five minutes going through Debbie's files, he could have learned all this days ago. Rushing around trying to keep up with the fast-evolving events, he had failed to do the basic due diligence.

"Debs lived with us until she was fifteen."

"What happened?"

"It was awful. She started visiting her birthmother just after turning fourteen. She would go one weekend every month. The woman was better, but still not fit to be a mother. Debbie wanted to get to know her. She kind of forced the relationship. We couldn't really stop her, but I'm sure you can imagine this change was of significant concern to both Stan and me. Every time Deb's returned from a weekend with her, she was a little bit more withdrawn. I don't know what that woman was doing to her, but it was clearly damaging. Then after about eighteen months of this, she phoned me from her mother's place. She said Stan had attempted to have sex with her and would not be returning." Rufus shot Hill a sideways glance. The detective sat unmoved as if he had expected the curveball statement.

"Was there any truth to her claim?" Hill asked compassionately.

"No. Absolutely not. Stan may have been many things, but he was a good father. In our whole time together, I never witnessed anything that would concern me in that respect. It was that spiteful woman that put Debs up to this. She got her claws into her and turned her against the family that loved, clothed and fed her. It was devastating for all three of us."

"When was the last time you had contact with Debbie?"

"A few months after her false accusation. As you can imagine, the whole relationship immediately fell apart. I haven't seen or heard from her in years." Barbra reacted as a thought came to her. "You said Debs had been helping you with your enquiries. Is she here, in Santa Rosa?"

"Yes." Hill confirmed. Barbra's face dropped in disbelief.

"Does the name Annika Smith mean anything to you?" Barbra considered the name for a few seconds.

"No. I don't think so. Should it?"
Hill ignored the question.

"Do you think Stan was ever unfaithful to you again?"

"I hope not, but he was away on business frequently. So yes, before you ask, every time he was gone, I wondered if he was with someone else. There was never any evidence of it, so I guess I gave him the benefit of the doubt. I tried not to torture myself with the suspicion that hung like a bad smell in my life. Was Annika another conquest?"

"No." Hill started to get up, Rufus followed his lead.

"Thank you for the information. It has been useful. I need to move now but I'll explain more when we locate Katelyn."

"Yes, of course." Barbra agreed. Desperate for more information, but also aware while Hill was here talking to her, he was not looking for her missing daughter.

Neither spoke until they were alone in Hill's replacement vehicle. Hill sat staring straight ahead, both hands on the wheel but had not even started the engine. Rufus debated for a period before adopting a direct approach.

"I know you're angry we didn't learn all that for ourselves." He ventured.

"Not we, but me. I'm the detective and I'm not even doing the basics right." Rufus pulled an exasperated expression before saying his piece.

"It is we. Regardless of my job title and experience, on this investigation we're a team. I'm here with you now because you give a crap. You can't shoulder the blame, all to yourself when something doesn't go right. At the end of the day, what harm has been done? If you knew this two days ago, would much have been different?"

"I wouldn't have released Debbie and more than likely I would have Katelyn sat in the neighboring cell, so yes, we are worse off, and I have fucked it." Hill fired back, the anger in his words directed back at himself. "You asked me what the hell I was doing when I released her."

"That doesn't matter now. This is the play we've been dealt so let's make it work." Rufus turned towards Hill, getting his face in the periphery of his line of sight. "Hill? Hill?"

Eventually the brooding detective turned his gaze towards the officer.

"What?"

"We've come this far, are you going to let it all fall apart now?" Rufus held his stare, much to Hill's annoyance.

"Yes, okay." He conceded. Rufus returned to a normal position.

"So boss, where next?"

"I think we need to swing by and check up on Chris. I've got no idea where either Debbie, Katelyn or Annika are heading, but I would say there's an outside chance one or more might pay him a visit."

"Agreed, it's worth a punt."

Hill started the car and pulled away down the Fisher driveway. As they reached the gates, Hill's cell rang. He answered on the vehicle's Bluetooth system.

"Hill."

"Detective, this is Officer Walsh. I've found something else of significance."

"I thought you'd be in bed by now Matt." Hill answered.

"So did I. I sent the rest of the team home, but just wanted to check a few other things before calling it a night, or a day in this case."

"Go on." Hill invited.

"I looked up the registered vehicle for Dr Rose, then using the license tag software ran it on the day of Stanley's murder. I had numerous hits. Again, it's difficult to clearly identify him, but looking at the image on his driver's license, it's a good match."

"Interesting." Hill commented.

"Agreed. As far as I can track, he arrived in Santa Rosa at around six in the late afternoon. Drove towards Debbie's apartment until we lose him on the coverage of the network. Shortly afterwards we pick him up on a route back towards the Fisher residence. If that's where he went, I would put his time of arrival at approximately quarter to seven. Just before seven, his vehicle is again picked up on the Sonoma Highway heading back towards Fremont." Hill and Rufus exchanged glances.

"Good work Matt, remind me to buy you a beer sometime."

"No problem detective, but there's more."

"Go on?"

"I started playing around some more with the license tag software, just to see what else popped up. I entered Annika's tag details onto the footage of Katelyn driving to Riverfront Park. I didn't notice originally, but Annika's car follows Katelyn from a distance all the way from when we pick Katelyn up until the camera network ends near the park."

"Matt?"

"Yeah?"

"Let's make it a pitcher of beer."

"Thanks Hill."

"Anything else?"

"Nope, that's it for now."

"Okay, get yourself to bed. That's some mighty work my friend."

"Will do." Hill hung up the phone. Firing up the vehicle's concealed emergency lighting and siren, he accelerated hard towards the station.

"I think we need to have another chat with our friend, the good doctor."

Chapter 40

Hill slammed his hand powerfully down on the interview suite table maintaining his trademark fashion. Brian, already wincing, flinched at the sound of the impact.

"Enough stories. Enough lies. Tell me the truth." He shouted at the cowering man. Rufus sat uneasily from his adjacent table perch. He wondered how Hill's performance might be perceived if this section of the interview recording was played out in court. "We have you on camera. You thought you were clever, didn't you? Driving up from Fremont all the way to Santa Rosa. No plane tickets with your name on? No security check points to identify your movements." Brian said nothing, his head just hanging low, defeated. "I'm going to guess you already had possession of the Tetrodotoxin, but you still had to stop by Debbie's apartment to pick up the key fob for the gates. We've got you driving to her apartment, then travelling straight to Stan's house. Shortly after your arrival time Stan received a lethal dose of the toxin. As he lay on the kitchen floor, his wife and daughter watching him die, you're captured driving away straight back to Fremont. As if you were never here." Hill grinned at the doctor. "Look at me. Look at me." Brian slowly raised his gaze to meet the detective. "We've got you now. There's no way out. You're done."

Brian started to gently weep, remaining silent. Hill stood up dramatically, walking around his target.

"Doctor Rose?" Rufus gently interrupted. "Did you kill Stanley Fisher?" Both law officers braced inwardly for the answer. Despite the strong evidence they knew everything they had on Brian was circumstantial at this point. Without a confession, a half decent lawyer would have them on toast in a court of law. Brian continued with his intimate emotional breakdown, but the indispensable words did not arrive. "Brian Rose, did you kill Stanley Fisher?" Rufus repeated, increasing his tone and weight of delivery.

"Yes." Whispered Brian, so quiet it was barely audible.

"What? Speak up." Hill blasted.

"Oh lord, what have I done?" Brian called out to the room. "Yes, I murdered that man, but you don't understand why." He snapped back angrily at Hill.

"I can think of three million reasons why." Hill quipped.

"Don't get hung up on the bloody money." Brian replied as his temper raised in the relief of finally confessing. "It was never about the money. Yes, we took advantage of his wealth, but that was always a side benefit. It was all about stopping a dangerous, sick, evil man." Hill let out a long, exaggerated exhale before retaking his seat. "I guess you had better explain." He offered genuinely.

"The Fishers know all about Debbie. She lived with them for years, as part of their family. Only Stanley wanted more from Debbie than a father's love. She told me it began when she was eleven or twelve. She said when nobody else was present he would start play fights and touch her oddly or make her sit on his lap. Debbie told me she immediately knew something was off about his behavior but didn't really understand what was happening. As she started to develop into a young woman the unwanted attention increased. He began making lude quips, accidentally exposing himself to her. All sorts of disgusting acts."

"Do you know how far he took this behavior?" Hill enquired sensitively.

"Debs told me he never took it beyond something which could be argued as her misinterpreting events, but it was getting progressively worse. She no longer felt safe in that house. At the same time, she had established a relationship with her estranged mother. Eventually confessing to her what was going on. From that point Debs never returned to the Fisher home. She escaped him, ironically safer with her alcoholic junky mother." Hill intensely studied the doctor's body language throughout his admission, previously establishing his obvious patterns when telling untruths. Whatever the truth was, Hill was satisfied Brian believed every word he spoke.

"That's a pretty serious situation."

"Yes. I believe Debbie's behavior towards other men all stems from the damage he did. Inside, she is a shattered individual."

"Okay. I can understand why you wanted to stop this man, but why do something so outlandish and attempting to profit from it to boot? Why did you not just contact the police?"

"Lord, I wish I had, believe me. Debbie and Annika talked me into agreeing to the blackmailing. I did not want to add that aspect, but I guess I was kind of a passenger. It was a runaway train and if I tried to jump off, I would end up badly hurt."

"They threatened you?"

"No, not like that. Hurt metaphorically." Brian corrected.

"But why kill him? That doesn't make sense to me."

"Because of Annika." Brian returned. "He had been undertaking the same repulsive behavior towards her. For years it went on. Her mother knew but turned a blind eye, pretending it wasn't happening. Annika tried to put a stop to it, moving out as soon as she could afford to, so she didn't have to suffer his visits.

Even then he wouldn't leave her alone, using her mother as leverage. One day Annika exploded at her mother for not protecting her. Allowing this sick bastard to prey upon her, in her own home. I think years of pent-up anger came out in one massive outburst. Annika stormed out leaving her mother alone with her thoughts. Annika calmed down, so a few hours later returned to attempt to discuss the topic in a more civil dialogue. Annika discovered her mother had hung herself."

"Jesus." Hill exclaimed soberly. The room sat in somber silence. The gravity of the freshly shared information required a moment of self-collection. After what appeared an appropriate length of hiatus, Brian continued.

"Stan was a predator. He didn't stop his pursuit of Annika. Now she didn't have her mother to get in the way, he elected to tighten the net, relocating here to be always near her. When I learned of his current tactic, I suggested going to the authorities. Debbie talked me out of it. Stating all the incidents she suffered were just his word against hers. Nothing could be proved.

"What about Barbra or Katelyn? Surely, they must have had their suspicions with Debbie?" Rufus added in.

"He was pretty careful. Ensuring events only took place when nobody else was about to witness it."

"And Annika?" Rufus continued

"Again, once the mother was dead, nobody else was aware. Stan was never named on her birth certificate, never legally her father. As long as she failed to stand up to him and try and take the case forward, he could pretty much do as he pleased. Annika isn't stupid, Debbie said she knew he could afford first rate lawyers. Annika didn't really have a chance if she took that route."

"What did Annika tell you about this?" responded Rufus.

"Nothing. Annika is completely unaware I know about his misdemeanors. Debbie swore me to silence. As far as Annika is concerned, I only committed the murder for the money. That was the only reason I eventually agreed to the extortion aspect."

"Hmmm." Hill came back in. "What reason did Debbie give for not involving Annika in your comprehensive knowledge of events?"

"She was worried Annika would feel betrayed. She told her everything in confidence. As far as Annika was concerned, they were using me to do their dirty work on the pretense it was about the money. The reality was the payoff was just a circumstantial bonus that gave my involvement credibility."

"Tell me about the murder."

"Okay." Rose paused while preparing himself to profess the details. "I drove from Fremont as you already know. I had the Tetrodotoxin already, which Debbie took for me before leaving Foundation. I had to go to her apartment to pick up the stolen fob for the gate into the Fisher compound. We didn't speak, she came down to the entrance door, handed it to me and then went straight back up. I drove directly to the house. Parked a short distance away and let myself in through the gates. It was a short walk to the house. I sneaked around the back, found an unlocked door and let myself in. I had never been at the premises before, so it was difficult to find my way around. Purely by luck I came across a lounge, Stanley sat alone inside watching television. His back was to me, so I didn't waste any time. I just crept up, jammed the needle in the back of his neck and pushed the plunger down hard. Naturally he jumped up. As he moved away, the needle pulled out. I hadn't delivered the full load, but I knew what had been administered was more than enough to ensure the result. I immediately ran hard, back the way I came and exited the house…"

"Hold on a minute." Rufus interrupted. Brian and Hill turned their heads towards him in unison, unsure why the confession was being interrupted. "I'm sorry, but there's something here that just doesn't make sense. You just lucked out? By chance there was an outside door unlocked?"

"Er, yes. That's what happened."

"Really?" Rufus's tone spurious.

"It's not that unlikely officer. I think they thought they were safe in the confines of their walled estate. Without a fob, it's not an easy building to gain access to. They were probably complacent about security within." Brian answered with such certainty, it reeked of overcompensation. Hill knew it, happy for Rufus to pick it apart.

"Complacent? Well, there's a thing. Let's talk about complacency." The officer continued. "In fact, let's talk about your complacency. Thought and planning went into concocting the blackmail scheme, significant complication into putting the whole thing together. The lengths Annika went to, to make Debbie's job untenable, so she was cornered into this scheme. The theft of the toxin, the CCTV on the gate taken out, the stealing of the fob, driving into town to arrive undetected. Debbie going for a burger to appear on the citywide CCTV at the time of the murder. So much of this scheme was carefully formulated into a tight precision operation. But one key aspect, access to the premises was left completely to chance? What were you going to do if all the doors were locked? Just go home?" Hill turned his gaze from Rufus to Brian. Color noticeably draining from his face. He stammered, shifting awkwardly, before delivering his response.

"Well, I tried my luck, but if no way in was found I would knock on the door and inject him as he answered." Hill could see it was clearly a fabrication, sure Rufus was reading it in unison. The man was not an accomplished liar. Hill kept his mouth shut, confident in Rufus to further stick the knife in.

"That does not make sense. How do you know it would be Stan who answered the door? Barbra and Katelyn were both home. It's a one in three chance. Were you planning to undertake this act with one or two witnesses watching? You are not a stupid man. This was a preplanned act, not a spur of the moment undertaking. You know full well we would track you down in no time. So, no. Knocking on the door was not your plan. You knew with certainty you could access the building. How did you know that Brian?"

"Your wrong officer." The doctor retorted without substance.

"Doctor Rose. How did you know you could get in through an open door?" Brian did not answer, knowing he was trapped. Terrified of providing the information the law enforcement pair knew was there. Instead, he mentally shut down. Hill looked at Rufus, giving a short discreet nod to signify Rufus had done well, but for now the point would not be explained by the subject. He wanted to move on before Brian completely imploded.

"Alright Brian. Let's move on. What is Debbie's total involvement?" Hill asked.

"She hasn't really had any involvement apart from knowing. Annika was the driving force. It was her idea. Debs was reluctant to move forward. It was Annika, it would appear who manipulated Chuck into confessing to the team at Foundation about her antics, ultimately forcing her out of her job. I pretty much pressurized her to steal the tetrodotoxin knowing she could use the money to set herself up for the rest of her life. It was Annika who tampered with the camera at the entrance gate. Annika who stole the fob, only passing it to Debs to give to me. It was Annika and me who threatened Stanley with the loss of his investment and moving forward with the police involvement on his sick sexual preferences. I can honestly say, Debbie is guilty of the crime of knowing, but not instigating. Her only active participation is assisting under coercion from either Annika or me."

"What was the whole episode with Chris about? Annika and Katelyn's colleague, who she stalked like a woman possessed. The motivation does not make sense to me." Hill tested.

"I'm sorry detective. I am trying to be open with you, but I'm not sure I understand that move myself." Brian replied with sincerity. Hill recognized the man would not be able to assist in rationalizing those events.

"Okay, we need to discuss all of this in more detail, I trust at this point I can rely on your full cooperation from here on in?"

"Yes." Brian answered.

"In a minute I am going to stop this interview and officially charge you with the murder of Stanley Fisher. Afterwards, I am going to request immediate legal representation for you, then I am going to continue my search for Katelyn, Debbie and Annika. Do you understand what I have just told you." Brian dropped his head like a naughty schoolboy facing the principal.

"Yes. I understand."

Rufus looked expectantly at Hill in the corridor outside the interview suite.

"Well, what's the next move?" He asked his commanding officer.

"We're close." Hill agreed, reading Rufus's facial expression. "We have the murderer. We know most of the story, but not all of it. As you picked up immediately, Brian knew a door would be left unlocked or he had a key. My instinct is telling me someone in that house was involved and deliberately left Brian an easy entrance. That means either Barbra or Katelyn was involved."

"Yes, that's my thoughts. At this point, I'd place my chips on Katelyn." Rufus concurred, inwardly pleased for Hill's recognition.

"That would make her disappearance and Annika's confinement in the trunk, more logical. Whether her life is currently in danger is debatable. Beyond that, we have the question of what each of the daughters knew, corroborated on and where they are currently located. Plus, the whole scenario with Chris. Finally, there is the question of who has the three million dollars?"

"Maybe we should go back to speak with Barbra, put her under some pressure and see what comes out." Rufus suggested.

"It's one possible tactic. However, I may be wrong, but I have another idea to try first."

Chapter 41

Chris paced his living room, desperate to be out searching for Katelyn. The search team's lead officer instructed him to stay at his apartment. Clutching at straws, he suggested Katelyn might turn up there. It was necessary to remain present, just in case. Frustration bore in, considering this a complete waste of his time and possible resource to assist in the manhunt. The aggravation dissipated rapidly when a knock wrapped on his door.

Chris bolted over, flinging it open in anticipation. Disappointment enclosed in surprise greeted. It was not Katelyn who stood before him, but Annika. Chris froze, unsure what this meant. Anger she was not locked up fizzed inside.

"Please, Chris. Let me in, before anyone sees me." She begged in desperation.

"Where is Katelyn?" He fired back angrily, not permitting her entry.

"Chris, I don't know. Please. I need your help. I need to stay out of sight."

"Tell me what is going on. Right now."

"I will. Please let me in and I will tell you everything I know." Chris remained motionless, physically blocking the doorway and her ability to push past, as he considered his options. Eventually relinquishing, Chris stepped back permitting access. Without hesitation, Annika stepped inside. Closing the door immediately behind her.

"I should call Detective Hill, right now." He threatened with full intent.

"No, please don't. Let me explain first. Then you can decide what you want to do." Chris held a firm stare before extending his arm towards the couches. "Can I get some water? I need a drink."

"Okay." Chris surveyed her before turning to the kitchen. Annika was visibly in a poor condition. He wondered again why she was not secure in police custody, providing crucial information on the current whereabouts of Katelyn. If she was on the run, it was already noticeably taking its toll on her. Chris quickly filled a glass, joining her on the couch. He waited impatiently while she desperately gulped back the much-needed fluids.

"Well?" He shot at her, the moment the glass parted from her lips. Annika did not know where to start. So much information necessitated explanation, all to a man who only cared about a single aspect. The current location of Katelyn. Something Annika could not answer.

"Chris, I do not know where Katelyn is. I think I've been duped."

"Duped?" Chris scoffed. I'm not falling for anymore lies. Not from you and certainly not from Debbie." Annika opened her mouth to speak, but before any words came out, someone else knocked on Chris's door. Both Chris and Annika jumped up.

"Shit. I've been followed or they were watching your door." Annika whispered. Her tone panicked. Chris stepped forward, towards the doorway. Annika jumped into his path, placing both hands flat on his chest in a vain attempt to halt his progression.

328

"Please don't answer it Chris, it's a trap." He threw Annika a dismissive expression before pushing her aside. "Chris, please." She begged in futile desperation, but he continued towards the door. On arrival, Annika's warning, her panic, penetrated his thoughts. Caution superseded anticipation, instigating the quiet use of his spyhole. Disbelief instantaneously filled him. The figure standing before his door was Katelyn.

Chris flung the door wide open, a massive smile forming on his face. The relief of knowing she was still alive overriding any other conscious thought. A second later the elation converted to alarm. Katelyn stood before him, large as life. Not with arms outstretched, instead wearing blue nitrile gloves, she bestowed a handgun. Aimed directly at his chest.

"Step inside." She ordered. No emotion in the command, her face calm. Chris walked backwards reacting more to the lethal threat of the firearm, rather than conscious compliance to the instruction. Katelyn stepped forward, prompting Chris to maintain his retreat. Once inside she trained the gun on Annika, stood trapped by the couches, lacking any option of escape. "Both of you, sit down. Now." She motioned with the gun for Chris to move over to the couches. "Sit together. Quickly." Katelyn barked.

"What are you doing?" Chris asked as he moved across, thoroughly confused.

"Shut up and sit down. Hands where I can see them." She responded, ignoring his question. With that, Debbie, also donning nitrile gloves, entered from the stairwell, shutting, and locking the door behind her. Annika's head dropped. The substantiation of her suspicions formed in the last twelve hours, abruptly confirmed in a single moment.

"Debbie?" Chris mouthed in astonishment.

"I knew it." Annika blurted out angrily. "You two faced, backstabbing bitch." Debbie turned from locking the door to face Annika.

"I might say the same about you Annika, only I'm a little better at this than you." She sneered, triumphantly.

"You both played me, didn't you? And Brian? We were patsies in your dark scheme." Annika's voice filled with fury. Chris took his seat next to her as instructed, remaining entirely bewildered. Katelyn elected on an armchair, a safe distance away from her two adversaries. Maintaining the aim of her weapon directly between them both. Debbie continued to stand close to the doorway.

"The plan is totally fucked." Debbie announced from her remote position. "It's everyone for themselves now."

"Maybe so." Annika replied without turning her head to Debbie. "But I now see if everything had gone to plan, I would still be trapped. There never was a happy ending for me, was there?"

"Ha." Katelyn scoffed. "Don't get nasty because we saw right through your own trap. You were planning to stitch us both up and walk away with a fortune. Now you've had a taste of your own medicine, don't start complaining about how bitter it is." A brief silence ensued, stark tension engulfing the room.

"Can someone please explain to me, what the hell is going on?" Chris spoke as calmly as he could manage.

"What do you think Debs? Should we enlighten him?" Katelyn asked in a droll tone.

"Up to you. It's not going to matter shortly."

"What does that mean?" Annika fired angrily.

"Nothing. Shut up." Katelyn aggressively shut her down. Chris had never heard Katelyn speak like this before. "So, this all started many years ago when Debs and I were fifteen. Debs is my half-sister, which I believe you are now aware?" Chris nodded to confirm. "At five years old, Debs moved in with us after the child protection agency took her from her mother. At that age I didn't understand about the implications of having a secret half-sister. It was amazing to suddenly be gifted a surprise sibling. I was so lonely. We bonded from the get-go and have been as close ever since. Neither of us were aware of Annika, yet another sister here in Santa Rosa. All was well for years. We were happy sisters. That changed when we began to become young women. Daddy never did anything improper to me, but when I look back, I guess he always viewed me as his legitimate daughter. Treating me as a father should. Unfortunately for Debs he took a different approach, he viewed her as his possession. I didn't see it at the time, but when I remember back, there was a clear distinction. Daddy considered Debs as an object, to do what he wanted with. Would you agree Debs?"

"Damn straight. I knew my place in the pecking order, and that was fine. I understood Katelyn was oblivious. I never raised it with her or Barbra. It changed when he started touching me, I wasn't gonna allow that." Debbie agreed.

331

"Debs took the only reasonable option available to her, she went back to live with her mother. It was awful, my own flesh and blood, my own sibling, taken from me. Just to shelter herself from the person who should be her protector. The whole family dynamic was shattered. I hated him for that."

"It never broke our bond though." Debbie piped up from her sentry post at the door. Katelyn nodded silently, clearly fighting personal deep-seated emotions.

"Debs and I maintained a clandestine remote relationship with each other. It was difficult, but our love for each other never changed. Anyway, fast forward to eight months ago. Daddy announced he was quitting his job and wanted to relocate for a more peaceful life in Santa Rosa, he expected mom and me to just give up our lives. To come with him. The only saving grace, the only reason I agreed to relocate was Debs. I knew she was living in Fremont, just a few hours' drive away. It meant I could meet with her, face to face on a frequent basis. Just before we left, I was sent an email with application forms for a position at Haskins & Wilcox. I had no idea at that time, Annika had sent them. I was still oblivious of her existence, but she knew all about me. I took the position innocently. Unaware this was a part of her dark planning."

"You're wrong Katelyn." Annika interrupted. "I just wanted a relationship with you, even if you didn't know we had shared blood."

"That's complete crap Annika and you know it." She vehemently fired back at her, holding a look of utter disgust directly at Annika. "All you were interested in, was getting your claws into Daddy's wealth." Katelyn calmed her tone and continued. "Annika was also aware of Debs, tracking her down in Fremont. She falsely set up a chance meeting between them in a local coffeeshop, asking if she could join Debs, who was sat alone. From there she engineered a friendship under false pretenses."

"She told me she had been abandoned by her father, never knowing who he was, just to strike a chord." Debbie clarified. "She never once mentioned it was the same father or that she did indeed have a relationship, albeit a secret one. That he had regularly visited her, her whole life. That he moved to Santa Rosa, for her."

"Annika had a single objective. She wasn't interested in the continuation of the relationship with Daddy, suffering the same illicit attention as Debs. Only keeping it going in the hope of tapping into his money. Annika decided she needed to force her hand to make that happen. She prayed on Debs, playing on her emotional pain and animosity towards Daddy. When Brian came into the mix, she worked the pair of them to formulate a plan against him.

"No, I did it to help her." Annika pleaded.

"Whatever." Katelyn snapped. "She also manipulated Daddy. Permitting his behavior, to introduce him to Foundation Pharmaceuticals. Annika had obtained inside information from Debs regarding the cerebral palsy medication. It was an investor's wet dream. Due to Annika's maneuvering, Daddy didn't realize he was being played, left thinking Annika had purely by chance put him on the scent of a goldmine. He did his own research, recognizing the potential. Shortly after investing almost all his wealth, a cool ten million dollars into the project. She persuaded him to change his will, to set up a trust in her name, to take ten percent of the shares, in the event of his death. Daddy was so delighted he agreed. Those shares would be worth a tidy sum once the product received FDA approval. Debs had no knowledge of any of this. Completely unaware of who her new best friend's father was."

"Chris, this isn't the true facts." Annika protested.

"Annika, shut up or I will shut you up." Katelyn snarled. "Annika then influenced Debs and her boss, Doctor Brian Rose into coming up with a scheme to end Daddy, on the pretense of stopping him targeting young girls, and taking a tidy sum of cash to boot. Threatening to crash his investment and expose his dark behavior unless he paid them three million dollars. Annika just so happened to be in possession of a bank account opened under a false identity so could receive the payment without risk. She influenced them to agree to inject Daddy with a deadly toxin, which would mimic his epilepsy before he died. She sold this under the guise of ensuring no other girls suffered at his hand, while simultaneously removing the risk of comeback on the embezzled finances. Annika hoped, if it looked like he died of a seizure, no formal police investigation would follow. You got that bit wrong, didn't you Annika?" Annika said nothing. "The final aspect of the plan, which she neglected to share with Debs and the doctor, was she intended to retain all three million to herself and disappear into the night. Safe in the knowledge she would also inherit ten percent of Daddy's shares, almost certainly worth in excess of another three million down the road. It was a tidy nest egg to live off for the rest of her sad lonely life. The other big mistake Annika made was not realizing Deb's and I had a relationship. Unaware we knew each other existed, let alone in frequent contact. It didn't take long for us to discover the new friend Annika in Fremont, was the same Annika who I worked with in Santa Rosa. With that established, after further investigating, it soon became clear we shared more than a workplace, we shared the same father."

"Not so clever now are we Annika?" Debbie cackled smugly. Annika grimaced but said nothing.

"Debbie resisted helping in the scheme after initially agreeing. It helped buy us some time to work out an alternative plan. Annika, unhappy with the delay, showed her true colors. Accosting married Foundation employees, Debs had revealed in confidence to Annika she was sleeping with. She eventually forced one to come clean in a big meeting, naming others currently engaged in relations with her. Debs was forced out of her job, making it easier for Annika to coerce her back into participating. Before leaving, Debs committed her only crime, stealing the toxin required to poison daddy. She in turn passed it onto Brian. Annika stole my key fob for the gates at home from my desk. She was aware of the CCTV but risked the move. As she thought no murder investigation would ensue, she was confident the footage would never be reviewed. I recently made sure it was, raising the incident with Detective Hill."

"You Bitch." Annika fired out, unable to contain her anger. Katelyn ignored the insult, carrying on.

"Annika damaged the CCTV on the gate and then we were good to go. The only question mark remaining for Annika was how Brian would access the property. Debs spoke with Brian to assure him she had sorted this aspect out, but to just keep it to himself. She said he should spin Annika a line saying he trained as a locksmith back in England and could make his own entry. Obviously, Brian was confused but his eye was completely on the money, and with his loyalty biased towards Debs, he did as he was told. On the Friday he drove up from Fremont, stopping at Debs's apartment to collect the fob. Debbie informed him, a back door would be left unlocked to permit his entry."

"He obviously questioned it, but I didn't elaborate." Debbie explained. "I just closed the door and went back upstairs."

"In case you haven't already worked it out Annika, I unlocked the door." Katelyn announced proudly.

"You participated in the murder of your own father?" Chris questioned in disbelief.

"Yes I did. That man took away my sister, because of his own perverted needs. Then he offers the inheritance that should have been put aside for Debs, to this piece of trash. Not on my watch, not ever."

"But?" Chris stammered as his mouth attempted to catch up with his thoughts. "But, if he's now dead, won't she get this any way when the will is read?"

"Not if she's incarcerated or worse."

"Don't threaten me." Annika growled, edging up from her seat. Katelyn focused the gun directly up at her.

"Go on, try it." She teased. A second later Debbie, quickly stepping forward forced her arm firmly around

336

Annika's neck, pulling her back into the seat. She applied pressure cutting off Annika's ability to breath.

"Stop it." Chris shouted, his hands attempting to prize her arm free of Annika's neck. Eventually Debbie backed off again, but not before landing a firm punch onto the back of her head. The very same spot, Katelyn had impacted the previous day. Point made; Debbie retreated back to the doorway.

"We had hoped to keep it simple. The money had been transferred into Annika's account. The time Debbie spent as Annika's best friend, living with her, before getting her own apartment was mainly spent on establishing how to access the account. Eventually she cracked it. Debbie moved out and we then just let everything play out. All we needed was your cellphone to make the transfer. You made that very easy for me Annika."

"Shit, yesterday." Annika understood instantly. "I only followed you to try to locate Debs and find out what the hell was going on. I can't even remember what happened."

"Yes. I was aware you were tailing me. I knew I would reach the park before Chris so I sped there as fast as I could, making sure you didn't lose me. As soon as I arrived, I went to the trunk and readied the tire iron in my hand. As you approached, I swung around and smacked you hard on the top of your head, knocking you out. It was all a bit spur of the moment, but it worked. I took your possessions including your cell. I knew I didn't have long as Chris was imminent. I needed to buy time, so I just pulled you into my trunk, locked the car and then left you in there. I took your car back out. You drove straight past me Chris, entering the park. I couldn't believe you didn't even notice."

"You're not going to get away with this Katelyn. Hill and Rufus are onto you both. It's now just a matter of time before they catch up with you." Chris fired back, anger rising within him.

"Oh? I don't think you've got that one correct. They know nothing about my involvement. I'm just the poor daughter, a victim. They're not onto me."

"Well Debbie then?"

"Sorry Chris." Debbie called out from behind. "My only crime was to steal the toxin from the lab. I signed a waiver from prosecution on that one to give information on Annika and Brian's involvement. So they already know, but can't do anything with it. I'm innocent on everything else. I made sure I was captured on CCTV during the time of the murder in town so I'm clear on that aspect. As you might imagine I painted a pretty dark picture of Annika and Brian to those bumbling detectives. They were like putty in my hand. I even played them to believe I was unaware you were my sister Annika. They ate it all up."

"You're sick, the pair of you. Totally sick." Chris whispered in disbelief. Katelyn and Debbie exchanged a triumphant smile.

"It wasn't supposed to be this complex, those two cops have caused significant trouble. We had to improvise a bit, but I think we're now home and dry." Katelyn announced to nobody in particular.

"I just don't get what my involvement was in all this? What was the point in doing what you did to me Debbie." Chris asked, braving turning his head towards her.

"Face back round." Katelyn commanded. He did so. "Yeah, on reflection, that was the pair of us getting a bit too cocky. Annika was totally in love with you Chris. Pitiful really. She can plan a fucking murder scheme of her own father, with the intention of ripping off her own sisters but can't fucking say hello to someone she loves like crazy." Laughed Katelyn.

"When I was going through all your stuff, looking to access your secret account I found your letters to Chris." Debbie cackled cruelly. Annika dropped her head, even in this situation she could not prevent her cheeks turning bright red in embarrassment.

"Letters?" Chris asked.

"Enough." Annika shouted angrily. Debbie ignored her.

"Annika has written literally thousands of letters to you, telling you how much she loves you. I guess she could never pluck up the courage to give you one. It's really sad. She has planned out your marriage, named your would-be kids, the dog. Described the house you would live in. It goes on and on." Chris gave Annika a sideways look. Her head down, mortification broadcasting outwardly from her face. This was genuine. "The last few letters take a slight change in tact, stating she had inherited three million dollars and wanted to leave town. She asked you Chris, if you wanted to join her and share the money together. We knew she intended to steal all the money, with or without you. We also knew Annika wanted to rip out Katelyn's eyes for her closeness to you, so we decided to play a little game, just for our own amusement. We had to quickly put a stop to it when the homicide investigation started up, but it was great fun until then."

"Jesus, all that was just a bit of fun? What the hell did I do to you both. It all centered around me. I was the one suffering." Chris fired back.

"Yeah maybe. I don't really care Chris. Like I say, it was fun. We didn't get chance for it to fully play out to its intended conclusion, thanks to Hill, but I enjoyed it while it lasted." Debbie continued in the same callous tone.

"Plus, you were actually a good lay Chris." Katelyn chimed in. "Annika you really should have had a go. You would have loved it." Debbie from behind them both caught Katelyn's eye. She tapped her watch. "Anyway, time is moving on. I think we need to get this all concluded so we can move on with our lives." Annika lifted the handgun in her nitrile gloved hand and cocked the hammer. In the same moment, Chris's cell, situated on the coffee table, began to ring.

Chapter 42

Hill parked his replacement sedan outside Chris's apartment. From their vantage point they could see the outside metal staircase leading up to his front door.

"We might be wasting our time here boss." Rufus commented.

"Maybe. My senses are telling me different. I've always listened to them, I'm not about to change that now."

"Are they ever wrong?" Rufus asked with a smile and a touch of sarcasm. Hill returned the smile.

"Often." He admitted. "But even a broken clock is right twice a day. Tell you what, give him a ring first. Let's see if he has anything to report before we go up." Rufus pulled out his cell, calling Chris. The ringing continued, on the loudspeaker. Hill and Rufus eventually exchanged a glance.

"He would be on tenterhooks with his phone while Katelyn is missing." Hill accurately observed. As the voicemail kicked in, Hill began to ready himself to exit the vehicle. "Something is wrong, let's go."

The phone rung off. Katelyn looked at Debbie, concern etched on her face.

"Let's get this done before we encounter more trouble." Katelyn said to her. Without further comment

Debbie pulled a hypodermic syringe out of her pocket, removing the safety cap. Annika following Katelyn's eyes, glanced around to catch sight of the offending item.

"You're gonna kill us? That's crazy. You'll never get away with it." She spluttered out breathlessly.

"No. You're going to kill Chris, then yourself. Wrap this sorry affair up like a neat package with a bow on top." Katelyn laughed to herself."

"What? No."

"During my confession with immunity, I told Hill the stolen tetrodotoxin was split into two vials. One went to Brian and the other to you, Annika." Debbie announced proudly. "Painting the damning picture of you as the instigator I made sure I slipped that important detail in. We have your phone, remember? I've composed an eloquent suicide note on it, detailing your involvement as I've reported to Hill. Adding you know it's the end of the road, the net is closing in on you. Read it out Katelyn."

"I don't think we should waste any more time Debs." She cautioned.

"Come on, let me just enjoy this one last moment." Katelyn huffed slightly. She removed Annika's cell from her pocket. After several attempts to unlock it, with her nitrile donned finger she began to dictate.

"Set to send to all your contacts." She introduced.

"Dear Brooke family,

I have no family or friends to send this to, so I have addressed it directly to you. I hope one day you can forgive me.

I murdered my father to stop him abusing me and certainly other women and girls. I collaborated with Dr. Brian Rose and forced my half-sister Deborah Green to help. Debs was unaware we were sisters and while Brian shares my guilt, Debs was manipulated by us both. She should be regarded as a victim rather than a perpetrator.

The police are closing in on me and it is only a matter of time now. I cannot continue down this road. I am taking control of my own fate.

Beyond this act of vengeance. I have been obsessed with your son Chris for years. I can't stand to think of him living on, beyond me. Living a life without me in it. I have taken him with me so we can always be together, for eternity. A love stronger than you will ever know.

I plead for your understanding.
Annika."

Debbie laughed out loud as it was read to the room. A loud riling shrieking cackle.

"Think about it Annika, when the cops find all your weird stalker letters to Chris, it's not going to take long for them to settle on you were a total nut job. It's all going to fit together nicely. Katelyn and I will walk away untarnished." She tormented. Meanwhile Katelyn moved to a standing position away from the couches, in front of the wall mounted television.

"Annika, move to my chair." She commanded.

"No. I'd rather you shoot than inject that shit into me. You can't pass that off as a murder suicide so easily."

Hill and Rufus crept up the stairs. Not an easy task without generating plentiful, audible noise. Although from inside Chris's apartment, the noise did not radiate through. Hill put his ear to the door. He could not hear anything, then just as he was about to pull his head away, caught sound of a loud female laugh. Debbie. Hill shot Rufus "the look," removing his firearm. Rufus followed suit. Positioning was awkward on the staircase. In such a situation, Rufus was trained to take a position off to the side of the lead officer. Providing instant cover, without sharing the potential assailant's line of aim. This would not be possible here. Rufus retreated down a few steps, crouching as best he could. Hill watched Rufus secure a suitable position before using the butt of his gun to bang loudly three times on the door.

"Police. Open the door." He bellowed loudly. Hill stepped to the back of the landing return, training his gun, chest height on the closed doorway.

"Annika, move now." Demanded Katelyn. She realized it was unlikely she would play ball but wanted to maintain the distraction as Debbie stepped forward to deliver half of the injection into the back of Chris's neck. Ironically mirroring the circumstance of Brian's attack on Stan. Chris's attention firmly locked on Annika and Katelyn's actions, unaware of Debbie's approach. Just as she was about to deliver the killer act, a loud purposeful knock occurred on the door. Debbie stopped inches from her target, immediately retreating back a few steps.

"Police. Open the door." The call could be heard loud and clear from inside the apartment.

"Shit." Katelyn spoke in panic. She looked at Debbie, who mirrored her concern. "Just do it anyway." Katelyn directed. Debbie hesitated, unsure if it was in her interest now. Katelyn aimed the gun directly at the door. "Debs, do it now." The opportunity Chris had been waiting for materialized. Katelyn, fully distracted by the unexpected new threat, her direct aim removed from him. Without further thought, he leapt straight off the couch, springing headfirst over the coffee table smashing his shoulder straight into her midriff. His arms wrapped around Katelyn as she fell backwards straight into the television. This time, the crash was terminal for the expensive electronic device, a large crack forming straight through the screen. Katelyn slumped to the floor, Chris's motion and weight forcing her down. The gun flew from her hand across the room, clear of the dazed young woman. Chris smashed his head onto the hardwood floor, rendering both individuals inactive.

Reacting, Annika made an attempt for the gun. She jumped down from the couch on all fours reaching out for the precious item. Unfortunately for her, Debbie had also responded to the change in affairs. Charging around the couch, her foot reached the gun as Annika made a desperate grasp for it, kicking it free of her clutch, back towards the incapacitated Chris and Katelyn. Before Annika could think about her next move, she felt the cold sharp prick of a needle entering in the side of her neck. Freezing instantaneously, knowing what it meant. Debbie wrapped her free arm around her, pulling Annika up to her feet. Her thumb positioned over the plunger, threatening but not deploying the dose of certain death, regardless of anything else that could now happen.

Hill, realizing the door was not going to be answered did not bother to repeat the instruction. Despite the short run up the landing return offered, he launched himself forward burying his left shoulder into the door. It was an impressive thump, causing the entire doorframe to judder, but the door did not give. It was solid.

"Fuck this." He uttered to nobody. Taking a quick couple of steps down, Hill pointed his gun at the lock and let off four rounds in succession. The area splintered wildly. Wooden debris flew back at him. Without hesitation he jumped back up to the door, kicking it firmly with the sole of his shoe. The gun had done its job, weakening the integrity of the door to withhold the lock itself. More wood splintered and fractured as the locked area ripped free of the body. The door swung open wildly.

Without thought for personal preservation, Hill burst through into the apartment maintaining the gun level to hit head or chest.

Before Rufus had chance to follow in to provide back up, Hill had clocked and assessed all occupants in the room. Chris and Katelyn lying on the floor, dazed and incapacitated. A firearm lay beside them. Debbie hauled up in the far corner, behind Annika, using her for immediate protection. While Hill further reviewed the situation he aimed his gun directly at Debbie's head, marginally past Annika. The third sister appearing vulnerable, under threat. Rufus finally entered, dropping back to provide cover. Hill spotted the needle, quickly understanding the lethal danger.

"Steady." He called out. Whether to Rufus or Debbie, only he would know.

"Drop the gun." Debbie instructed. "Both of you, or she is dead." Hill pointed his gun up into the air, raising both hands in surrender. "And you Rufus." She screamed. Rufus shifted his feet slightly but maintained a clean head shot in his sights. "I'll take her with me." Debbie affirmed, twisting the needle slightly in Annika's neck. Annika could not help but wince and cry out in pain.

"It's okay Rufus, hold off." Hill called out in front. Sight maintained on the target, reluctantly the officer bought his gun down to point at the ground.

"Both guns on the floor." Debbie pushed.

"That's not going to happen Debs." Hill spoke calmly. "Let's all take a minute here." He advised. "The guns are not aimed. Please remove your thumb from the plunger." For what seemed a lifetime nobody moved.

Everyone assessing their options. Rufus's gun pointing at the floor. Hill's, aimed at the ceiling. "Debbie. Please remove your thumb." Hill pleaded coolly.

"Not until both guns are on the floor and kicked away." Debbie repeated. Rufus followed Hill's lead. He did not move a muscle, maintaining firearm to hand but without direct aim.

"This is not a good situation Debbie. You press that plunger, I shoot you in the head, before the delivery is complete." Hill threatened in a tone so soft, he could be a father soothing his infant child.

"You need to listen." Debbie fired back. The situation held station for a few seconds more. Katelyn still lying with Chris on the floor discreetly made a move. Reaching for her own gun lying inches away from the hand. A single objective in her mind. Take out the detective who had caused so much grief to her and Debbie. As Katelyn made her play, Hill caught the movement. His gun aimed up in the air, too late to react, to stop Katelyn getting the upper hand.

He attempted to counter the move, bringing his gun down towards her, two successive loud cracks sounded. One behind him, one in front. A whistle past his ear, before blinding agony engulfed him. Falling to the floor, white hot pain swamping his upper body. Hill had failed to achieve credible aim, knowing he had taken a direct hit. Rufus, however reacted with superior speed. Not quick enough to prevent Katelyn getting off a single shot, but as he watched her head jut back with the direct impact of his gun. He understood his reflex had achieved a direct and deadly blow in the fleeting moment of exchange. Dead before her finger even left her trigger.

Debbie squirmed slightly, her natural recoil of the firing weapons. Reacting now on pure instinct her thumb tightened over the plunger. Yet for all her effort to retaliate, conscious or otherwise, Rufus's second shot came too soon. As if an expert marksman, trained on Debbie, within a microsecond of a direct hit on Katelyn, he took her, clean in the midpoint of her forehead. Her thumb pressed against the plunger, but before any movement was achieved, it fell numb, along with her body and conscious thought. Her frame slumped clumsily to the ground, lifeless before she even fell. The needle ripped from Annika's neck. Screaming in pain as the needle tore through flesh and muscle, crucially failing to deliver even a drop of the lethal toxin. Annika jumped forward and clear of her dead sister. Neck bleeding but very much alive.

Without hesitation Rufus stepped forward kicking the gun well away from the lifeless hand of Katelyn, his own weapon moving onto Annika.

"Lie face down." He shouted. "Hands out in front." Knowing better than to trust anyone from this family. Annika complied. Any ambition of walking away from her personal involvement long since dissipated. "Hill? Hill?" He called desperately. His body lying still, behind the couch.

Outside of Chris's apartment a barrage of police vehicles and ambulances resided. Hill sat out of the back of an ambulance. Very much in defiance, he was not about to take the gurney as the paramedics had insisted. Shirt off and his shoulder temporarily strapped. Surgery was imminent to remove the bullet lodged in there. Taking a personal moment, he studied Rufus. The cop working well above his paygrade, consoling Chris, before the young man was taken to the station in a black and white to provide his official statement. The poor kid had been through the mill, emerging out of the other side, a survivor. As for Rufus, Hill could only concede a level of respect he rarely experienced for anyone in his profession. He possessed the knack, something that could not be taught. A skill, he shared with Hill. A sixth sense, for lies, motives, danger, for the evil within anyone. The two had worked together, understanding, and reacting to each other. A level of natural perception normally requiring years to obtain between partners, if ever.

Rufus finished his conversation, stepping back towards Hill, fully aware he was being observed.

"What?" He asked.

"I was just thinking you would make an excellent police marksman. You should give it some thought."
Rufus raised his eyes up to meet Hill, a wry smile etched on his handsome face.

"Nah." He returned. "I thought I might train for detective." His smile broadened. "I presume I could ask you to make a recommendation?" Hill looked down, shaking his head, taking the smile from his colleague.

"And there I was thinking this kid's got some brains in his head. Looks like you're just as stupid as me."

Printed in Great Britain
by Amazon

36056638R00198